Chose the Wrong Guy, Gave Him the Wrong Finger

Also by Beth Harbison

Shoe Addicts Anonymous

Secrets of a Shoe Addict

Hope in a Jar

Thin, Rich, Pretty

Always Something There to Remind Me

When in Doubt, Add Butter

Chose the Wrong Guy, Gave Him the Wrong Finger

Beth Harbison

ST. MARTIN'S PRESS
New York

This is a work of fiction. All of the characters, organizations, and events portrayed in this novel are either products of the author's imagination or are used fictitiously.

www.stmartins.com

LIBRARY OF CONGRESS CATALOGING-IN-PUBLICATION DATA

Harbison, Elizabeth M.
    Chose the wrong guy, gave him the wrong finger / Beth Harbison.—First U.S. Edition.
        pages cm
    ISBN 978-0-312-59913-3 (hardcover)
    ISBN 978-1-250-03190-7 (e-book)
    1. Triangles (Interpersonal relations)—Fiction.   2. Love stories.   I. Title.
    PS3558.A564C48 2013
    813'.54—dc23

                                                                    2013009104

St. Martin's Press books may be purchased for educational,
business, or promotional use. For information on bulk purchases,
please contact Macmillan Corporate and Premium Sales Department at
1-800-221-7945 extension 5442 or write specialmarkets@macmillan.com.

First Edition: July 2013

10 9 8 7 6 5 4 3 2 1

Happy birthday, Connie Atkins!
Thanks for being the best Mommy ever!

Also, to Jack Harbison—I am more proud of you
than you will ever know! I love you!

And John Harbison, thanks for
the memories and the beautiful children.
I will always remember you with love.
Good-bye, old pal.

Acknowledgments

Thanks to Devynn Rae Grubby, for a million things. You are the coolest chick I know!

Jami Nasi, I don't know what I'd have done without you. Here's to many more happy trips to the Grotto, and the place with the apple dumplings, and nights on the porch with champagne and witchcraft.

Connie Jo Gernhofer and Stevie Brown, you have made my house look gorgeous and saved my sanity quite a few times in the process. However, our shopping trips are making me broke.

Annelise Robey, thank you for always going above and beyond, and for being such a great friend!

Jill Jacobs Stilwell, I want to be just like you someday.

Kate Farr Clark, you are an awesome neighbor and friend, and I'm so lucky to have you there. Thanks to Brian Clark as well, for occasionally weed-whacking my side too.

Thanks to Bob, Brenda, Bobby, and Kat Walsh for so much more than I could ever say here.

Jocelyn Friedrich, you were a good friend to a guy who needed that. Thank you.

Mimi Elias, there are no words. You are an amazing friend—I am so grateful.

Chandler Schwede, thanks for stepping up so many times and reassuring me you're a few minutes away.

Jacquelyn and Elaine McShulskis, I am so lucky for sisters like you.

Thanks and hugs to Denise Whitaker, my long-lost cousin and friend—I have enjoyed our correspondence so much and look forward to meeting soon!

Dr. Michael J. Will, thank you for fixing those things so brilliantly. . . .

Greg Rubin, I hear you and I'm *trying!* Haha. You've been a godsend, seriously, I am so grateful.

Jordan Lyon, you crack me up. Russell Brand was a brilliant answer. You're still getting points for that one.

Paige Harbison, there is too much to say to try to put it in one pithy comment. So I'll just thank you for coming along, for being such an entertaining child, and for not getting arrested more than once.

Happy eighteenth birthday, Taylor Lyon! Here's wishing you every happiness and dream come true (especially the flying one, which will never, ever not be funny!).

Bigosi, you're still the big It. I think you always were, and I know you always will be. I love you.

Chose the Wrong Guy, Gave Him the Wrong Finger

Chapter 1

June, Ten Years Ago

There are five stages of heartbreak.

The first is Denial (He didn't! He wouldn't!), followed by Fear (What if he did? What will happen to me if I dump him?), a variable period of Rationalization (He didn't even have *time*! I would *know* if he'd been with someone else!), and eventually Acceptance (Okay, he did it, I have to move on, he doesn't deserve me).

Then comes Revenge.

Unfortunately, all too often these stages mix themselves up or repeat, repeat, repeat like a film on a loop, and sometimes another person gets thrown into the mix.

Once upon a time, that was what happened to Quinn Barton.

. . .

"Quinn, Frank's at the door. He says he needs to talk to you. He says it's urgent."

Quinn Barton turned to her bridesmaid, Karen Ramsey, and lifted her veil, an act that was soon to seem very prophetic. "He needs to talk to me *now*?"

Karen nodded. "He's *insisting*."

This was weird.

Something was wrong. Had something happened to Burke? Had he been hit by a car? Killed minutes before their wedding?

Heart pounding, Quinn pushed past Karen and hurried to the door, holding her skirt up enough so that she didn't trip, but otherwise unconcerned about what she might knock over on her way past.

"What's wrong?" she asked Frank as soon as she saw his face.

His eyes darted left and right. "I need to talk to you privately."

"Is Burke dead?"

"What? *No!* No one's dead, there's just something I need to tell you about."

All of Quinn's anxiety immediately melted into disproportionate irritation. "Really? Hm. I'd love to chat, but maybe now isn't the best time. I'm about to get married."

His expression hardened. "That's exactly why it has to be now."

Something about the way he said it, or maybe that granite set of his jaw, gave her pause. "Fine. We'll go out the back door. There's probably no one out there. I don't want Burke to see me in my dress before the wedding, it's bad luck."

Frank made a derisive noise.

They stopped on the sidewalk a few yards outside the church

and Frank said, "I think you need to consider stopping the wedding. Or at least postponing it."

"You think I should stop the wedding now?" she asked, vaguely aware of a hint of feeling, deep inside, that she'd been waiting for something like this. Then, numb, afraid to hear the answer yet looking for it like a rubbernecker in traffic looks for severed limbs and decapitated heads at the scene of an accident even though those details could never be forgotten or less horrifying, she added, "Why?"

"Come on, Quinn, you *know* why. Surely you know why."

"No, I don't! Tell me, specifically, *why.*"

"Because he's *cheating* on you, that's why!" Like she was stupid for asking. Like she already knew it, like *everyone* knew it, and he was just tired of watching her silly game.

She felt her hand go reflexively to her chest. What is that gesture? Why do people do it when they get a shock? To make sure they're still alive, that there's a heart beating under there, that they haven't died and gone to hell?

Because this revelation certainly made Quinn feel like she was in hell. Quite suddenly and unexpectedly.

"No, he's not!"

Denial.

"He wouldn't do that," she went on. Her voice was small. Childlike. But that didn't make him any gentler on her.

There was no compassion in his voice. "He would and he did."

"I don't believe it."

"You want proof?"

Fear.

What kind of proof? If it existed, would she want to see it? Or would that just be the kind of thing that, once seen, could never be forgotten and would gnaw at her forever?

"I don't believe it." She swallowed and leveled her gaze on Frank. "When did this supposedly happen?"

"Are you kidding, Quinn? You know he did. *Repeatedly!* Probably different girls. Probably even last night. Definitely in the last month. Does that answer your question enough?"

It felt like she'd been punched, hard, right in the gut. That's the cliché, there's a reason for it. Felt like she'd been punched in the gut. Shorthand for the myriad emotional, intellectual, and physical ramifications of being stunned.

Punched in the gut.

Except that was *exactly* how it felt—the unexpected blow connecting to the solar plexus, forcing the air from her lungs, tripping her heartbeat, curving her shoulders over in the time-immemorial position of, *Stop! I give up! I can't take it!*

Uncle!

No mas.

In short, his words immobilized her. It was like crazy sci-fi technology in action—he said it and she was instantly frozen into complete inaction at the very moment the church bells began to ring their call *to* action.

It's true, her most fearful inner voice said. *You know it's true.* But fear is such a liar, isn't it? Always there for you, louder than anything else inside, always pretending to be on your side. It's just looking out for you, right?

"When *exactly*?" she challenged, but she knew she wasn't going to like the answer. This wasn't fear she was talking to, or at least it wasn't fear who was going to answer, this was a real-life person who would *know*. Her hands tingled and she balled them into and out of fists as she paced on the sidewalk in front of him.

Frank. Francis Albert Morrison. Named, by his mother, after Frank Sinatra, despite his distinctly English ancestry and complete lack of creative talent, musical or otherwise. He wasn't a romantic either, or at least he'd never demonstrated anything resembling that in the six years she had known him. Why he was suddenly Dustin Hoffman yelling, *Elaine!* at her would-be wedding, she didn't know.

Well, that wasn't quite fair. He wasn't yelling *Elaine!* He was yelling *Cheater!* Not *to* her but *at* her, and actually he wasn't even yelling it so much as he was *condescending* it, and he was talking about someone who, right up to that moment, had been her fiancé.

Someone who, at that very moment, was waiting for her at the altar of the Middleburg United Methodist Church to become her husband.

Unless, of course, he was fucking her maid of honor behind the pulpit, which perhaps Frank would have her believe was equally likely.

Or which, god forbid, *was* equally likely.

"Give me the details." Her knees went weak. She sank down onto the curb next to Frank and took off her wedding shoes. Her grandmother's wedding shoes. Something old. It took some effort. Her feet were dented and grooved where the material of the slightly small shoes had cut into her flesh, which had swollen in the heat and stress.

Later she realized that "Give me the details" are some of the most ill-advised words anyone can ever utter. Details *never* make anything better.

"I don't want to say . . . I can't do that to him . . ."

"*Him?*" she raged. As if he could just go this far and let her handle the rest on her own?

"I wouldn't do it to *you* either. Maybe even *mostly* you." Like that made it better. "It's none of my business at all, I'm just trying to help you before you make the biggest mistake of your life."

"Then *help* me! You cannot make this implication *while I'm supposed to be walking down the aisle* and not tell me exactly what you're talking about."

He looked pained, it had to be said. A good actor, or just a guy with a conscience? She didn't know. She realized, all in that one moment, that she'd *never* known. Because she'd actually always thought he was a good guy. Solid. Not one to whip up some sort of dangerous passion inside his soul and use it to potentially destroy someone else.

"*Frank.*" She stood and continued pacing in front of him even though her bare feet were killing her. Her feet always swelled when she got really stressed out. It was weird, but it was her *thing.* Maybe weirder since she wasn't really into shoes like her mom was. She'd spent a lot of time barefoot as a teenager, pacing her feet into a size that, as her father always said, was better suited for the box than for the shoes that came in it. At this moment, every tiny pebble of the street pavement felt like it was cutting into her feet like glass, but she couldn't stop and try to wedge her Jurassic feet into her wedding pumps now. "I don't believe you."

He looked surprised. Hurt? Maybe insulted, maybe just worried that she'd dismiss something important. Ego or altruism, she didn't know. But he went forward boldly. "I saw her," he said. "I saw them. Together."

"You saw her," she repeated dully. A foreign student learning the language by repeating.

He nodded. "Yes. I saw her."

"*And . . . ?*" She didn't want to know. She really, really didn't want to know. But she *had* to. She wanted every single awful detail. She was ready to hear it all and slice herself with each tiny detail again and again for the rest of her life, regretting it each and every time. "Where? How? Elaborate!"

"A few times, she was at the farm," he began.

Her throat went so tight she nearly gagged.

Eight words that held so much. The shortest longest story ever told, at least to her.

A few times = there were too many to count. Not one single betrayal, possibly drunken, possibly mistaken, possibly—somehow—forgivable.

A few times . . .

But, worse, *the farm = her* place. The place she loved more than any other. His family's farm went back generations. But she'd been going there since she was fourteen, so it was part of *her* as well. She grew up in town, but Burke's family had a farm—actually, it was a huge horse farm to her, ninety acres of the most beautiful rolling green hills you can imagine, with stables so pristine Thurston and Lovey Howell could've moved right in. It was a place she'd always loved. Middleburg was horse country, and, as a girl growing up, she'd loved horses and always wanted one of her own. Her family weren't particularly wealthy, despite their zip code, so that dream remained an impossibility for her.

But when she'd begun dating Burke at age fourteen—which was still young enough to cling, if only in some vaguely subconscious way, to those childhood dreams and wishes—the place might as well have been Disney World to her.

There was a five-page entry in her high school diary describing the farm from the first time he took her there. Every detail was still correct, from the ebony bookcases in the den to the crocheted bedspread in the guest room. And everything she wanted to change, on the day she was certain she would eventually move in, was also still in line with who she was and what she wanted. It seemed so much like fate.

It wasn't just a place to live out her childhood fantasies of horses and stables and whatever old *Spin and Marty* episodes were shown on *The Mickey Mouse Club* reruns they played on Channel Five. When Burke and she started to date and fall in love, it became *their place*. Burke and his grandfather and often his brother as well, would work around the place while Quinn would sit on the patio with his grandmother Dottie, drinking iced tea and hearing tales of the old days while the wind hushed across the long stretches of green nothingness that were increasingly rare in the D.C. suburbs.

The farm was sacred space.

Surely Frank knew how much it would hurt her to bring this up this way. Surely he wouldn't do it if he didn't think he *had* to . . . would he?

"He took her *there?*" she said. Her voice sounded so much stronger than she felt. Her throat was so tight she felt like someone was strangling her, yet it sounded like she had the conviction and anger appropriate to a woman who has found out, *just in the nick of time*, that she's been betrayed. She'd ask the questions she had to ask, even though she didn't want the answers. She *needed* the answers, and she'd get them. She was a detective, she was fucking Columbo or something, with a pretend pad and pen in her hand, saying, *And what, exactly, do you know about that?*

"I really don't want to say more. You know enough. Ask him now. How could he deny it?"

"Apparently he has for some time!"

Frank shook his head. "I can't betray him anymore, it goes against Guy Code."

"*Fuck Guy Code!*" How could anyone look at a woman in the pain she knew was contorting her face and burning in her eyes, and think it was sufficient to give a small, yet powerful, detail without follow-up? "What. Else. Do. You. Know. About. Her?"

Long pause.

"She's a stoner," he finally said with a shrug, though his tone was one of disgust.

Ah.

That should make her feel better.

She was lesser than Quinn, because Quinn wasn't a stoner. Quinn was the opposite. How comforting. She was totally anti-stoner. But so was Burke! Burke was as straight and narrow as they came! She'd never seen him have anything stronger than a beer, and he usually opted for milk at that.

Yet he'd taken some stoner chick to the farm and banged her there? This was either a huge flaw in Frank's story or it was the detail that dropped the *Price Is Right* Plinko chip into the $5,000 slot of her lingering doubt about Burke's faithfulness.

Her throat tingled and she thought she might pass out, a big white unidentifiable splash in the street gutter that people wouldn't even slow down before running over.

What was that? A sack of sweet feed?

She straightened, with some effort in the now-ridiculous dress, and tried to breathe and walk off the shaking that emanated from a spot in the center of her being.

Her heart.

Then Frank delivered his final blow, which she'd never have time to figure out whether it was an incredibly clever manipulation via lies-so-weird-they-had-to-be-true or just truth-is-stranger-than-fiction.

"Actually, she got stoned there with Rob." He looked at her earnestly, his wavy dark hair short and controlled just like his demeanor, versus Burke's wild mane. And Frank's eyes were a serious amber brown, in contrast to Burke's heartthrobby blue.

It made Frank easier to believe somehow.

He considered for a moment before adding—as redemption for Burke?—a lame, "That did piss Burke off."

"But . . ." Her mind couldn't compute. Couldn't make sense of this. Couldn't do the math. Yet couldn't stop trying. Rain Man trying to add every single number in the phone book. Rob was a hired hand who'd moved out, what, a year ago? *Ages* ago. It was weird enough to say that Burke had somehow condoned this, but adding the detail—Rob—that conceivably had credibility *and* the vague insinuation of a time frame . . . well, honestly, she just would never have given Frank credit for being that creative. He was *very* smart, but in a left-brain, numbers sort of way.

Weaving these perfect, weird details for her just seemed out of his league.

Hell, it was even out of *her* league, and she was what she would normally consider a fairly wily woman.

"But he hates . . . ," she tried, then lost her voice. Or her point. Or her soul.

This just sounded too true, if only in its very falseness. It didn't matter what Burke hated or approved of, maybe there had even been some perverse fetishish pleasure in going for someone deliberately opposite Quinn. Still, it was the timing that stung like lashes from a whip. "It's been going on *that* long?"

Frank gave a half shrug. In cynical retrospect, she would believe it was meant to look sympathetic. Or maybe *commiserative* was the better word. *Hey, I know, it sucks,* that shrug implied. *I'm so sorry you're going through this, but give the jerk what he deserves.* Because he *clearly* expected her to be outraged by this news.

As pretty much any self-respecting woman would be.

But all she could think about were weird little clues, tiny things that she'd ignored—though consciously—time and again. There had been scratch marks on Burke's shoulder once when she was massaging his back. She'd noticed them, thought the curve of them seemed pretty distinct and specific, yet she didn't even *question* him about them because she *completely* trusted him. She just figured there had to be a reasonable explanation.

Because there's *always* a reasonable explanation for things, right? How many times had she been worried about something and been 100 percent sure the only possible outcome was that something awful had happened, when, in fact, a little series of innocuous things had happened?

She didn't enjoy being angsty and upset. She didn't want to be Jealous Girl. Jealous Girl is just so uncool. She's Walter Mitty's wife, the harpy nag who gains power with a wedding ring, then demands an accounting of every moment her man isn't with her. The fat actress in every old movie who lost her guy to Marilyn Monroe or Myrna Loy or Katharine Hepburn. Jealous Girl was Insecure Girl, and she did all kinds of ugly things that turned life into drudgery for everyone around her.

Quinn wasn't Jealous Girl! She honestly thought she was a good catch *because* she didn't freak out about every little thing! Once upon a time, she would have been all, *Ugh, I* hate *those girls!*

But here she was, pacing on hot, rough pavement in what was once a beautiful wedding gown, her mind racing with angry, suspicious, painful thoughts.

A couple of times he's told me the same story more than once, without remembering he'd already told me. Is that because he thought he'd told her?

Those times he said he wanted to stay in because he was "tired," even though he obviously *would have had hot sex with me if he'd seen me—was he having hot sex with her instead?*

*Oh, my God, hott*er *sex with her?*

Was that even possible?

The pain of imagining it was awful. Him touching her, stripping her, her hands on him, her *mouth* on him—that was *Quinn's* man, that was *Quinn's* body to love, he reserved it for *her.* She knew every single millimeter of it, knew which muscles hurt just by touching him, he never even had to say a word. No one else would know, or care probably, that he held his tension in his shoulder blades; that the arch of his foot tightened when he ran, and that that turned his calves to tight painful ropes; that for some reason his left upper body was usually tighter than the right but his right lower body was tighter than his left. . . . All those meticulous little details that Quinn had so proudly believed proved she loved him better than anyone else ever could.

Had he cupped this other girl's face and kissed her while he was on top of her, moving inside her? God, that was the worst of all. Him *kissing* her. Kissing was so much more intimate than the rest. Emotional.

Not that *the rest* didn't matter. Not that the rest didn't exist. Apparently it did. This puzzle had so many more pieces than she'd anticipated. Had he ever been with her the same day he was with Quinn? Had her kisses still been on his lips when *she*, Quinn, kissed him?

She felt like she was going to puke.

"Why would he do that to me?" she asked Frank, though she wasn't really looking to him for an answer. How could he have it?

"You know him. He did it because he *could*. He did it because he always wants more. More money, more attention, more pizza, whatever, he's like a six-year-old who thinks of no one but himself."

And she did know Burke. She knew he was completely capable of being a child. Wild, irresponsible. His sense of humor was sometimes raunchy, his timing sometimes inappropriate. Sometimes he laughed too loud, drove too fast, pushed too hard. But in spite of that—perhaps even *because* of some of it—he was wildly charismatic.

And *she* had won his heart. *She*—Quinn Morgan Barton— whose Awkward Phase had gone on longer than many other girls' in junior high, who had always thought just a little too much about things, and tried just a little too hard to do everything right— maybe sometimes erring on the side of being too dull for a guy like Burke—*she* had won his heart in ninth grade and had been with him ever since, almost seven years.

Yes, they'd had their challenges now and then. There *was* that time they'd broken up because he refused to go to the homecoming dance, and then, while they were broken up, he went with Tammy Thomas, whose stupid name made her sound like a brand of shoes and whose stupid face could probably model for the ads. That had sucked. But he'd done it to spite her for dumping him and, in some weird way, that was better than him doing it without regard for her at all.

At least he was thinking of her.

But for the most part everything had been good between them. No, they'd been *great*. The two of them were the best of friends, they had a long history, god knew they had amazing chemistry.

They *loved* each other.

He'd loved her enough to propose. She hadn't even seen it coming, but he'd done it, he'd proposed, and here it was, their wedding day.

Or was it?

"Why are you telling me all this now, Frank? Why now?"

"Because you need to know before you go in there and marry the wrong guy."

She sank down next to the curb again, her own private rise and fall of service, and hugged her knees closer to her, her feet stinging against the hot pavement of the gutter.

There was a steady drumbeat of, *This isn't true, this isn't true, this isn't true, this isn't true,* thrumming in her head.

But she didn't buy it.

"But why now? Why at the last possible minute?" She met his eyes. "Why not, I don't know, yesterday? Last week? Last month? Just how long have you known all this was going on?"

"I've known it all along. I thought you knew—I mean, how could you *miss* it?—but I guess you didn't want to know. It wasn't until today that I realized maybe you really didn't get it. You missed every hint."

"Hint?"

"There were a million of them. Hell, *I* gave you a million of them!"

"Jesus, Frank, you might have a million thoughts in your head, but if you throw me a balloon, all I'm going to catch is the balloon!" She threw her hands in the air and came perilously close to hitting him in the face. Which she wouldn't have been sorry for at all. "Who wants to leap to conclusions only to have their heart broken?"

"I understand," he said, in an infuriatingly calm voice. "But sometimes you need to be realistic."

"I thought I was, *Frank*." She practically spit his name. "Right up until this moment, I thought I was. Because no one gave me the benefit of, apparently, the facts."

"But you knew them, Quinn. Come on. Deep down, you must have known."

Had she? Her stomach tightened at the thought. Had the occasional worry or moment of mistrust been significant, or just paranoia? Didn't everyone have doubts in a relationship now and then? Didn't *everyone* occasionally think the person they loved might be . . . attracted to other people?

"I think you're mad at the wrong person," Frank concluded.

"No, I'm not! I'm mad at all the *right* people. I'm mad at you, I'm mad at that sonofabitch in there"—she gestured toward the church—"and I'm mad at myself most of all. Myself and you. And him." God, she hated everyone.

He gave a soft laugh. "I guess that about covers it." He looked as if he wanted to reach for her, to comfort her, but thought better of it. "I've known you a long time, Quinn. In fact . . ." He held a breath for a moment, pent up, then expelled it. "I . . . well, I kept hoping you'd see what was going on. The truth. I would never treat you like this."

She looked at him incredulously. "You are not seriously making a pass at me."

"Quinn, I want you to be treated the way you should be treated. You know me, you know who I am. There's no need to sell myself to you, I'm not right either, I'm sure, or you would have seen it a long time ago. That's not what this is about. I told you what my conscience said I had to tell you. What you do with it is up to you." He stood up and dusted off his pants. "I'm going in now. I'll let them know you're on your way, no matter what you decide to do once you're in there." He shrugged. "And, Quinn, I'm really sorry to have done this . . . this way. Or at all. I just didn't know what else to do at this point. I couldn't sit on it without giving you a straight shot."

Then he went into the church, his gait certain, if not confident. And why wouldn't it be? *He* wasn't the one whose life was just shattered. *He'd* be okay no matter what. Obviously he'd made something of a confession to her, but it was equally obvious that his life—his heart, his sanity, his well-being—didn't *depend* on what *she* did.

She didn't know how long she stood there, staring at the carved wooden door after he'd gone through it. It felt like forever. She was completely numb. Part of her wanted to never move again. To never have to do anything again. Her world had been shattered, and she wanted to just collapse into a million little pieces on the ground, the million little puzzle pieces she would otherwise have to put together in order to make sense of this.

Then she heard her mother's voice calling to her. "Quinn! Come on! Come in here! Everyone's waiting!"

And that was duty's call.

Mechanically, she got up and started to walk toward the door, aware that her veil was askew, that she'd sweated her makeup into something of a blur, but unaware of the gum she'd sat on that was now sticking to her dress, and marched to the internal beat in her head, morbidly in tempo with the "Wedding March."

It can't be true, it can't be true, it can't be truuuue, it can't be true.

That beat carried her all the way up to the altar. She was aware of eyes on her, but she met no one's gaze. Not even Burke's, though she knew—she could just *feel*—it was questioning.

What's wrong? What's going on?

No clear answer formed in her head. She didn't know what was going on, exactly. She was dazed, being carried on a rickety raft by an ocean of adrenaline.

She didn't know what she was going to do until she was right there by his side.

That's when it all came clear.

She drew her hand back and slapped him with all the power of every unacknowledged hurt he'd ever inflicted on her.

Then she turned and ran back down the aisle, out of the church, followed, not by the undoubtedly stunned Burke, but by his best man. His brother.

Frank.

Five hours later, as the night crept over town, Quinn sat alone in her shop—she had refused her friends' well-intended offers of help and support, half ready to strangle the next person who offered either—opening presents, writing awkward *thank you anyway*'s for them, and repackaging them to ship back to the sender.

And all the while, her anger grew stronger and stronger, like hoofbeats from an oncoming calvary.

She couldn't believe she'd put so much trust in Burke. Couldn't believe it. Everything seemed so clear now.

Yet, as clear as it was, she still worried about how she'd struggle when her current anger dissolved tomorrow, or the next day, into sadness.

She put her pen down and cracked her knuckles. Her hand was *killing* her from all this writing. If it were thanks for wedding gifts it would have been a lot more fun. But this? Explaining. Apologizing. Wondering which recipients would understand and which would be angrily tucking into their returned gifts, wondering if she'd opened them and made toast with them first.

And why did *she* need to do the explaining anyway? Apart from the million things he should have done to prevent this catastrophe to begin with, *he* should have gone straight to the pulpit and done the one gentlemanly thing there was left for him to do: tell the guests that the wedding was off, it was entirely his fault, and . . . whatever. Offered them cake to go or something. Gotten Ziploc bags and plastic forks and let everyone have at it at one of the many traffic lights along Route 7 on the way home.

And maybe assured them right then and there that their gifts would be returned *by him*, so she wouldn't have to be sitting here wondering which guests thought she was the kind of inconsiderate runaway bride who thought the damn Vitamix was her right just for letting them sit their butts on the pew for an uncomfortable forty-five minutes while she dithered about whether or not she actually *wanted* to have the party she had invited them all to.

How many of them thought she was a flake who just had second thoughts for no good reason?

Now she'd have to spend the whole damn night packing stuff up for UPS to get the next day.

When she was *supposed* to be in Jamaica!

Middleburg, Virginia, was most definitely not Jamaica. It was just the same old scenery she'd been looking past for twenty-one years.

She'd *wanted* more. She'd wanted to broaden her horizons, open her world, grow with him. With Burke. The man she'd loved since he was a boy of sixteen and she was a girl of fourteen.

That was laughable now, given the truth.

How many other people had known the truth before she'd even put on the blue silk garter?

What were they thinking about her now?

What would *she* be thinking about her now?

An uncharitable part of her saw that she would be shaking her head and clucking her tongue at the dumb girl who'd ignored every sign that had been offered to her on a silver platter because she was so damn eager to wear a gorgeous dress and saunter down the aisle to a gorgeous man who was waiting there to take her hand in marriage.

Oh, the sucker, she'd think to myself, *she sold her soul to the devil, then tried to marry him in God's house.* Actually, no, she wasn't that religious. Or that kind. *Stupid bitch*, she'd more likely scoff. *Um, hello! It's not just about the* hand *in marriage on the* one *party day, it's about a whole lot of stuff, a* lifetime *of stuff, including "keep thee only unto her." Look at her crying like she's really surprised by all this! She wanted the nice sheep so badly she didn't care that she could see his wolf fangs behind the mask.*

Well. Maybe Metaphorical Mean Quinn was right.

She looked around at the wedding announcements—*Joanne and Bernard Barton proudly announce the loving union of their daughter, Quinn Morgan Barton* . . .—and the clouds of white satin and tulle that filled Talk of the Gown, her family's bridal shop, where she had spent the past *six months* lovingly sewing her dream wedding gown, which now had dried mascara tears down the front of it and fucking *gum* on the back from when she was sitting on the curb outside the church, trying to figure out her life.

That's how all great decisions are made, right? Winston Churchill probably ground his coattails into three hundred years' worth of grime on a Downing Street corner and questioned, *Should we just give up and have some bratwurst? Ja or nein?*

But, actually, she didn't even have her own last-minute thoughts and hesitations. She couldn't even hang her hat on that small an accomplishment.

Her decision was handed to her by someone else instead. Well, not her *decision*—even though she was essentially left with only the one possibility, it was her own. But her options were certainly presented to her by the wrong person, in the wrong way, at the worst possible time. There she was, *literally* on her way to the altar, and her options were practically hand-engraved and sealed in an envelope that read *Pride*—clearly marked so she could take it or leave it forever.

As long as she lived, she would never forget the way it felt when Frank said she should stop while she still could. She'd thought it was a joke at first, yet she'd known—in that horrible gut way you sometimes know things—that it wasn't.

And now here she was, writing note after note after note, the same nine words; her only explanation to the two hundred guests who had come to see the fairy-tale wedding she'd dreamed about for years:

Chose the wrong guy, gave him the wrong finger.

She stopped. With maybe twelve more notes to go, she just stopped. And she went to the phone and dialed the number that was more familiar than her own.

It rang twice before there was an answer.

"Hi," she said, out of habit more than salutation. "It's me. I hate how everything happened today. And I totally hate how I feel now. I don't think I can get through this going back to my house and going to sleep and picking up my life like . . ." Her voice wavered and faded. She closed her eyes tight for a moment before taking a steadying breath. "Can you come to the shop and pick me up? I need to get out of here. Just get in the car and drive as far away as possible. Let's go to Vegas."

She only had to wait a moment for his answer.

"Yes."

"Good," she said, and swallowed hard over the lump in her throat, looking at the work she'd done and knowing she was going to just pick up and go and leave it for her mother to clean up. Right now she just didn't care. She couldn't. "I'll see you out front."

She hung up the phone and picked up a few pieces of silvery wedding gift wrapping and tossed them in the general direction of the trash can. Some fell by the side, but she didn't pick them up.

Instead, she took a length of receipt paper from the cash register, pulled it out, and wrote a note to her mother on the back:

Gone away for a few days. Don't worry, seriously. I'm okay.
I'll be back. Sorry to leave the paper all over.

Then she set it down on the counter and went out front to wait for Frank.

Chapter 2

Present Day, Ten Years Later

"Misssss Quinn!"

I'd know that voice anywhere. Dorothy Morrison—grandmother of Burke and Frank Morrison—the biggest, brightest character in town. Everyone's Auntie Mame. She had more energy than a toddler, and I didn't think there was a person in Middleburg—or in the world—who didn't love her.

But I hadn't seen her for a while. Actually, I'd wondered what she was up to. "Misssss Dottie," I said, in her same tone.

She bustled over to the counter, behind which I was sorting threads, and leaned down on her elbows. Which, actually, wasn't such a far *lean*, since she was five feet tall, tops.

"I have got news," she said. "*Big* news."

I set down the threads I was sorting, careful to keep the greens in order—Kelly, mossy, sea. "Do you?"

Now, Dottie *always* had something to say, so a declaration like this didn't necessarily prepare one for a bombshell. On more than one occasion she'd circled the town with pronouncements about saving a robin that had fallen from its nest or finding a "bone" she was sure was a relic from the Civil War, despite the fact that it looked a lot more like a Meaty Bone dog treat to the rest of the world.

Dottie was *eccentric.*

And delightful. Truly. Never mind that her grandson had completely broken my heart, I had nothing but happy associations with her. It was impossible not to. She was just that kind of person.

"You will never guess," she said, peering over the counter at me. A waft of Estée Lauder's Beautiful nudged over me. One of her only nods to the past couple of decades.

"Did you save another robin?" I asked.

"No." She smiled. "Well, *yes*, but that's not the news. This is *big*. Guess again, Quinn, go on!"

"You got the parlor wallpapered?" Maybe she forgot she'd told me that last month.

She looked at me as if I had just told her I was giving up the shop to join the circus. "That was quite a long time ago." She screwed up her brow. "I'll give you one clue: I may need to *borrow* something."

So, okay, in retrospect I see why she thought it was a good clue, but at that moment, she could have meant *anything*. She could have meant she'd smashed some Waterford and wanted to borrow my vacuum cleaner; she could have meant she was picking up her ancient sister from the airport and wanted to borrow my car; or she could have meant she was about to sneeze and wanted to "borrow" one of the embroidered handkerchiefs in the case before her.

"I just don't know, Dottie," I said, shaking my head. "I give up. Tell me."

She pressed her lips together, and her cheeks bloomed like apples. "I'm getting *married*!"

"Married?" I echoed dumbly. I hadn't seen this coming. At all. This was crazy. Dorothy had rattled around that old farm for almost twenty years since her husband had died, without one date that I knew of, without any hint or gossip in town about her fraternizing with any man. "What do you mean?"

She gave a spike of laughter and her expression sharpened into absolute clarity. "How many things could that mean, Quinn? I'm getting married. M. A. R. R. I. E. D."

I didn't want to insult her by letting out all the confusion that came first to mind. "To *who*?"

"Well." Apparently satisfied that I was taking her seriously now, she gave a secret smile. "I met him online."

"You're online?"

"Good lord, child, I'm not that out of touch! Just because I don't carry an ePad around, doesn't mean I don't understand what's going on in the world of technology!"

I had to smile at that. "Point taken." I stood up and ushered her over to the sitting area—i.e., several very comfy boudoir chairs outside the fitting room—that we had set up for those who generally had to sit and wait for brides to try on hundreds of different dresses, then try them again, and dither, and beam, and hope, and dream. "Have a seat and start from the beginning."

This was what I'd done almost every day of my life for more than a decade—I welcomed nervous/happy/excited/terrified/etc. women into my place of business and tried to make them feel good about themselves. Most of them were brides-to-be, some were prom dates, and there were smatterings of other Honored Guests of Special Occasions, but almost without exception their roles all carried high emotion of one sort or another.

Usually it was happy excitement.

Not always, though.

In this case, I wasn't sure at first.

"I didn't want to tell anyone." She perched on the edge of the chair, so excited she could clearly barely contain herself. "You just know they're all going to say there's no fool like an old fool."

"No!" But yes. I could imagine people saying that.

Dottie knew too, the look she gave me showed me that. "Well, one night after perhaps a little too much whiskey"—no delicate sherry or brandy for Dottie, she was a whiskey girl all the way—"I decided to click on one of the dating advertisements next to my list of Facebook friends."

Dottie had Facebook too?

This was too much to process.

For one thing, if she was on Facebook, why hadn't she friended *me*?

"It was for Silver 'n' Gold Singles," she went on, then turned the corners of her mouth down in a mock frown. "Doesn't that sound absolutely ghastly?"

It kind of did.

Fortunately I didn't have to commit to my agreement, as she

kept on talking. "But I figured, what the hell, I'm silver *and* gold at this point, and most definitely single."

"Okay . . . ?"

"Oh, stop looking at me like I'm making up stories! I know that look! Do you think I don't see it all the time? Heavens, girl, I am not a fool, I know people are skeptical about some of the things I say, but I never, *ever* tell a lie. I may have embellished here and there, possibly obfuscated, but have you ever known me to tell a *lie*? Come on, be honest."

"No, of course not."

"Good, then we can move on to business. Because I, Quinn, am telling you the truth when I say I am going to need the fanciest dern wedding dress you have ever made, and I'm going to need it a month from yesterday."

"Wow." Such an understatement. She wasn't kidding. I couldn't swear she wasn't *crazy*—this still wasn't adding up to the Dorothy Morrison I knew.

"Wow indeed." She reached into her purse, an old black leather cavern of a bag that Thelma Ritter might have carried and called a *pocketbook*. She pulled out a smartphone and started moving her pudgy fingers across the screen as quick as a kid playing a video game. Then she triumphantly turned it to me and said, "Here he is! Lyle! Isn't he handsome?"

Lyle. This was becoming real before my very eyes and it was cute *and* disconcerting.

Lyle *was* handsome, actually. And easily a decade and a half—maybe more—younger than Dottie. Not exactly a baby, he was in his late fifties, close to sixty or just over the mark, I'd have to guess, but he wasn't the octogenarian I might have expected, had I expected *any* of this.

He had salt-and-pepper hair, more salt than pepper, and the smooth forehead of the fully Botoxed. But his eyes had a kind crinkle to them and a certain sincerity in them that I wouldn't have expected if someone had just been telling me this story without showing me the picture.

There's no fool like an old fool. Poor Dottie, she was right. People were bound to leap to the worst conclusions first. But maybe this was on the up and up. I kind of got that feeling looking him in the photographic eyes.

Not that I hadn't been fooled by eyes before, of course, so what did I know? But those revealed a man who had smiled a lot, laughed a lot, and it was hard not to see a smiling, laughing man as a kind one.

"He's hilarious," Dottie said, as if reading my mind. "Does the best Bob Barker imitation."

I laughed. Bob Barker? I guess you *would* know a Bob Barker imitation if you heard it, though who would ever expect it? That was almost like doing an excellent Kristy McNichol—it would be familiar to some, but why bother?

Then again, the answer was right there in Dottie's eyes. Bother because the *right* person is going to think it's hilarious.

The *right* person would get it.

In my business I see a lot of *right* people, and a lot of *wrong* people. It's terrible when there's one of each in a couple, because you know someone will end up with a big heartache. At one point I started doing an x-stitch (idea being I was pre-disastering them so they'd be okay) on the back hems of gowns I imagined were going to lead to disaster, and though I didn't know how *all* of them ended up, and *some* of them were still playing out, I knew enough to know I'd been more right than wrong.

I'd stopped that, though, because my friend Glenn called me a ghoul and said maybe I was jinxing people and, believe me, I always, *always* hope my clients have a happy ending.

It's just that, all too often, one person is getting more out of the relationship than the other. There are obvious cases of wealthy men and shallow younger women—though who's using whom more in those cases is hard to define—but sometimes it's a wildly enthusiastic, nurturing bride I see, eagerly asking a distracted fiancé's approval for all of her decisions about the wedding, and I just know what that's going to look like down the road. Excessive attention to the seasoning of a pot roast, followed by the subtle but distinct letdown of disinterest. High-thread-count sheets, carefully washed with lingerie fabric softener, only to be met by the exhausted, beer-breathed body of a husband who falls asleep during foreplay. Clock-watching primping with the anticipation of greeting him at the end of the day, dressed in something he once called pretty, only to see the hands wind around the clock like something in a cartoon, until finally she calls him and is told he's working late.

Is he?

It's not just women I see headed for doom, though. Marriage is an equal opportunity for disappointment. Sure, obviously I've seen the lithe young brides, ordering custom dresses and paying with a black Amex card bearing a man's name, while talking on their cell phones to someone whose male voice is decidedly younger and sexier than their intended's.

But there are more subtle disappointments showing themselves in the shop every day as well: the girl who *insists* on extracting her fiancé's opinion, only to trounce it the minute he produces one. The bride who bullies her mother and bridal party so much they're like head-shy dogs, flinching at her every gesture and word.

And then there's my favorite: the Ace Manipulator. It was so subtle at first I didn't detect it: the bride who seems so meek initially that her groom brings her in with the gentlest lead, his chest puffing out bigger with every small, modest objection she makes to "fanfare."

These are women who will do whatever it takes to please that man until her retractable nails are firmly in his back. You'd be amazed at the subtle but steady trajectory of their steeliness, from acquiescent at first, to what can only be described as *testing* ("What if I can't make lasagna like your mom's, you won't call off the whole wedding, will you?"), to the last I see of them before they start their life together: "You agreed to this, and this is how we're doing it! God! What is your *problem*?"

It doesn't take long for people to get beaten down.

Which was why I never tried the whole relationship/marriage thing again. Once burned, and all that. Look, I went into my relationship with Burke with a *completely* open heart. It was all his for the taking. I didn't read, or follow, *The Rules*, there was no hard-to-get in my playbook. I loved him, I loved touching him, tasting him, pleasing him, nourishing him in every way I could. You could even call it selfish in a way because *I*, myself, got so much out of being indispensable to *him*. It never felt like I was sacrificing myself in *favor* of him, but more that everything I did for him was rewarded with adoration.

To this day, though, I don't know if I was even the only one who felt that way.

And that, right there, is the problem with betrayal. For five minutes of your life you're pissed at the other person, but the bulk of the response is to the doubt you have left in *yourself.* In your own judgment.

In your trust in *anyone* else, *ever.*

Because who are you left with at the end of a relationship? Only you. The other person is gone—their choice, your choice, mutual choice, whatever, they're gone—and you have only yourself to fall back on.

And if you have given yourself—whole heart, mind, body, and soul—to someone who betrayed you, perhaps spent months or even *years* betraying you, well, how do you even fully trust the meter on the gas pump at your local Shell station?

Everything becomes questionable, because you went so long *unquestioning.* Making idiotically sincere declarations like, *"Oh, he's home tonight because he's tired, poor thing. He worked outside for so long today. . . ."* Then you have to wonder if the person you were talking to knew better, was laughing at you behind your back.

Poor little fool.

Nope. For me, it wasn't worth taking the chance. And I mean that seriously, not bitterly, not with crossed arms and a snarl, but it was just the decision I had made for myself. I had great friends and I got *plenty* of relationship drama—and intrigue and even the occasional truly romantic story—at the shop.

Like now.

For Dottie, I didn't know if this was going to be truly romantic or *drama*, but so far it was certainly *intrigue*.

And I was damn glad it wasn't my own.

"What does Lyle do for a living?" I asked, bracing myself for just about any answer, including "magician."

Actually, I think I was kind of *expecting* magician. He had the kind of face that would love looking at itself under a top hat and over a cape.

She fidgeted with a screen display of earrings on the counter. "He's independently wealthy. Doesn't have to work at all!"

Red flag.

Worse than magician.

"But he is a wonderful artist. He calls it a hobby, since his job is selling furniture, but I think his paintings could sell for a lot of money."

Still—red flag.

"Well, that's very romantic, isn't it?" I said. It did have romantic potential. Imagine having been Renoir's love interest!

She pointed a pink-lacquered fingernail at me. "That's what *I* said. Tell *that* to the boys, though." She snorted.

The boys.

The boys.

Burke and Frank. I hadn't seen them, either of them, in ten years. Somehow I'd always been lucky enough *not* to be at the same place at the same time as them if they were in town. I heard about them from Dottie, of course, so it wasn't one of those taboo subjects either. Frank was a lawyer at a firm in D.C.—a once-venerable firm now more famous for one of the partners having written a crazy bestselling novel about the U.S. president going on a Jack-the-Ripper-style murder spree in Georgetown.

Burke owned a contracting firm based in Leesburg, Virginia. I had no idea how big or small it was, how successful or toppling he was, it was a Google search I would not allow myself to do. It was enough to know he was just about twenty miles up Route 15, but it might as well have been a world away. I think he lived in Reston or something, but I tried not to get too many details about Burke because Thinking About Burke was not one of my favorite activities. It was a deep rabbit hole and there was more pain than fun in that.

"They don't approve?" I asked Dottie.

She shook her head, her gray fluff of curls wiggling like springs. "They think he's a gold digger."

I opened my mouth to offer some sort of supportive outrage, but she pointed that finger at me again.

"*You* thought the same thing, missy, don't say you didn't. I saw it in your eyes."

Reflexively I blinked. Erase. Delete. "I have no idea what you're talking about. I'm just taking it all in."

She smiled. "And speaking of taking things in, I have lost four pounds and hope to lose at least another couple before the wedding." She was not a thin woman and I admired her for allowing herself the accomplishment of losing four or five pounds instead of starving herself into a wedding dress she'd spend the rest of her life flogging herself for being too big for, like most of my clients. "But this is the dress I have in mind." She reached into her purse and produced a cutting from a magazine. It was an old magazine. I remembered piles of old *Good Housekeeping* magazines in the back room of the farmhouse. I pictured her there, leafing through them, looking for a picture of the perfect dress to start her new life.

There was something cool about that.

She handed me the picture and I smiled when I saw it. It was *very* her. Ivory satin, drop-waisted, modestly hanging down to mid-calf, with a square neckline. The only thing that kept it from being completely conservative was the fact that it was positively festooned with small pink fabric roses. Little pinwheels of color that twisted around the dress in a way not unlike the little curls of her hair.

"It's *perfect*!" I breathed.

"Can you do it?"

"Absolutely!"

"By June twenty-fifth?"

"You will be my *highest* priority."

She beamed. "You always were such a doll to me. You're *family* to me, Quinn." She took my hand in hers. Her fingers were cold and dry, but the gesture still warmed me.

"So I'll leave the picture with you, shall I?" She closed her purse.

"Please. Now, if we can just get a few measurements, I can be off to the races before you know it."

"Virginia Gold Cup!" The annual early May race was her favorite because until about ten years ago she had always hosted a grand party in the field, her way of heralding spring.

"Virginia Gold Cup," I agreed, and got out my tape measure.

"By the way," she said, lifting her arms for me to measure her bust, "do you know of a good local mover?"

I jotted the measurement on my pad. "Mover?"

"You know, one of those big trucks to move furniture from one house to another."

I wrapped the tape around her waist. "Not that I can think of off the top of my head." I wrote the measurement. "But I could ask around. Why?"

"Well, the *boys* are going to do the packing, of course." She shook her head and looked heavenward. "They are *thrilled* about that, let me tell you."

I ran the tape down her arm. "What packing? I'm lost. Who's moving?"

"Honey, *I* am! Haven't you heard our conversation? Lyle and I are getting married"—she gestured at the tape measure, as if to point out the obvious fact that I was making her dress—"and, of course, we're going to move out, get a place together."

I paused, midmotion. Of course. I mean, that *did* make sense, most people got married and started a new life together. It just hadn't occurred to me, not even for a moment, that she might have been planning to leave the farm. She was part of the place, and together the Morrison family were a big part of the town, and the town's history. The idea of her not being there was just . . . it was unthinkable.

And I could well imagine that Burke and Frank felt the same way.

There was no way *not* to.

That place without Dottie, without all her stuff . . . Wait a minute. "Who's going to stay at the farm?"

She made a dismissive gesture. "Selling it."

"Oh, my god."

"Time to move on!"

Suddenly I hated Lyle. I hated his smirky, smug face and his stupid "artist" act when he was really a salesman, and I was pretty sure his Bob Barker sounded just like Lyle using a funny voice, and not like Bob Barker at all. I'd never met the man, of course, but I *hated* him because apparently he thought he could come out of nowhere and steal Dottie and just make her get rid of a place so special, so historic in so many ways (many of them personal for me), just *get rid of it*, sell it to—whom? Some developer? In two years would those ninety acres be some fussy neighborhood full of one-acre McMansions on half-acre lots? Perhaps with big stone gates at the entrance, announcing the *neighborhood* as "Grace Farms," a tiny, tacky nod to what had once been a noble tradition?

"What's the matter, Quinn?"

I found my voice. "Dottie, I just can't imagine you not being at the farm. I can't imagine the farm belonging to someone else." And it wasn't like I could ever have any hope of buying it. My business was variable at best, but it would never generate half the income required to buy that amount of property.

She chuckled indulgently and put a hand on my forearm, apparently thinking I was just being altruistic, thinking of her instead of panicking at the dissolution of *my* old dream, which should have died ten years ago when I put my gum-and-grime-dotted wedding dress on a bonfire and vowed to never look back.

It was a lie. I looked back all the time. And the moment the tulle caught fire—like a *News 4* demonstration of the dangers of flammable Halloween costumes—I'd wanted to drag it out and bat the flames down. But I'd already made my big "To hell with Burke Morrison!" declaration and couldn't risk my life and limb to turn back on a stand I'd made for my own dignity.

"Honey, that place has become an albatross around my neck, I'll tell ya. I am so damn tired of thinking about who's doing the work and how much it's going to cost. Lyle and I want to get a little place on Lake Michigan and then travel the world, see things we've never seen before."

I flinched at the sound of his name, and I was afraid that was rapidly going to become a habit, but I could see in her watery blue eyes that she had dreams that didn't involve remaining in a life that didn't fit her anymore. A dream that wasn't hers.

And I couldn't be such a baby as to whine that the world wasn't accommodating me by staying exactly in place so that I could take out my little box of ancient wishes every now and then and turn them over in my hand like some pretty bauble in a consignment shop.

Besides, I had no voice here anyway. No horse in the race. But I knew Burke and Frank would fight for it. Somehow. They'd keep this from becoming the catastrophe it threatened to become.

"I don't blame you for that," I said, trying to picture her in some "little place on Lake Michigan," but failing. I could, however, picture her traveling the world, a feisty old cat, eager to see, hear, taste, and try everything. If that was what she wanted, she deserved it. Not everyone gets a second chance. Believe me, I knew it. "I'm sorry, Dottie, it's just so sad to think of you going that I'm probably raining on your parade."

"Don't you worry, missy." Another indulgent pat on my arm. "This is nothing compared to the stink Burke put up."

"Just Burke?"

"Mmm." She nodded absently. "I don't think Frank is eager to stop what he's doing in the city and come here for manual labor, but he gave me a few bits of practical advice about the financial aspects of selling and I think he's going to be all right with it."

That surprised me, but what did I know? I hadn't seen Frank or Burke for a long time, I had no way to know or guess what their positions might be on *anything*. "It's good that he can help you with that."

"Oh, he's a financial *whiz*, he truly is. You should see his place up in Northwest. It's like a palace. All from his clever investing."

And, undoubtedly, Burke's design and contracting, but I didn't want to ask. For some reason, Frank had always seemed to be the favorite in the family. Certainly he was viewed as the smarter of the two brothers, which was important in a family that valued cunning over something as unreliable as physical beauty, which Burke had in spades. But whenever the accolades were handed out, they went to Frank first, then leftovers were nudged in Burke's direction.

I'd often wondered if he noticed that, but I hadn't wanted to ask him, for fear that he hadn't and my pointing it out would create paranoia about something previously unconsidered.

"I'm glad he's doing well," I said sincerely, setting my book of measurements down with the picture of the dress she wanted.

"And I'm very happy for you, Dottie. It's wonderful to see you so happy." Impulsively, I moved toward her and gave her a hug.

Morrisons aren't huggers—actually, Bartons aren't really either—but she patted my shoulder awkwardly, just as she had my arm earlier. The same way she would have any of the fine-bloodlined horses they'd once raised. "Quinn, I appreciate your congratulations. I wish things could have worked out back then, but . . ." Her voice trailed off, leaving the echo of her implication: *You had to go and ruin it. But I forgive you.*

"But they *did* work out," I said, more brightly than I felt. "Everyone's doing great. Every one of us is doing great."

She made a noise of disagreement, but I didn't know what it meant.

"Well, the boys are coming over for supper on Saturday night to talk about the details of the move and the sale. I wish you'd come join us. You're always so lively and fun and I have a feeling, with Burke there being surly about it all, it's not going to be that much fun."

Oh, I had a big picture of how that would go. Suffice it to say, I wasn't going to be improving Burke's mood anytime soon. Nor he, mine. We hadn't talked since I'd tossed, *"And the horse you rode in on!"* over my shoulder at the church that day, after the guests had left and he'd offered qualified denials and made admissions I think I'd still, to that moment, hoped he wouldn't. Couldn't.

No, I didn't want to see Burke Morrison.

Ever again.

And I couldn't really imagine facing Frank either. It seemed like 90 percent of my moments with Frank had involved profound humiliation on my part.

"I'm tied up Saturday," I lied. "But thanks. Plus, as you know, I have a very important project to work on now, so I need as few distractions as possible."

"You really think you're going to have enough time? Those little bitty roses look like they're going to take *forever* to glue on there!"

I shook my head and followed her to the door. "A couple of stiches each, it'll be fine." Though she was right, it was going to be time-consuming.

But with what was apparently going to be a sustained amount of time with *the boys* in town, I was thinking my being otherwise occupied was going to be a very good thing.

"Oh! One more thing!" She stopped and opened her purse and pulled a small piece of blue ribbon out of it. "Can you sew this inside somewhere? Maybe the hem or something?"

I took it. It was soft, well-worn satin. Like the kind of thing you'd find in tatters on a well-loved baby blanket. "Sure. Like maybe in the hem?"

"That sounds grand."

"What is it?"

She hesitated and sighed. "That little blue ribbon was on the front of my dress when I married Joss," she said.

"Oooh." Involuntarily, I put my hand to my heart.

"I know that's probably inappropriate, that's why I want it hidden, but"—her voice grew quieter—"we had forty happy years together. If Lyle and I can have a few years half as happy, I will be over the moon."

"Wow," I said. "I think that's really nice."

"You think we Morrisons aren't very romantic, and you're probably right for the most part. We're bullheaded, selfish, and too prideful for anyone's good. But inside, we *do* have hearts. Sometimes tender ones, at that."

With that, she winked and went out the door.

Chapter 3

The legend of Bridezillas is not exaggerated.

We've all seen the shows, the viral videos, etc., where the overly tanned, thin, white-toothed bitch shrieks and yells at her bridesmaids, mother, and hapless fiancé over stupid things like whether or not the icing bow on her shower cake is Tiffany blue, as she requested, or just robin's-egg blue.

And those brides exist, trust me, I've seen plenty of them.

But there's another breed that is much more subtle, and much more dangerous.

Mindy Garrett was one of them.

Her gown was a simple sleeveless wrap of cream satin, with a fitted bodice and heavy drape from the waist down. It would have been beautiful on anyone, but on her it was particularly gorgeous because she had a body so sarcastically hot, I wouldn't be surprised if MATTEL was stamped on her spray-tanned ass.

But, as she stood on the bridal stage looking at her perfection from all angles in a triptych mirror, her little bow mouth turned down at the edges.

"What's wrong?" her maid of honor, Wendy something, asked.

"I'm so fat." Mindy raked a mean glance over her own image and took a small, wavering breath.

I exchanged a look with Becca, my right hand at the shop—a harried mother of three boys under eight and who had little patience for foolishness or b.s.—and she was clearly trying not to laugh.

"No, you're *not*." Wendy hurried over to her and put her arms around her. "You are *so beautiful*. Do we really need to go over this again? You were the homecoming queen two years in a row, which you *know* never happens, you won Junior Miss Virginia a year younger than anyone ever did before, and then your boss, who *everyone* thought was so handsome, fell for *you* and took you out of the office and gave you that gorgeous ring!" She lifted Mindy's limp left hand—which must have taken some muscle, given the size of the rock on it—and tipped it so the facets dazzled under the light. "You have a charmed life."

Mindy looked at her friend with big, liquid blue eyes, her lip trembling ever so slightly. "You're just saying that. He's going to realize I'm a fatty and dump me."

I hoped he'd realize she was a manipulator and dump her, but both eventualities seemed to have the same zero likelihood.

"Do we need to let the waistline out some?" I asked helpfully.

Her response was predictable. She turned a sharp eye on me (actually her friend did too; she had a better fiancé *and* a better best friend than she might have deserved) and said, "No, I don't need you to let it out. It fits fine. For now. But I'm just worried about what's going to happen." She looked down at the floor and I wondered if she used Latisse or something like that to make her lashes so long and dark.

Honestly, she knew all her angles, knew just how to look her most fetchingly attractive no matter what she was griping about and who was viewing her.

I wanted to tell her I could elasticize the waist, but she knew I was on to her, and that would have been unprofessionally obnoxious, so I held back.

Business had been somewhat rough lately and I couldn't afford to alienate *any* customers, not even ones who popped in to buy a single pair of silk stockings.

Talk of the Gown was the only job I'd ever had, and all of my money was tied up in it. If it failed . . . well, I didn't know what I'd do. I couldn't bear to think of it.

The bells over the door tinkled, and we all looked at the tall, dark, slightly funny-looking man who walked in. I mean, I'm sorry to say it, but it was true. His lips were a little too bubble-ish for a man, and his nose seemed like it was placed slightly too far to the left.

But his bank account was, I imagine, a very beautiful thing to behold. He walked with the swagger of a man who'd never had to care much how he looked.

"Oh, thank goodness Lee's here," Wendy cooed.

"No!" Mindy shrieked. "He can't see me in my dress! Close your eyes, Lee!"

He stopped and made a show of putting his hand over his eyes.

Becca took a shawl over to Mindy and she covered herself with it, at least enough so that he couldn't see more than a peek of satin at the bottom, and there was no giveaway in that, almost anyone expects a wedding dress to be made of fabric something like that.

"Can I look?" he boomed.

"Yes, but not too closely," Mindy cooed.

He took his hand off his eyes and Wendy immediately said, "Lee, please tell Mindy she's not fat!"

Lee furrowed his brow. "Fat? That's crazy."

"Quinn just said she should let the waist of my dress out some." Mindy gestured limply toward me, but didn't look in my direction. She didn't need to. She, like I, felt all eyes land on me like bugs.

You're welcome for the shawl, Whinestein, I thought.

"What I said"—I met Lee's eyes, because I knew, no matter what a snot she was going to be to me, Mindy flipping *loved* that dress, knew it looked amazing on her, and wasn't going to take a chance on having to find another one three weeks from the wedding—"was that if the dress was uncomfortable in any way, as she was saying, we could make alterations to accommodate her no matter what."

Understanding came into his eyes and he turned to his bride. "Mindy, honey? Are you thinking you look anything less than stunning in your dress?"

She pressed her lips together for a moment, then said, slowly blinking her dewy eyes, "I just don't want to disappoint you."

"You could never disappoint me," he said, moving in and putting his big bear paw around her, patting her awkwardly as he did so.

She began to weep delicately. Tearlessly.

With dry sniffles.

Wendy looked fretful and gnawed on her thumbnail. I'd actually noticed she did that a lot when she got uncomfortable.

This was not the first time I'd seen it.

"Stop this now," Lee said, exchanging a quick panicked glance with Wendy. "Honey? Min, listen, how about you go over to Calloway's and pick out something so sparkly you won't be able to see or think about anything else?"

Calloway's was the town jeweler. It had been here for eighty-some years, and people came from the entire metro area to get their jewelry designed and reset by Dick Calloway, now the third-generation owner, because he'd taken the little place and put it on the map with mentions in *Vogue*, *People*, and *Vanity Fair*.

Calloway's was an excellent cure for whatever ailed any spoiled rich woman.

Mindy was no exception. I saw the smallest shift in her posture. A straightening he probably didn't notice or perceived as cuddling in. But that wasn't what it was. It was triumph.

It was clear in her still-dry eyes when she looked at him. "Are you sure?"

"Am I— of *course* I'm sure!"

She gave what I was sure was meant to look—and *did* to him and Wendy, I was certain—like a brave little smile. "Ohhh, you are so good to me."

He gave an indulgent chuckle. "I hope you're still saying that when we're in the poorhouse."

She didn't answer. Of course she didn't answer. She was not accompanying *anyone* to the poorhouse. If things started to look like they were heading in that direction, she would turn her Christian Louboutins in a new direction and keep walking, without looking back, until she'd found a new mark.

Lee took a black card out of his wallet and handed it to her.

She looked at it, poked her bottom lip out a little farther, and asked, "When am I getting the one with *my* name on it?" The nontears threatened again.

Talk about an artist!

"As soon as you have your new name," he answered, begging the question of whether or not he knew the deal he was making as well as she did. There was no way to tell for sure. He gave her a final squeeze and came over to me.

She didn't even watch him go, but, instead, looked down at the card, then shared a smile with Wendy, though I honestly think, where Mindy's smile looked calculating, Wendy's just showed relief that her "poor, sweet friend" was feeling better now.

Lee indicated I should follow him to the door, and when we got there, he asked, very quietly, "*Does* the dress need alterations?"

"Of course not." I couldn't believe he'd actually fallen for that for even a moment. Didn't he see her body in the buff every night? I felt like that was part of the price she'd be paying for this marriage.

At least until it was over.

But maybe he didn't. Maybe the promise of it was the prize he was expecting for marrying her.

"If that need should arise," he said, so quietly I almost had to move in to hear him, though I didn't want to get any closer than I had to, thanks to his mildewy breath, "I want you to tell her it's loose and you need to take it *in*, not out."

"If the dress gets too tight, she's not going to believe me if I say it's too loose."

"Then tell her you did something wrong. Cut it wrong or something. Made it two sizes smaller than it's supposed to be. Whatever it takes. I don't want her upset about *anything* before her big day."

Which told me, right there, she was probably going to be "upset" about a great many things before her big day.

"I'll do my best," I told him.

"See that you do and I'll make it well worth your while." He gave me a look like we were sharing a secret, then, before I could object—because I do object to idiotic bribery—he gave a conspiratorial nod and called, over me, "Get on over there before it closes, babe."

"I will," Mindy said, then, for good measure, sniffled.

Lee gave me a wink and went out into the night, just as my friend Glenn Ryland came out of the door of his shop next door—a cheese shop called the Mouse Trap—and headed for mine, holding a bottle of wine and, as usual, a platter of cheese.

I held the door open for him and he came in.

"We'd better hurry," Mindy was saying urgently to Wendy, all of her meekness gone. Wendy was apparently taking too long to unzip the dress. "Come on, come *on*."

"Got it." Wendy pulled the small zipper down and the dress fell from Mindy's perfect body and pooled on the floor at her feet. She didn't even care that Glenn, a complete stranger and a man to boot, was here, she was just determined to get to the jewelry store before it closed. "Pick that up for me?"

"Sure!" Wendy scurried to do her friend's bidding.

I guess all these people got a charge out of pleasing Mindy, maybe because it was so hard to do that it felt like an accomplishment for them every time.

At that point, Mindy went into the dressing room and got her street clothes on so quickly it seemed like a magic trick. Her maid of honor put the dress back on its hanger and carefully hung it up, gently tugging it so it wouldn't wrinkle. For a moment, the gesture was so soft and loving that I was struck by what felt, or at least looked, like raw longing.

But the moment was over quickly when Mindy bolted from the dressing room and grabbed her friend's arm. "Let's go, this is going to be *so* much fun! Thanks, Quinn," she singsonged, then, spotting the platter Glenn had brought, "Oh, yum, cheese! Can I have a bite? I'm absolutely *famished*."

So much for her supposed weight concerns.

"Go right ahead," Glenn said.

I'd tell him the story later.

I was pretty sure he'd regret having given Mindy the free cheese then. He didn't have much patience for ninnies.

Both of the women took little handfuls of cheese and left, all traces of accusation and misery blown away by the wind of commerce that would carry them down the block and around the corner to the land of diamonds and platinum.

Chapter 4

Thirty minutes later, after Becca had left for the night in a frenzy, shouting, "Find the ipecac and make him puke it up, the little idiot!" into her phone, I'd locked the door and was halfway into my second glass of wine, beginning to unwind. "Oh, my god, this is *amazing*! What *is* it?"

This was how I began almost all of my deep conversations with Glenn, because after closing—my shop, and his next door—he always brought over either the leftover samples he'd had out during the day or something new I'd never tried before.

"Fromager d'Affinois." He put a smear of it on a little square piece of toast and handed it to me.

"So, it's like Brie?"

"It's Brie on steroids."

He was right. It was Brie-times-twenty in the "creamy" department. I was sure it was worse than drinking melted butter, but it tasted *amazing* and I needed a little distraction. Culinary distraction was all the better.

"Have you heard," he jumped right in, "about the dry cleaner across the street?"

A dry cleaner had gone into a space that had been empty for *years* about two months ago. I'd hoped our businesses could be complementary, but the owner was a real jerk. Truth be told, I'd expected them to have gone out of business as quickly as they'd gone in, but for some reason they had a lot of traffic in and out.

"What, are they a front for the Mafia?" I asked, only half kidding. There had to be a reason such a sour man could stay in business.

"*No*, they have a *seamstress* in there who is making knockoffs of celebrity dresses!"

This didn't compute. "What?"

"You know, like Stella McCartney's Colorblock dress, everything Kate Middleton ever wore, *including* her wedding dress . . ." He raised an eyebrow.

"Oh, my god, they're taking my clients?"

He nodded. "Bringing people in from far and wide for a cheap version of an expensive designer gown. You should look at the reviews on Yelp." He shook his head. "We've got to shut them down."

"But . . . I make *personalized* one-of-a-kind dresses. I've built my reputation on figuring out the perfect look for every special occasion. I was in *Southern Living*, for Pete's sake. . . ." I was arguing, but there was no argument. A dress shop with high overhead and stock probably couldn't have come in across the street to

compete with me, but a tiny hole-in-the-wall dry cleaner with an underpaid seamstress?

Maybe that was the reason my revenues were going down.

How had I missed that?

"Her name is Taney," Glenn said. "We need to run her out of town."

"Stop," I said, but laughed. "I consider this a call to action. I've got to do better than my best. If I up my game, cheap knockoffs can't possibly compete."

He nodded. "They shouldn't. But I'll keep a baseball bat around just in case you want me to go for her kneecaps. Or, better still, her knuckles."

"I don't think that'll be necessary. That reminds me. You will never guess who came in today *for a wedding dress*."

He looked immediately intrigued, his brow furrowed slightly over his piercing dark eyes. He was hot in a way so classic that most womens' gaydars didn't even blip. "Is it worth even trying to guess?"

"No."

He laughed. "Tell me."

"Dottie Morrison."

"Dottie Morrison?" He looked blank. "What's the punch line?"

"No punch line." I smiled and shook my head. "I'm being completely serious."

"*Who* is she marrying?"

"That's the best part! Some younger guy, claims he's independently wealthy and an artist and blah blah blah." I had more cheese. I was going to gain ten pounds tonight alone unless the inner

trembling that had begun when Dottie told me about the farm burned it all off. "I mean, I don't know, maybe he's totally on the up and up. There was something I kind of liked about his face, and she's certainly charming. . . . There's no reason a handsome younger man *wouldn't* be interested in her." I shrugged. "But of course it has all the hallmarks of a Very Special *Golden Girls* episode, doesn't it?"

"Or a *48 Hours* mystery. 'She was the town character in a town full of characters, but two weeks after she married Juan deHotti, she vanished, leaving nothing behind but a broken bottle of illegal absinthe and questions. . . .'"

"Absinthe?"

He nodded. "Dottie Morrison would never do anything in an ordinary way."

"So there would have to be a hallucinogenic involved?"

"Obviously." Another smear on another toast, another inch on my hips when he handed it to me. "So this begs the obvious question. Are you going to the wedding, whereupon you will finally see your Achilles' heels again?"

No point in pretending I didn't know who or what he was talking about. "No. Well, *probably*."

"And that's why there's this subtle little shadow in your eyes tonight?"

Leave it to a gay man to be so perfectly attentive. "Yes, but it's not just that. She's selling the farm"—I felt an unexpected catch in my throat as I said the words—"and they're going to be here for the next month or so cleaning it out."

He held up a finger. "Hang on. This is going to require wine." He looked at what remained of the cheese. "And Stilton. None of

this wimpy stuff. I'll be right back." He got up from where we were sitting cross-legged on the floor of my shop and slipped out the front door, leaving the bells to tinkle emptily after him.

And I felt alone.

Sometimes it would come over me. Not often, but sometimes the Monster Thought I tried to avoid would sneak up on me and roar to life when I was just sitting there minding my own business, thinking about something else entirely.

I was alone. Not just at this moment, but in my life. Yes, it had been a choice. A decision I'd made after the Burke-Frank fiasco. Yes, I'd had *dates* along the way, I wasn't a nun, but I never got too close to anyone. Truth be told, I was never even tempted. Maybe in some small space deep inside I *wanted* to be tempted. I couldn't imagine myself being the kind of woman who, faced with the perfect man who could offer a lifetime of fun and companionship, would put her hands up and say, *Whoa, no way. I am not interested in being happy.*

But I didn't know. Because at thirty-one I still hadn't met someone who came close. And I knew thirty-one wasn't old, even though crossing the line of thirty had felt significant to me, and I knew it wasn't too late, it's never too late, Dottie was proving that right now. I knew all the things I'd say to a friend who was saying the same things I was right now, but here, in the dim quiet of the shop, I was very aware that I might spend my whole life just exactly like this. Seasons passing predictably. Perfect fall days, icy winter nights, muggy summer mornings, I'd see a million of them. I'd already seen a million of them. Some of them brought good things, some bad, most *meh*. But *years* could slip away like that.

When I was growing up, the only thing I ever really wanted—my only *dream*, if you will—was to be just like my mom. To get married and have children and shop for back-to-school clothes, and bake Christmas cookies, and dye Easter eggs, and plan birthday parties, and have peaceful nights and sitcom neighbors. I thought I'd have a husband I could count on as a partner, the way my mom could my dad, someone to watch TV with, play tennis badly with, read in bed with before switching out the lights and sleeping the sleep of the contented with.

And, of course, work in the shop during the day. Very often my mother would take her handwork home and do it while watching *Survivor* or *The Amazing Race* with my dad, but there never seemed to be a lot of stress or friction in her life. She lived exactly the way you'd imagine the perfect woman in a detergent commercial lived—simple, easily satisfied, always wise, rarely disappointed.

They still lived like that now, though they'd moved to a suburb of Tampa four and a half years ago, leaving me to take over the shop. Now Mom puttered around the house, making projects of repurposing objects and turning them into shabby chic works of art. She got ideas from magazines and HGTV, and from the many overpriced shops that sold those kinds of things all along the wealthy corridors of beachside towns of Florida's Gulf Coast.

I'd given up the dream of having the same idyllically domestic life a long time ago, but I'd never really replaced it with a *new* dream. I carried on day to day, and I was doing fine, but there were no huge *ups*.

I wanted a few huge ups.

Yet I was never an *Eat Pray Love* kind of girl. My adventurous spirit had its only roots in digging around old "haunted" houses in the neighborhood as a kid and taking the occasional weekend in New York or Atlantic City or Rehoboth Beach now. I wasn't a soul-searcher.

I was boring. I wasn't dead, of course, but I wasn't really *living* either.

The bells over the door chimed and Glenn came in with a large bottle of white wine; two glasses; and a tray of cheese, crackers, and cured meats that looked like it had been put together by Martha Stewart herself.

"I need to go to an ashram," I told him as he sat down in front of me.

He scoffed. "You wouldn't even make it out of Chhatrapati Shivaji."

"Huh?"

"The airport in Mumbai." Glenn didn't often flaunt his worldliness, but he'd been all over the place and he'd seen and done more in his thirty-two years than most people did in a lifetime. Every once in a while, after a couple of drinks, he'd tell a story of something that had happened to him or someone he'd met that would be so outrageous there was no way to *not* believe it.

Me, on the other hand . . . say "Mumbai" to me and I think *Hey Mambo*. He was right, there was no way I was ever going to be any sort of adventuress, when I couldn't even book a flight knowledgeably.

He pointed to a blue cheese and added, "Try this with the fig jam."

I did. It was fantastic. Of course.

"You know what you never talk about?" Glenn was assembling little samples of cheese, condiments, and crackers and pushing them in front of me.

"Charpi Shivaji?"

"*Chhatrapati* Shivaji, and yes, but no. You never talk about Frank Morrison. Or Burke. What the hell really happened there?"

Glenn had grown up here and gone to high school with all of us, he'd even been on the football team with Burke, but he'd gone to college abroad and spent a couple of additional years living in Manhattan before moving back and opening the Mouse Trap. We hadn't really been that close in high school, but we'd been the best of pals since his return, so it was hard to remember sometimes that he hadn't been here for it all. That he didn't already know it.

"You know what happened. I was on my way to marry Burke when Frank told me he'd been cheating on me and I couldn't trust him. Called off the wedding, had a brief, ill-advised relationship with Frank, and, boom, end of Morrisons. End of story."

"There." He pointed at me. "That right there. Elaborate on this brief, ill-advised relationship with Frank."

I sighed. I just hated thinking about this stuff. Which, okay, right there was probably a clue that I hadn't really worked it out. But I was happier not thinking about it. Why keep poking the bruise?

"You know how they say the best way to get over a man is to get under another one?"

Glenn laughed. I think he'd said that himself on more than one occasion, though sometimes making lewd variations of the expression. "I am familiar with the expression, yes."

"Well, it ain't always true. When I left the church that day, the day of the wedding that would have changed my whole damn life, I was beyond heartbroken. I was numb. That day, and for a lot of days afterward, I wished, more than anything, that I hadn't heard anything, that I'd gone on with the wedding and with my life in ignorant bliss. If the stories were true but he was faithful once we were married, was there ultimately any harm?"

"Hard to say. If you never knew and it never happened again, it's like that stupid tree falling in the woods, isn't it? If the next chapter, or the next six chapters, or however you look at a married rest-of-your-life and all the things that follow, was what you thought it was, maybe it *didn't* matter what happened before."

I shrugged. "I don't think I'll ever know the answer to that."

"But you knew, for sure, that what Frank said to you was true."

"Actually, to this day I don't know the extent of it. But I do know that in the heated five minutes we spent in the rectory, he admitted that he *had* had one or two indiscretions. He said it was while we were broken up, but we were *always* breaking up and making up, there was never any reason to believe it."

"The old 'we were on a break' from *Friends*."

"Exactly! Now it's in our lexicon forever. Shorthand for someone fucking up and someone else either having to forgive or not forgive."

Glenn put a piece of cheese in his mouth and chewed thoughtfully. "There is another possibility. Maybe he bought it every time you dumped him. Maybe he *believed* you every time you got fed up, or had a drama queen moment, and walked away. Some guys do, you know. Guys see what's directly in front of them and act from there. It's a biological difference between our brains."

"Yeah, there are a *lot* of biological differences in our brains. Men can have meaningless sex too."

"True." He put his hand on my arm and made me look into his eyes. "That's *true*."

"I'll never understand that."

"No, you probably won't. When you filter the act through your own brain, you cannot make it mean anything less than love, and, honey, that hurts so much more as a betrayal, doesn't it?"

A lump formed in my throat. Why, after all these years, I didn't know. It embarrassed me and I swallowed hard. "No."

Silence bloomed between us.

"You know what the last thing he said to me was?"

"What?"

"There's gum on your ass."

Glenn laughed. "*What?*"

"There was. I'd sat in gum and it ruined my dress. It and everything else I'd sat in, but the gum was the biggest insult and that was his parting shot of, and *at*, me. *There's gum on your ass.* It was so typical of him I almost laughed. But he was *always* able to make me laugh, even when I was most livid at him, so if I'd laughed, that would have been like giving in, saying it was all okay, when I knew it would never be okay again."

"I'm sorry. This iceberg goes deeper than I thought."

Deeper than I'd thought too. I couldn't think about that day with Burke. Couldn't do it. Right or wrong, good or bad, it was too painful. I closed my eyes for a moment, then said, "Anyway. Frank. I don't think he meant to be as artful as he was, manipulating me, I think he really thought he was being sincere in trying to warn me not to make a mistake."

Glenn raised an eyebrow. "But he got the girl?"

"No. I moved back home. Didn't run off down the aisle with him, as great as a *fuck you* as that would have been to Burke—"

"Which I'm sure he offered to do."

I shook my head. "No, he didn't, actually. He didn't." I thought about it. I'd always thought he would have, given the chance. He was interested, probably, but he never actually *said* so, so maybe that was all my vanity in play, no reality at all.

"So how did you feel about him?"

"Well, it's funny, I had a crush on Burke before I discovered Frank. I was fifteen at the time, so he seemed much more sophisticated than Burke or me. And he *was*, actually. Did you know him in high school?"

"I really didn't."

"Well, he was pretty much always sixty-three years old, you know? Very serious. Very *smart*." I shook my head. "Man, that guy is *smart*." That was part of his appeal for me, and I realized why at this moment. "He was the kind of guy who seemed like he could take care of things. Anything. Everything. So when I was broken and vulnerable, I think I wanted him to take care of me."

Glenn handed me a cracker. "It would have been an easy way out of heartbreak."

"If it had worked."

"It never works."

"No easy outs."

We laughed, but neither of us really meant it. Heartbreak sucks and we both knew it.

"So you guys, what, dated? Was it serious?"

I shook my head. "One night. Well, I don't know, it was a few drunk nights in a row, but only one . . . *night*. You know."

He looked nonplussed. "I have no idea what you're talking about."

"We drove to Vegas and I started drinking, starting with some Bud Lights from the 7-Eleven on 15, and didn't sober up till we got back. The first night, in some Hampton Inn off the highway, I was hammered and upset and I just . . ." I shook my head and gestured. "We did it, and . . ." I shrugged.

Glenn raised an eyebrow. "And it was good?"

I nodded. It was. "It *was*."

"But you didn't do it again."

"Well . . ."

"So the next night in Vegas you did it again."

I felt the pink rise into my cheeks. "Okay, yes, but that was *it*. That was all. After that I began to feel really guilty for doing that to Burke."

"After what he did to you."

"I *know*!"

"So . . . how *was* Frank? Any good?"

Oh, yeah. That was both my private shame *and* my private glee. "Frank Morrison is hotter than you think. He was hotter than *I* thought. Very . . . *skilled*."

"So it wasn't a mistake."

I shrugged. "I was young and hormonal and angry." I laughed. "And I think it kind of helped. It didn't *cure* me, obviously, but . . ." I shook my head, remembering. Pretty vividly. "It sure didn't suck."

"Wow! Why didn't you stick with it, then?"

"That wouldn't have been fair to Frank. How could it be, really, coming right off an engagement to *his brother*? Almost a marriage. Certainly a life I had been planning on for years. It was crazy to think I could just switch gears that way and pretend Thing Number One had never existed and just go with Thing Number Two. Especially since they were so close, obviously, so that Burke would always exist. I'd always hear about him, which would forever keep him between Frank and me. This wasn't exactly like taking off and starting a new life."

Glenn nodded. "That is the worst thing about having mutual friends after a breakup. Hearing about the person. Wanting to, not wanting to, sometimes happening upon information you never wanted or needed to know."

"Like that Burke was dating Sarah Lynn."

"He did not!"

Sarah Lynn was my archnemesis in high school. She was a regional tennis star, I was hopelessly shy. She had glossy dark hair, versus my yellow-blond. There was an air of money about her, which was because she came from a moneyed, aristocratic family, while I was in the right zip code with the wrong tax bracket. Which, I think, was what she didn't like about me. I wasn't up to her standards, even just to be a classmate or neighbor. It was as simple as that.

I'd ferreted her out on Facebook not too long ago—we had thirteen mutual friends, so I was sure she got, and ignored, the suggestions that we might know each other just like I did—and she looked spectacular.

Of course.

"I think they went out for, like, three weeks or something, but yeah, he did that."

"I can't think of that girl without remembering that party at Chris Stein's house."

I was drawing a blank. "What party? What happened?" I was imagining her getting up in front of everyone, doing something spectacular that no one knew she could do. Sing like an *American Idol* favorite; flip like an Olympic gymnast; save the life of a choking guest better than Dr. Oz could have.

"Oh, you know this story," Glenn said. "When she went behind some bushes to pee and didn't realize she was right under a spotlight and being projected on one of the security cameras? Which, as it happened, were being projected onto a big screen as live party shots?"

My jaw dropped. I loved this story unreasonably, given how long it had been since this had happened, since we had any sort of "rivalry" at all, and how mature I really should be now. "You're making this up."

"Could I make this up?"

"No one could make this up."

"Certainly not me."

We were a sitcom. A well-timed duo of shorthand, back and forth. In a way, it was a shame he was gay, because we might have been the perfect couple.

I took another sip of wine. "I like that story."

"I'm not surprised." He tilted his head and assessed me, à la the RCA dog. "Why does he still get to you? How could Sarah Lynn possibly still matter to you?"

It was a good question. Was my life, my *world*, so small that what happened ten years ago might as well have happened last week?

Yes. Yes, it was.

Because, like I said, I'm not an *Eat Pray Love* girl. I'm not an adventuress. I am, I hate to say it, in too many ways timid. Ten years ago could feel like last week because last week wasn't that different from ten years ago.

I was in a rut and I said that to Glenn.

"I am *so* glad you finally see that," he said, sounding insultingly relieved. "I've been worried."

I frowned. "I'm sorry?"

He obviously got it. "No offense."

"Oh, none taken," I said dryly.

"Quinn, when was the last time you left this town?"

"I was in Dupont Circle last weekend!"

Exasperated sigh. "This *whole* town." He gestured broadly. "When was the last time you left this country?"

"You know I can't do that! I have the shop to take care of!"

"Well, you need to do *something*, because you're becoming Grandma Walton here."

"Thanks."

"What about just a weekend trip? A weekend in Paris?"

It didn't even appeal to me. Can you believe the words "a weekend in Paris" could not appeal to someone? That was me! I felt homesick just thinking about it.

He was right, I needed a change. Quick.

"Among other things," I said, "I have Dottie's dress to make, and the time is already going to be tight."

He pressed his lips together and thought for a moment. "Here's what I'm going to do," he said, in a voice that told me I wasn't going to be able to argue. I'd heard that voice before. "I'm going to give you a task a day for the next month, just a little something you have to do during the day. Sometimes it will be an all-day thing, like wearing clown makeup . . ."

"I'm not doing that."

". . . and sometimes it will be something quick, like throwing a tomato at a passing car."

"You're crazy."

"Those aren't *real* examples. I've got to come up with thirty of these suckers, so it's going to take some consideration."

I laughed. "And what is the point of all this?"

"To broaden your horizons. To make you do things in a different way. Think differently. Just be something a little bit different than Quinn. Not that I don't love Quinn," he was quick to add. "I do. But she needs a little change."

"It's true, she does." I had to agree.

He stood up. "This seems like the perfect note to end on, then." He stretched and looked at his watch. "I'll have your first assignment for you tomorrow."

Chapter 5

September, Seventeen Years Ago

The entire school smelled like the church rectory: a mix of new carpeting, cheap cafeteria food in tin containers, some good intentions, and a whole lot of fear.

High school.

Quinn took a deep breath outside the blue front doors, ignoring the rush of bodies bumping past her, and tried to gather her courage.

Middle school had been hard at first too, she reminded herself. All the new people from three different elementary schools pooling into one. Lockers. Linoleum floors. No paste, scissors, construction paper, little kids. There were no hand turkeys taped to the wall at Thanksgiving there, though a little room had still been allowed for ugly parent-chosen clothes and cardigan sweaters, at least at first.

But in high school, she had to get it right and she was already afraid she had it wrong. Was her Blink-182 T-shirt all wrong for this crowd? Were her faded Levi's from Gap uncool? She should have gotten new shoes, because she'd had these running shoes for so long they were more like slippers now.

"Quinn!"

Oh, thank god! Someone she knew! She turned to see her friend Jackie coming toward her, all tan and leggy and Jennifer-Aniston-y in cutoff shorts, slip-ons, and a plain white T-shirt. That had been a good choice. Who could criticize plain white?

"Hey," Quinn said, putting on a smile even though she suddenly felt like crying. This was too much. She was overwhelmed. There were going to be more people she *didn't* know here than she did, and she wasn't very good at being outgoing.

"Are you just *so psyched*?"

Quinn grimaced. "I'm nervous."

"Oh, please. Why? Do you know how many new hotties we're going to meet? You know you haven't had a boyfriend until you've had your first *high school* boyfriend."

Easy for her to say. She'd had, like, four boyfriends in middle school.

"I haven't had a boyfriend at all."

"Oh, that's right." Jackie shrugged. "So you're going to have your first boyfriend. Come on, don't stand out here like a freak, let's go in." She tugged on Quinn's arm.

"What's your locker number?" Quinn asked.

"Um . . ." Jackie paused to open her purse and took out a piece of paper. "Eight-fifty. What about yours?"

"Eight twenty-nine. Hopefully they're near each other."

"God, I can't believe how scared you are! This is *awesome*. We're in *high school*! Stop being such a wimp!"

They followed the signs on the wall to the eight hundred corridor and, fortunately for Quinn, their lockers *were* near each other. Opposite sides of the hall, and maybe six yards apart, but that was better than being on totally different floors.

Quinn went to her assigned locker and used the combination she'd memorized, though she noticed everyone else had brought their orientation papers and were referring to them. Apparently she was the only one who had been so nervous about today that she had committed every single thing they'd sent to memory. She knew where each and every classroom was, on A days and B days (today was B, weirdly), and she knew every teacher's name. She'd even looked up the lunch menu in advance so she knew what she'd pick and exactly how much it would cost.

She put all her books but math in the locker, then took the Disney World magnet from her purse that she'd brought to stick to the door. It was Woody and Buzz from *Toy Story*. When she'd chosen it, it had felt familiar and comforting, it had made her smile, but now it just looked babyish. She considered it for a moment, then decided she just wasn't cool enough to pull off the retro act, so she pulled it off and was about to put it in her purse when the girl at the locker next to her said, "Oh, I love Buzz!"

"I'm sorry?" Quinn asked, not quite connecting the obvious dots. Her first thought was that maybe drugs were as rampant here as her mother had warned.

The girl gestured at the magnet. "Buzz Lightyear. That was my favorite movie when I was a kid."

"Oh." Quinn smiled. "Mine too." Then she had the vague thought that maybe the girl was baiting her, setting her up for some sort of Mean Girl prank.

But that would be just so lame as far as pranks went.

"I'm Rami, by the way." The girl smiled and pushed her hand through her thick red hair, though it fell right back in front of her face. "What's your name?"

"Quinn Barton." Whole name. She might as well have extended a stiff arm and asked, *How do you do? Would you like some crumpets and tea?*

Rami nodded like that was something to understand and she understood it. "Looks like we're locker roomies this year. Are you in ninth grade?"

Quinn's face colored. Of course it was obvious she was in ninth grade, but it still embarrassed her that it was *that* obvious. Like she was wearing a beanie with a spinner on top. "Yes."

"I'm in tenth. I hated ninth. Well, the first couple of weeks of ninth. I came from Montessori school, so I was freaked out about all the people here."

"I know what you mean."

"Don't worry," Rami said, shrugging. "You'll get used to it." Her eyes darted behind Quinn. "There's a lot of good stuff here." She nodded toward something in the hall.

Quinn turned and saw nothing but people. Just teenagers. All from central casting. "What am I looking at?" she asked.

"Ummm . . . hottie alert. *Burke Morrison.*" Rami sighed dramatically. "Yummy."

Quinn looked again, at faces this time, rather than the intimidating throng, and it was clear there was only one person Rami could have meant. A guy with dark hair, tanned skin, bright blue eyes, and a confident swagger that could have made up for the lack of any and all of the rest.

As soon as she looked at him, his eyes met hers, and she looked down quickly, knowing that, as usual, her face had gone bright red in that instant. She was embarrassed way too easily and the fact that it showed up so quickly and unmistakably embarrassed her further.

"Who is he?"

"Seriously?"

What could she say to that? "Yes."

"He and his brother live on Grace Farms with their grandparents. Fastest horses and coolest guys in Middleburg. I can't even believe you've never heard of them."

"I'm not really part of that . . . set." Was *set* even the right word? The Horsey Set. Maybe that was something only old people said. She'd certainly heard it quite a few times. From old people.

If that was a faux pas, Rami didn't seem to notice. "They're kind of hard to miss here. Oh, there's Frank." She pointed. "Blue shirt, black backpack."

Quinn looked. She never would have picked Frank out as Burke's brother, that was for sure. Where Burke's face was square-jawed and chiseled, Frank's was thinner and almost pretty. Undeniably masculine, but there was something slightly more delicate about his features, though his eyes were harder by far. Kind of that Clint Eastwood thing, when he was threatening people in a Western. It was attractive, but also a little intimidating.

Which was interesting, because his eyes were the thing that took his look from soft to hard, where the warm light in Burke's eyes was the thing that took his look from hard to soft. Or soft*er*.

Both of them were attractive. It just depended on whether you liked your hotness in guys obvious or more subtle.

The bell rang.

"That means I'm already late." Rami laughed. "You too. Nice to meet you! I'm sure I'll be seeing you around quite a bit!"

Quinn fumbled with her math book while at the same time closing the locker door without everything spilling out. "Nice to meet you too. Thanks for the rundown!"

The doors to the cafeteria were closed until the second bell rang. Quinn stood in the crowd in the hallway, looking anxiously for Jackie or for *anyone* she knew from middle school who might sit with her. She'd always hated musical chairs, and that was exactly what this felt like. A game of musical chairs that would determine her standing for the next four years of high school.

Sit with someone and you can, at the very least, go unnoticed until something calls attention to you.

Sit alone, and you are a Loser for Life. Or at least a loser for the lifetime of your school tenure, which might as well be life. She'd seen it happen to Barbara Klepding in sixth grade and she didn't want to be the Barbara Klepding of high school.

Of course, Barbara Klepding had provided herself with plenty of other fodder for mockery, it had to be said. Her constant and all-too-public hula performances of "Pearly Shells" after her family trip to Hawaii—no matter who asked or how many snickers accompanied the request—didn't help her popularity much. Nor did her incessant harping about sodium nitrates in the school lunches, when no one knew what sodium nitrates were but everyone liked hot dogs.

Still, standing in the crowd outside the cafeteria, Quinn couldn't quell the thrum of fear that beat in her chest.

"Excuse me."

She felt a hand on her arm as someone moved to push past her.

She was already automatically backing out of the way as she looked up and recognized one of the only faces, besides Rami's, that she could put a name to.

Burke Morrison.

"Sorry," she said.

He smiled. He hadn't smiled earlier, so when she'd thought he was cute, she'd had no idea just exactly *how* cute he was.

So cute.

Seriously, even though his face was gorgeous to begin with—those sweet, warm blue eyes, dark lashes, sharp cheekbones—when he smiled, it transformed into something of guileless friendliness.

She had to smile too.

"You're new here, right?" he asked.

She nodded. Mute.

"I'm Burke."

She met his eyes, though it took courage she kind of felt she didn't normally have, and said, like she talked to cute guys all the time, "I'm Quinn."

"Quinn." He repeated it like he was trying it on for size. "Quinn what?"

"Barton?" She knew it was Barton. She didn't know why her answer came out as a question.

He shrugged. "Never heard of you."

Well, *that* was rude. "I've never heard of you either." Then, even though she knew the answer full well, she asked, "Is Burke your first name or your last name?"

There was that smile again. "You never know. It might not be my name at all."

"That's true." Though she knew it was. "You could be making the whole thing up. But that would just make you a jerk. Burke."

He laughed. "Well, I'm not that."

"Which?"

"A jerk. I am Burke. Morrison," he said. "Burke Morrison. And you win, Quinn Barton."

"I do?" She was seized by an uncharacteristic surge of confidence. "What's the prize?"

He thought about it for a moment. "Hmmm. An ice-cream sandwich?"

"I love those!"

"Guess you're going to have to sit with me, then, to make sure you get it after you eat your lunch."

Her face flushed with pleasure. She had not seen this one coming. Not at all. Today was turning out better than she ever could have even imagined.

"I don't know. . . ." Where this was coming from, she could never say. She never had nerve at all, much less the kind that went head to head with a guy. But something about him made her want to play along. "I *was* going to sit with my friend. . . ."

"Boyfriend or girlfriend?"

"Girlfriend."

He looked pleased. "I think she'll be okay for the day."

And, in fact, she was. Jackie had met a guy in her civics class, whom she ended up dating for all of a month and a half, so, though of course she and Quinn would compare boyfriend notes, neither of them turned out to be as socially needy as Quinn had feared she would be.

By that time, Jackie had made other friends and didn't care that Quinn spent every single lunch period for the next two years—until his graduation—sitting with Burke Morrison.

Chapter 6

Present

The first few days of Glenn's challenge were relatively easy. Side Ponytail Day (I felt ridiculous, as he knew I would, but got a *ridiculous* number of compliments). Wear All Black Day (I never wear black, he had to leave a dress shirt and his black formal pants for me to borrow, since we wear the same size). Run a Mile Day sucked, but it had the codicil, "It doesn't all have to be in a row, I don't want you to *die*, just make sure you run a total of a mile no matter how much walking you need to intersperse"—so that took longer than it might have for most people. And my favorite was Sit in the Sun for at Least an Hour Doing Nothing Day. That one was good. It really wasn't something I normally would have allowed myself, but under Glenn's rule, I had no choice and relinquishing some power felt good.

There was probably something in that fact alone that was beneficial to me in terms of this thirty-day program of his. I was always in complete control of everything in my life and I was just so *tired* of having to do that alone. Not that I wanted someone else to take over my life for me or tell me how to do things, but when you're the only one accountable for *everything*, that *can* get old.

Doing silly things because I was being instructed to in order to get out of my rut was fun.

Until day six, when I arrived at the shop in the morning and found the small red envelope taped to the door as usual. It was addressed to *Wonder Woman*. He always had a different name on the envelope. For instance, Run a Mile Day was addressed to Bruce Jenner, whom we had a morbid fascination with, thanks to *Keeping Up with the Kardashians*. Side Ponytail Day was addressed to *The Real Housewife of Middleburg*, since all the stars of the *Real Housewives* franchise seemed to, at one time or another, end up with a side ponytail in their diary interviews.

But *Wonder Woman* . . . that was a strong statement for Glenn. He *loved* Wonder Woman. At one point he had, with a straight face, suggested we stake out Lynda Carter's house in D.C. just to try to catch a glimpse of her and see if she had an invisible plane in the yard (I already knew he was planning to tell me he could see it "right there!").

I'm not gonna lie, I felt a little twizzle of dread in my chest.

I opened the envelope and took out a card that simply read, *Go Commando today.*

I laughed and looked around, half expecting Glenn to jump out and tell me he was kidding, but there was literally no one out yet on the sunny sidewalk.

Then my phone rang. Glenn.

"I'm serious," he said. "Take off your panties, miss."

"No! That's creepy and insane."

"*No*, if any *other* guy told you to do that, it would mean something totally different. *I* want you to do it because it's something you'd never, ever do, and you're going to be reminded all day long, as you squirm uncomfortably and think everyone knows or is somehow going to see through your jeans."

"How do you know—" I stepped back and looked in the window of the Mouse Trap. Glenn waved his phone at me, smirked, then put it back to his ear.

"This is an easy one," he said. "A little something to get you started. Trust me, these little things are going to make a bigger difference than you expect. Call it a Mind Adjustment."

"I call it *ridiculous*."

"Do it."

"It's so . . ."

"Do it."

"Fine." I clicked off the phone, made a face at him, and unlocked the door to the shop.

It *was* ridiculous, but what if he was right? What if little changes could add up to something bigger for me? Not huge. Not giving up all my wordly goods and going off to finish Mother Teresa's work, but just . . . maybe crack me open a little bit more.

I went into the dressing room and took off my jeans and looked in the mirror. This was worse than he'd probably imagined. I was wearing briefs that weren't all that brief. They weren't exactly Granny Panties, but I knew Glenn would have called them that.

They were more modest than most bathing suits.

He was right, damn it. I needed to stop being so stuck in my ways. I took off the briefs and wadded them up to put in my purse, but at the last second I just chucked them in the trash can.

Old Quinn would never have done that, but *new* Quinn was going to get some new lingerie.

Maybe.

We'd see. But maybe.

Oh, did I mention the Morrison boys were coming back to town to clean out the farm? I feel certain I did. So *of course* one would arrive, after he'd been gone for ten years, on Go Commando Day.

See, that's just exactly the kind of guys they were. The kind who would be inexplicably drawn right to the spot where a woman, sans underwear, was looking for frozen corn. Yes, it was the grocery store, but no, it wasn't the cucumber section of the produce department or anything else quite so ridiculously parallel.

I was just trying to pick up the frozen corn for an amazing-looking soup I'd seen someone make in, like, three minutes on *Top Chef,* when I heard a voice I'd never forgotten.

How could the grocery store be out of frozen corn? Corn was a staple! A boring one, at that. Not the kind of thing you'd expect them to have a run on, certainly.

Someone opened the door next to the one I had open. By then I'd been standing there so long the glass had fogged, so I couldn't see the person, but I saw a hand reach in and grab bag after bag of frozen peas.

That's how it happens, I thought. Some weirdo with a corn and pea fetish had obviously gotten to the corn just before me. I closed the door and stepped back to ask the person if they could spare just one of the bags of corn I expected to see in their cart (along, I imagined, with scads of other irreplaceable ingredients people might need—all the yeast, for example, or seventeen cans of garbanzo beans and twelve boxes of stuffing mix).

But there was no cart.

There was, instead, a familiar man.

My stomach dropped.

Of course.

Obviously this moment had been coming, I'd known it from the moment Dottie told me *the boys* were coming back to pack up the farm.

Somehow I think I'd imagined the eventual *meeting* would come at a more predictable time. A time, perhaps, when I might have been able to look my best and, I don't know, have underwear on so I didn't feel so *off*.

That, of course, had been Glenn's aim, to mix things up for me and take me out of my very narrow comfort zone. And that was fine(ish) in the shop, or on a normal grocery run, but not *now*.

At first it didn't register that it was *him*. I hadn't seen him in years and his features, while still young, were settling into a more granite masculinity. And he was wearing a really nice suit that I'd never seen him in, although the tie was loosened and it looked like he'd spent a long day in it.

Plus he smelled good.

I love when a man smells good.

So I noticed him before I *noticed* him.

He tossed the last of what looked like ten bags of peas into the basket he had hooked over his forearm and backed up, glancing at me and then doing a double take.

"*Quinn?* Is that really you?"

At least I wasn't the only one taken off guard.

"Well, hey, Frank," I said, all brightness and bluster. Like this wasn't incredibly uncomfortable for me under the best of circumstances, but even worse, as I wasn't exactly at my best. "I heard you might be coming around town soon."

It all came back to me, those neon-lit nights in Las Vegas, the way the shadows played across those high cheekbones and cleft chin, and the machinelike movement of his muscles as he moved onto me, naked, in the dark.

Those were my most vivid memories of *him*. Unfortunately, I was also aware that his memories of me would involve a lot of sobbing, sniffling, mascara smears, and, on one semi-memorable occasion, puking.

So who did he see me as now? Who did he remember me to be?

I expected him to put the basket down and come in for an awkward hug, and I wondered if I should do the same, but neither of us made a move toward the other. We just stood there looking at each other, both our faces registering what I could only imagine was a mirror image of surprise and discomfort.

He looked good. I had to admit it, he looked good. If I'd just spotted him in the frozen food aisle and he was a stranger, I probably would have thought he was hot.

He gave a short nod. Busy man, lots to do. "Lots to do here suddenly."

"I heard. I mean, Dottie said she was selling the farm and you and Burke"—my voice didn't actually change at all when I said his name, but even so I heard it as if I'd been bleeped by a censor—"would be coming here to get the farm ready to sell."

"That's right." He nodded. Didn't move.

"And apparently eat pea soup."

"Sorry?" He looked blank.

I gestured at his basket. "That's a lot of peas."

Finally he cracked. He gave a short laugh that showed the old Frank in his face. There had been a certain stiffness to his visage before he smiled that made me feel a little like I was talking to a stranger, but when he laughed I felt his warmth.

It had been a long time, but I'd always liked Frank.

So why I felt so nervous with him now, I couldn't say.

"Except I don't think those are the kind of peas you make into soup," I went on, lamely. "I don't know."

"Dottie sprained her ankle," he said, as if that explained it. "So she sent me out to get the peas."

"Peas help a sprained ankle?" She was eccentric, but there was no way anyone was going to make me believe eating peas magically healed bones.

"No, no." He laughed again. And I could see the handsome guy I used to know. Somehow, over the years, he had grown more and more dour and serious in my mind, to the point where I was picturing someone as grim-faced as Humphrey Bogart in *Sabrina*, instead of the real Frank. "She's supposed to keep it iced for a couple of days."

"Okay, you know that's peas, right? Not tiny green ice cubes?"

He took a bag out and held it up. It flopped over his hand.

"She prefers these because, she says, they form-fit to the injury. And the ice cubes she had in Ziploc bags just poked her bruises."

"Ahhhhh. That actually makes sense. Very clever." I shifted my weight from one foot to the other and was reminded of my commando status, which made me—if possible—feel even more self-conscious standing here talking to Frank than I had before.

He shrugged, oblivious to my internal struggle. "They make ice packs that do the same thing, but she wanted peas."

"You don't happen to have any corn in there too, do you?" I asked, peering at his basket.

"Nope. Not the same."

"They'd probably *feel* the same."

"Not quite."

And suddenly I felt like we weren't talking about vegetables anymore. We were talking about him and Burke and the fact that one could not easily replace the other. Though both, in my experience, were capable of turning ice-cold.

But they weren't interchangeable by any means.

My life probably would have been a lot easier and more comfortable if they had been.

"So is Burke in town as well?" I went ahead and asked, since I really believed we were both standing there as aware of him as if he'd been standing right in between us.

Frank shook his head. "Can't be bothered. He had to work. His work is more important than anyone else's, as usual. You know how he is."

Well, no, I guess I didn't know how he was. Arguably that had always been the problem. I didn't really know him as well as I thought I did. But I knew he loved Dottie and that farm, so I couldn't believe he would leave her high and dry instead of coming to help.

"That doesn't sound like Burke," I said simply. Lots behind those words, of course. What *did* sound like Burke these days? Had I ever known?

He looked me in the eye, the amber brown color expanding as his pupils narrowed. "When was the last time you saw him?"

"At our wedding," I answered, my voice dry. I could talk about this without crying, but it was a heavy emotional weight. "The happiest day of my life, remember?"

Now, I knew it wasn't Frank's *fault*. This was a classic case of shooting the messenger. And then *doing* him. So my feelings of anger at him for telling me—and telling me *then*—were all mixed up in this soup of good memories and bad. Mostly bad.

Obviously I was more pissed at what Burke had done, but that didn't necessarily let Frank off the hook.

"Yeah, well, you should have seen him at *his* wedding."

It didn't even take time for me to process the words. My core went rigid before I even digested the meaning. "His wedding?"

Frank nodded. "That's right."

Oh, god. Burke was *married*?

How had *that* little piece of information gone unshared? Dottie loved to chatter about everyone, but no one more than her grandsons. How on earth had she never mentioned Burke's *marriage* in all of her mindless blatherings?

Had she purposely avoided the subject, knowing it would affect me just this way?

Probably.

Wacky as she was, Dottie was kind of sensitive and intuitive that way.

"I didn't know," I said to Frank.

He looked genuinely surprised. I was glad. I didn't want to think he took inordinate pleasure from telling me upsetting things about Burke. That would be a pretty mean hobby, though apparently one rich with material. "I'm sorry, Quinn. I thought for sure you'd know. That he'd told you, or Dottie, or"—he shrugged—"someone."

"Oh, it's been so long, I don't think anyone even associates us with each other anymore," I said, in a voice much lighter than the boulder it felt like was sitting on my chest. "There's a lot of water under that bridge." The bridge we'd burned. "No one would think to keep me posted on things like that. I've got so many other things going on." I made some sort of vague hand gesture that I suppose was meant to illustrate how very, very many fascinating things I had going on.

What did she look like?

How tall was she?

What did she weigh?

How old was she?

Could she sing along on key with the car radio? Did she always take Paul's part when the Beatles came on?

Where did she come from?

"Yeah, I guess you're right," Frank said. "So all I meant was that Burke looked a little like he was facing a firing squad at his wedding."

So she'd trapped him? Oh, dear god, she'd gotten pregnant and trapped him into a marriage and now he not only had a wife but a child as well, and this was how I was finding out, here in the frozen food aisle of Giant, where I didn't have so much as a bag of frozen corn, much less a husband and child and blissfully fucking happy marriage of my own?

"I'm sorry to hear that." *Tell me more. Stop, don't say anything else, but tell me everything!*

I wished he'd never said anything.

Was that my *thing* with Frank in this lifetime? Was I always going to wish *he'd never said anything*? Would every chance encounter, however infrequent, bring some sort of news to make me sad?

"Anyway, that's not really the point," Frank was saying. "The point is, somehow we've got to get the entire farm cleared out in just a few weeks so Dottie can go on her honeymoon at least hoping someone bites on the property so she can spend with impunity."

"I can understand that."

"Obviously I'm going to have to hire outside help as well. That's one of the things Burke's in charge of."

He sounded so disgusted with his brother. They'd always had a certain distance between them, but they'd also been pals in a way. Obviously, when Frank broke up the wedding and subsequently kind of dated the bride, that had probably put a crimp in things, but I couldn't believe it would still matter to them today. Not enough to put that hard edge in Frank's voice when he talked about Burke.

"Well, if there's anything I can do . . ." What? Call me and I'll come help haul the refrigerator somewhere? I had my hands full making the bride's dress! Speaking of which, "Oh, my gosh, Dottie was supposed to come in for a fitting this evening. I guess she's not going anywhere, though."

"Not a chance. At least not in the immediate future."

Well, this was a pickle. I couldn't really progress too much without her. I could bide some of my time making the little roses, since they'd have to be made at some point or other, but I would much rather have gotten the dress itself done and fitted before I moved on to the embellishments.

"I guess I'll have to go to her," I said, picturing the farm and knowing exactly how I was going to feel when I went there. It was going to be hard. No question about it.

"Oh. Well, then. Problem solved, I guess."

I nodded.

"I'd better get these back to her, meanwhile," he said, lifting the basket. "She's already making noise about how she's only walking down the aisle twice in her life and she did it once without hobbling, so she has no intention of hobbling the second time. The sooner we ice her down, the better." He gave a half smile. "Come to think of it, it would probably be nice to occupy her mouth with some nice hot peas at the same time. I have a feeling this is going to be a long few weeks, at least for her fiancé."

I had to laugh. Dottie could be hard to take under the best of circumstances, when she was bustling about from here to there, like a little butterfly who didn't stay in one place for too long. Dottie laid up and in pain and worried that she might not be able to walk down the aisle was a different creature entirely.

"Is she taking painkillers?" I asked, trying to imagine Dottie on prescription pain meds.

He shook his head. "Just ibuprofen, thank god. I cannot imagine her on something that made her loopier than she already is."

We laughed, but the laughter dissolved quickly into another self-conscious silence.

Finally I said, "When you get back, please let her know she should call me to set up a time when I can come by."

"I will," he said. "Thanks. I know that's out of the way for you." There was an uncomfortable hesitation before we both tried to excuse ourselves at the same time.

"It was good to see you again, Frank," I said, and you'd never know, from the stiffness of the exchange, that I had been naked in bed with this man more than once.

"Likewise. And I guess I'll be seeing you around. At the farm or whatever. The wedding."

"Definitely the wedding."

"Okay, then."

More silence.

"All right. So." Why was he still here? Why hadn't he bolted? Why hadn't I? "Remember to tell Dottie to call me," I reiterated. "I've got to stay on top of the fittings or her dress won't be finished on time for the wedding."

He nodded and his eyes shifted just enough for me to gather he was also getting pretty sick of this discomfort. "I'll tell her. She's going nuts just sitting there, I'm sure she'll be glad for the distraction."

And with that, the exchange finally, mercifully, ended.

For now.

Chapter 7

"It just seems ridiculous to wear white, or anything like it, even *yellow*, to my fourth wedding, you know?" Nicole Sizemore looked *exactly* like someone who'd had multiple husbands. Perfectly highlighted blond hair, elfin but pretty face, tiny waist, round butt, and I never *ever* saw her in anything but heels. If she went to the gym, I bet she wore them there too somehow.

Men *loved* women who looked like Nicole.

"I agree," I said. Because what was I supposed to say? People came to me for my honest opinion and I was good at this. I sucked at my personal-life stuff, but I did have a reputation for coming up with all the right touches for wedding attire. I couldn't send Nicole out in a puffy white Bo Peep dress for her inauguration into Liz Taylor territory.

"Black?"

I shook my head. "Too ironic. Where is the wedding going to take place?"

She gave a grimacy smile. "His ex-wife's place on the bay, July fourth. We're really starting to sound like freaks, but they have a good relationship, a couple of kids together, and she offered. . . ."

"That's really nice," I said enthusiastically, thinking there's no way I'd ever want to marry a man in his ex-wife's presence, much less on her property, but whatever. That wasn't because I was *right*, it was just that I wasn't as mature as Nicole, maybe. Or as progressive. Or something. "I have an idea." I took out a scrapbook I kept pictures and ideas in and turned to the beach section. I'd gone through it so many times it took only a few seconds to get to the page. "Something like this?" It was a light cotton sundress, strapless, that flared slightly at the hip and had a swingy A-line skirt. It was a shape that hinted at a fifties sort of Grace-Kelly-on-the-beach-in-Monaco look that would be perfect on Nicole's figure. "Maybe linen, in a pale sky blue? A color that suggests optimism more than, say, *innocence* . . . ?"

She reached for the book with interest and gasped when she saw it. "I *love* it!"

"It's not totally traditional, but not out of the ballpark either."

Nicole smiled. "Like me."

"Exactly."

"You're a genius."

I laughed. "Hardly."

"Can it be done on time?"

This was a piece of cake. It could be done in a day or two. "No problem."

"Then you're better than a genius, you're an *angel*. Thank you so much!"

I know I'm not an angel, but every once in a while it's kind of nice if someone else thinks I am.

It was unusual for me to stop for breakfast on my way in to work, but since it was Watch the Sun Rise Day—the envelope had been issued the night before, on my windshield, in preparation (with a note saying he couldn't give me more notice because he didn't know if it would be cloudy till the last minute)—I had ended up with quite a long morning.

The dry cleaner's across the street was already alive, I noticed with some irritation. The people coming and going at this hour were probably just dropping off their dry cleaning, not looking to screw me out of business, but I couldn't help but feel annoyed, with the business and with everyone who patronized it. Which wasn't fair, I realized, so I decided I probably just needed to get some breakfast to quell my moodiness.

So it was both coincidence and yet not entirely shocking that I ended up at Blue Ridge Bagel Co. that morning when Frank was there.

He was at a booth, where I was just planning to pick up carry-out, but our eyes met as soon as I walked in and it would have been conspicuously rude for me to say nothing, so I went over to say hello and he invited me to join him.

It was still early, and, I'll be honest, I had a certain morbid curiosity about how his life had been going, so I did.

The waitress, Jody, came over and poured coffee in my cup the minute I sat down, and asked for our orders.

"Good thing you already knew what you wanted," Frank said when Jody walked away. "That was kind of a bum's rush."

"It's the best breakfast place in town," I said. "They try to keep the traffic moving." I snap-snap-snapped my fingers.

He nodded and looked at me evenly. "You look great, Quinn."

I hadn't expected that, and the blush I felt creep into my cheeks felt embarrassingly girlish. "Thanks, Frank. So do you." And he did. Really. He'd always been a classically handsome guy—even features, eyes as hard as flint, and wavy dark hair that always looked just a little tousled but still good enough for church.

By contrast, Burke always looked like he'd just rolled out of bed. Even at his conscious best, he looked like he'd just rolled out of bed. Burke was *hot*, where Frank was handsome. The kind of handsome that you had to see behind in order to see hot.

I'd seen him hot, though. That was hard to forget when I was sitting right in front of him.

"So you still live in town, huh?" he asked.

It was like the nerve was exposed and he walked up and said, *Hmm, what's this? You never got a life?* But I knew he didn't mean it that way, I was just hypersensitive to begin with and I knew he'd become a huge financial success, which made my contrast even smaller. "I have the business here," I said.

He took my meaning immediately. "I wasn't being condescending. To tell you the truth, you've come to mind a few times and I wondered if you were still here or if you'd gone off into the wild blue yonder somewhere. I hoped you'd still be here." He shrugged. "So I guess I'm glad you are."

I poured cream into my coffee and stirred the swirl into beige. "Well, I'm not exactly a wild-blue-yonder kind of girl."

He frowned. "No? You used to be."

I had to laugh. "I think you have me confused with someone else."

"Are you serious? Quinn, don't you remember how you wanted to go to Ireland and become a nanny?"

That was true. I'd seriously considered that once. I'd even looked up agencies. How had I forgotten that? "That was just during my brief and ill-advised Colin Farrell crush."

How would my life be different if I'd followed through on that?

"What about fishing in Alaska? You wanted to do that too."

I groaned. Wow, did he remember every embarrassing, hare-brained idea I'd ever had? "I just heard it paid a lot. Like working on the pipeline. I never would have done it."

He smiled. Nice smile. I remembered being very fond of that face for a while. "You were pretty convincing about that one. Remember? When I questioned how serious you were, suddenly you had a place to live and everything. You were going to leave in June and—"

"Come back in September and buy my own farm in Middleburg," I remembered. "I might have overestimated the pay *just* a little bit."

He sipped his coffee. "Probably a good thing you didn't go, then. Lots of disappointment in dark days, cold weather, and low pay."

"More disappointment than flights home," I agreed, but I

remembered seeing some extremely beautiful pictures of Alaska and being genuinely interested in going. It was only for a few weeks, but I honestly *had* checked flights, lodging, and, I'm afraid, I'd made more than one public declaration that that was my intention.

I'd said the same thing about becoming a blacksmith once too. Also a lucrative profession, by the way.

And an acupuncturist. I don't know why I'd thought that was going to be a quick study, though I am good with a needle, obviously.

"See, you had some blue yonder in you," he said.

The waitress arrived with our orders, and we both leaned back in our booth seats, as if that would make more room for the food on the table.

"I don't anymore," I said, picking up my knife and fork. "Now I'm *literally* the spinster with a sewing room." I cut into the sausage patty on my plate.

"Equally admirable." He'd gotten an omelet. Onions, peppers, and jalapeños. No cheese, though I remembered that was because he had a thing against thick, gooey cheese, having nearly choked on it on pizza as a kid. Still, he probably thought I was a complete porker. Which I was, actually, when it came to buying breakfast. I love restaurant breakfasts. "How's business going?"

"Really well, actually." I was glad to be able to say something I was proud of and have it be the truth. "Better than expected. I have an employee and two outside seamstresses for the foundation work."

"Dottie's really excited about you making her dress." He took a bite, then waved his fork in my direction and said, "She thinks it's going to bring her good luck."

We were making small talk when, after all these years, there were bigger questions and answers, and we both knew it.

"Because I'm so lucky with weddings?"

He hesitated before saying, "I'm not sure you're not."

Ouch. But good point. "What happened after you got back from Vegas?" I asked, knowing it could seem abrupt.

He didn't look surprised. He just leaned back and sighed briefly. "He was pissed."

"I'd imagine."

"He made a lot of noise about me hurting you, accused me of doing it callously in an effort to get to you, but he never owned up to his part in it."

The thought came to me immediately, and unbidden: *Had he played no part in it? Had he actually been falsely accused? Had I dumped him for no reason?*

As if reading my mind, Frank said, "I think he would now, if you cared to ask him."

I looked down. I knew enough. I didn't need more details to whip me back in time and make the small part of my old self that still existed in me feel even worse. "How long was he mad at you?"

Frank gave a small shrug. "Not very. He knew it was his own fault."

"So things just went right back to normal?" He couldn't know how horrible the thought was to me, given how much I'd suffered.

So when he answered, I knew it wasn't meant to hurt. "Whatever our *normal* is, yeah."

Does he ever talk about me? I wanted to ask. *Does he ever think about me?* But those were questions Frank couldn't answer, and, more important, they were questions that shouldn't matter in my real life now. It was my ego asking, not my heart.

"What about Dottie selling the farm?" I asked, making a conscious effort to change the subject. "How do you feel about that?"

"It's up to her." He didn't shrug, but he may as well have.

"But aren't you sad about it?"

He considered before answering. "There's no point in going to that place mentally. If I think about it, allow myself to feel attached to an outcome I have no control over, what's the good in that?"

Okay, now, I know that sounds really cold and impersonal, but I have to confess, that is one of the things I always liked best about Frank. His soft-spoken, hard truths, just like he'd just thrown at me about Burke. This one didn't hurt, though. It made good sense. If I could genuinely face my life that way, accepting the things I cannot change (to recite a phrase), I'd probably be a much happier person. Certainly I'd have a lot less free-floating anxiety humming along in the background all the time.

"But," I said, because I wasn't that laissez-faire person, "even though that's a good attitude, and definitely healthy in general, the thing is, she's going to sell the place and it will be gone forever. Someday maybe you'll have kids, or even if you don't, someday you might want some feeling of connection to your heritage.

Your history. Aren't you at least a little tempted to take it over and keep it?"

"Yeah." He cut off another bite of his omelet. "But it's not practical."

And if there was one thing Frank Morrison was, it was practical.

I didn't say it, but the sentiment echoed between us.

"What about Burke? Is he thinking of buying it?"

Frank took another sip of coffee and shook his head. "I doubt it. It's pricey. But I don't think he's all that happy about it being sold either."

"No?" That he felt the same way I did about it struck me in a more personal way than it probably should have. "Why not?"

"Same reasons you said, basically. I think he referenced *history*, but it all adds up to the same thing. What can we do? It's not our decision and we can't make Gran feel like she's letting us down by living her life. She should be commended for starting over at this stage. That takes a lot of courage."

"I agree." Then I sighed. "But I wish someone was going to keep it in the family. It would be weird for someone else to take it over and maybe change it. I honestly always thought Burke would end up there. I'm surprised he won't."

"You know how Burke is," Frank went on. His voice was even, despite the fact that his words were somewhat harsh. "He wants things, but he doesn't really want to do what it takes to get them. He expects everything to fall in his lap. I guess he thought the farm would too. Inheritance or whatever. Now that Dottie wants to sell, he's pissed, but I don't see him out trying to get a mortgage or investors, so he must not be that motivated."

"Do you think he could?"

"I have no idea." He waved his hand. "You never know with him. I gave up trying to help a long, long time ago."

Around the time he "helped" me get out of a relationship with Burke?

Or did he consider that helping Burke?

Obviously there was an element of helping himself. He wasn't entirely altruistic.

"That's a shame."

He shrugged. "He's my brother. But I'm not his keeper. And he doesn't want me to be. It works out fine. Not a shame at all."

I remember how they had always had this dynamic. There were times when they were pals, and I think in the end that will be the ultimate story of them, but there were many, many times when they had conflict. Frank was sharp and condescending, often treating Burke like an incompetent child. Burke, on the other hand, was wild and immature, often acting like an incompetent child.

In its weird way, it worked.

Certainly it wasn't an argument I needed to have right now. "As long as you're at peace with the relationship."

He was chewing his food and nodded vigorously before saying, "Oh, yeah, there's no angst there."

I sighed and probably shouldn't have said, "I do wish one of you would keep the farm. I really hate to see it go."

"That's a lot of money for a hobby I'm not really interested in."

"How much is the asking price?"

He told me, and everything in me deflated. Who could afford that? I could buy several nice houses in town for that. Not that it was an unfair asking price, but it was even more out of my league than I could have dreamed.

I wondered if Burke was too proud to admit to his brother that the price was just too much for him.

Then I chastised myself for even worrying about how he might feel about this.

Instead I changed the subject and forced myself not to ask any more questions about Burke, or anything tangentially involved with Burke, because I knew there was no point in going there. No good would come out of it, I'd just feel weird.

I'd moved past this a long, long time ago, and I had no intention of ever revisiting.

Not that it was all that comfortable revisiting Frank either. He did not loom large, as Burke did, in my heart, but he was a big part of my life, and of my memories. If I'd stayed with him, and he would have liked that at the time, it was possible that my life would have gone in a very different direction. Not that I was unhappy with how it was now, but, like I said, I really liked Frank. I'd always kind of loved Frank, though not in exactly the same way I'd loved Burke. Sometimes I wondered if we could have been happy together under other circumstances.

That is, if it was possible to have a happy life with someone when the relationship would necessarily involve someone else who had hurt you. If I'd met Frank independently, then sure, maybe we could have had a go of it. Or at least a longer relationship than the momentary blip we'd had.

But that couldn't have been realistically possible. Ultimately,

Frank implied Burke in too many ways. They didn't look alike, but they were brothers, and there were similarities that ran deep and subtle. The same vocal inflection now and then. The same laugh. A similar stance, weirdly enough.

To say nothing of the very real fact that holidays, funerals, and other family events would necessarily put us all together.

I could never give myself wholly to Frank because I could never fully let go of Burke. With someone unrelated, maybe Burke would have become a memory that dimmed to sweetness with time. Or, better still, dimmed to obscurity. From a photo to a watercolor.

But as long as I was with his brother, there wasn't a chance in the world I'd ever forget him and move on.

None of which is to say Frank would have actually *wanted* me. But there was no point in adding that to the mix, since I wasn't really stirring it anyway.

Frank and I made small talk after that. Nothing about the farm, the wedding, his family, nothing even remotely incendiary. He told me about his job, the renovations to his row house in D.C., the market in general, and I, in turn, gave him a few anecdotes about my life as a small-town bridal gown seamstress.

And, to be honest, that part of the conversation went really smoothly. It was comfortable. Like a really good first date. Had he been a stranger and it *was* a first date, I probably would have agreed to see him again, but it wouldn't have been with much enthusiasm.

I was sure he didn't have that problem with all women. Objectively speaking, this guy was a catch. Good-looking, successful, smart, self-assured . . . there was no doubt about it, he'd survive the dating marketplace better than most.

I finished my meal and pushed the plate away, the universal sign for *Uncle*.

"It was good to see you, Frank," I said, reaching for my purse and hoping I had some cash so we didn't have the awkwardness of splitting the bill onto two credit cards. I found a twenty and took it out, figuring it would cover both of us.

"Put that away," Frank said as soon as he saw what I was doing. "This is on me."

"No, Frank, that's not—"

"Quinn."

I put my money away. There was no sense in dickering over this and asserting my independence. If he wanted to buy me a breakfast I hadn't planned on sharing with him, fine.

"Thank you, Frank," I said.

He met my eyes and smiled. And for a moment I could really see the man he was, apart from his family and our history and everything else.

He put some bills down on the table and we both stood up and walked, a bit awkwardly, to the door, past townspeople who would undoubtedly be speculating about this later. Even people who didn't know about our history—that's how small towns are.

I didn't care anymore.

I couldn't.

We stepped out onto the sidewalk in the already-blazing sunshine of a late May morning.

"I guess I'll be seeing you around," I said.

All of the awkwardness of that first meeting we'd had in the grocery store was back. All of my self-consciousness, and my questions about his own impressions of me. Isn't that crazy? We'd talked about Burke, about the fallout from my Runaway Bride act, but I couldn't ask Frank how *he* felt about everything that had happened.

I think in a way I felt that if I didn't ask, it wouldn't remind him of all the humiliations of mine that he'd witnessed.

Without any seeming awareness of the push and pull within me, he gave a single nod. "No doubt."

"Please let Dottie know not to panic about her immobility, at least as far as getting fittings done. It's not that big a deal. I can go there if I need to, but the dress isn't all that complicated, as far as construction goes. It will still be ready well in time for the wedding."

A muscle in his jaw ticked at the word *wedding*. I wasn't sure why. "I'm sure she'll be very glad to hear it."

I nodded, and a tense silence ballooned around us.

"So . . . thanks!" I said again, this time with a forced cheer that might as well have screamed sarcasm.

"Anytime."

I put my hand out to shake hands—a gesture that always feels ridiculous and unnatural to me, like I'm pantomiming some businessman in a foreign language video (*"It was a pleasure meeting with you."*)—just as he came in for the cursory insincere hug, and as a result I effectively jabbed him in the stomach.

We both put our hands up in surrender and laughed.

"Sorry!"

"Let's give up," he said, flashing that smile again. "Before something seriously embarrassing happens."

"Amen," I said, shaking my head. "See you later."

And, at that moment, I wasn't dreading it.

Chapter 8

October, Seventeen Years Ago

W hat does it look like?" Quinn asked.

They were on their way to his horse farm about forty minutes down the road from her house. It was in a particularly wealthy part of the county and she had not been there before, despite having spent her whole life in the area.

He had lived there with his brother and his grandparents since his father had died and . . . he didn't talk about his mother. Quinn imagined a lot of sad scenarios to explain that, but few of them were even plausible. She had no idea if she'd ever know the truth.

But she was going to meet his grandparents, and she took that to be a very good sign that things were headed in a good direction with their relationship. You don't introduce your boyfriend or girlfriend to your family if you're not serious, right?

"You'll see it soon," he said, switching lanes to pass a slower car.

"But just *tell* me." She was unreasonably excited. It was a perfect October afternoon and they were set to have a cookout. Then she and Burke were going to stay over so he could get up early— seriously early, as in so early many people would just consider it "late"—to go fishing with his grandfather.

It was like he was giving her a really good peek at his life, and she was thrilled. Maybe she was actually going to be getting a look at her own future life!

"Is it fancy?"

"It looks a lot like that," he said, and gestured out the passenger window.

She looked eagerly and saw an ancient wooden barn collapsing on itself, grass and weeds growing through the slats by the foundation. "Smart-ass," she said to him, and rolled the window down to let the warm air from outside in. She leaned back against the seat and closed her eyes while her hair blew around her face and she sang along with the radio.

Burke drove, steady as always, patient with her loudness and constant CD-switching.

They drove for about twenty minutes and then he took an exit off the two-lane highway and pulled onto a narrower, tree-lined street. Almost immediately he pulled into a road-side bakery and drive-in parking lot. It looked like something out of the fifties. Or at least the movie and TV version of the fifties.

"The cookies?" she asked as they got out of the car.

"They also have snowballs that Frank and I used to get." He led her to the bakery display shelves and pointed at coconut-covered fluffy icing balls. "They have cake in the middle. You want one?"

"Yes!"

"Obviously you should save it for after dinner," he said, and then laughed.

"Oh, please." She had a terrible sweet tooth. There was no way that thing was going to be within six inches of her for two minutes before she devoured it.

He ordered snowballs and cookies from a man in a chef's coat with a face the color of seared meat, while she wandered around looking at the breads and the menu for hamburgers and hot dogs and other fast food. It was Saturday and there were a fair number of people there, eating at picnic tables that were set up next to the kitchen.

"How old is this place?" she asked Burke as he came to her with a bag in hand.

"I don't know. It's been here since I was a kid." He took out a snowball and handed it to her.

"I wonder if everyone comes and hangs out here on Friday night." She took a bite. The coconut spilled down her shirt. But it was good.

He watched her, looking amused. "Want a drink?"

"Mm-mm." She shook her head. "I'm good," she added, mouth full.

They sat at a picnic table while she finished. The landscape was green and lush, with lots of leafy trees throwing splashes of shade across swells of green fields. Across the street there was a huge old barn with a sign out front that read ANTIQUES. The people milling about outside were noticeably well dressed, so it was easy to imagine the antiques were pretty pricey. Not like the junk shop near *her* grandparents' house in Thurmont.

She could see living like this.

When she finished eating they went back to the car and turned onto a winding country road. In another five minutes he was pulling into the gravel driveway of a sprawling, pristine farm of green fields, white fences, and horses. So many horses. Gleaming, shining Thoroughbreds and hunters. It looked, for all the world, like the horse-and-stable set she used to play with as a child. It had been her favorite toy. Many times she'd faked sick so she could stay home from school and play with the horses and farm.

And here it was, blooming to life right in front of her.

"I love it," she breathed, wide-eyed.

He parked outside a low brick stable and they got out and headed toward the stately stone main house.

"What's that?" she asked, pointing to a bungalow in the shade on the edge of the property.

"Tenant house," he said. "Basically a little place no one really uses for anything but storage. My granddad wants to rent it, but Dottie, my grandmother, always says she wants it there for Frank and me when we get older and want to move out. She figures it'll keep us from moving too far away."

"I guess it would!" She wanted to see inside. Most people would be more enamored of the big house, but something about the little place captured her imagination right away.

A man who looked to be in his thirties came out of the barn, wiping his brow with a dirt-smeared arm. "Who's that?" she asked, as he was clearly too young to be Burke's grandfather.

"Hm? Oh, that's Rob. He's in charge of keeping up with all the horse business."

Rob stopped by the fence and took a pack of cigarettes out of his pocket and lit one.

"Isn't that dangerous around a barn?" Quinn asked.

"He's a total freak." Burke shook his head. "I think he's constantly stoned, but Dottie has ideas about rehabilitating him. She thinks the work and responsibility will straighten him out. *Face his demons and shoo them away*, she says."

"Dottie?"

"My grandmother."

"Why do you call her that?"

"It's her name." He laughed. "Everyone calls her that. She didn't like how aging *Grandma* sounded."

Quinn liked this woman already.

A black and tan dog ran and yelped excitedly at them in the yard, and the sound echoed across the fields.

It was perfect.

As they approached the house, the screen door swung open and an older man with thinning gray hair and a red-checked western shirt came out. He had a string tie around his neck and a leather belt with a big silver oval buckle cinching his generous waist.

This was obviously Burke's grandfather, though he didn't look nearly as intimidating as Quinn had imagined.

He was followed by a spritely whip of a woman with wavy

blond hair up in a half-done bun. She wore a tan skirt that might have been suede and a summery print sleeveless blouse. There was a certain elegance to her, even though she looked slightly disheveled. It was an *elegant* kind of disheveled.

Quinn's nerves hummed.

But her fears dissolved instantly when the older couple greeted them. Each gave her a hug in welcome and then introduced her to the dog, Zinger. When Burke's grandfather offered her a Coke, she accepted and he handed her a bottle that looked like it had been in the fridge since the late sixties. Quinn eyed it dubiously and sent Burke a questioning glance. Could Coke go bad? If it was past its expiration date, could it make you sick?

All she needed was to spend the night she met his grandparents for the first time throwing up in the bathroom. If she was lucky, that is. What if she didn't even make it to the bathroom?

Burke seemed oblivious to her unspoken question, so she carefully poured the Coke out a little bit at a time when no one was looking.

Of course Burke caught her as she dumped the last of it, and raised his eyebrows at her.

She grimaced and shrugged.

He looked at the bottle and nodded.

Apart from that little glitch, though, it was a perfect evening. They had steaks cooked over peach bark and they were the most delicious food Quinn had ever eaten in her life. She was in complete bliss.

When Frank showed up after dinner, Quinn felt even more at ease. She and Frank had really gotten to be friends, apart from her relationship with Burke. Sometimes he'd even call her himself, just to check and see how she was doing. Not because she was his brother's girlfriend but because he genuinely *liked* her.

He'd even told her that.

"I like you, Quinn. Apart from the whole Burke thing, I like you."

"Thanks! I like you too," she'd said.

He'd looked surprised, so she added, *"No, I really do."*

There was a long moment when he had looked at her, scrutinized her wordlessly. Then his gaze shifted and he had moved away, as if he had assessed something, and moved on to another task, and she was forgotten.

As twilight fell, they all sat on the front porch and Burke's grandfather told a ghost story while Quinn listened with rapt attention. When he had her completely engaged, he ended his story with a stomp of his foot at the punch line and both Quinn and the dog jumped. Both Frank and Burke laughed.

"Burke and I both fell for that one when we were kids," Frank said. "I think Burke fell for it more than once."

"Probably," Burke agreed.

"Burke, why don't you take Quinn for a walk in the field while we clean up?" Dottie suggested. "Show her the lay of the land."

"No, let me help clean up," Quinn protested.

"Absolutely not, missy. You're our guest. Frank will help out, won't you, Frank?"

"Sure," he said, though Quinn noticed his gaze darted away from her when she looked at him. Was he irritated that he had to clean up after her?

Burke slipped his hand into Quinn's and said, "Come on, guest."

They took the dog with them and walked through the cut grass holding hands.

"I want to live here," Quinn told him.

"Wouldn't you miss your suburbia?"

"No way. I could honestly live here. I'd learn to hunt and race and"—she shrugged—"whatever else you do with the horses."

"Breed."

She raised an eyebrow at him. "And you want to show me how to do that, right?"

He laughed outright.

"What's with Frank?" she asked then.

"What do you mean?"

"He seemed so pissy when we left."

Burke frowned. "Did he? More than usual?"

She laughed. "Frank isn't usually pissy!"

"You're kidding, right?"

"No . . . are you?" Frank was one of the nicest guys in school. It was really touching how he had always been solicitous of her.

Burke shook his head. "We must not be talking about the same Frank."

"Oh, stop it. Come on, he's a great guy."

"Okay."

"I don't get why you two don't get along better."

"This," he said, gesturing at the land, "is Civil War country. Maybe we just have a blue-gray thing going on between us."

"Which one are you?"

"Frank's got no shades of gray, believe me."

She had to laugh. "Clever."

They got to a line of trees and Quinn glanced back at the farm-house. Frank and his grandparents were carrying things into the house and she could barely see them for the dusk.

"Come with me," she said, and took Burke by the hand to the other side of a wide tree.

This was the kind of thing he loved. He gave her a rakish smile. "What are you up to?"

"Nothing. Just thought you might find something to do with some privacy."

Once hidden, she backed against the tree and he braced his hands on either side of her and leaned in to kiss her.

She slid her arms over his shoulders and drew him closer to her, deepening the kiss until they were pressed together so tightly that it would have been impossible to slide a sheet of paper between them.

The dog foraged around in the brush, occasionally taking off at a run, then trotting back.

She didn't know how long they stayed there, making out in the darkening night, but by the time they came up for air it was dark out.

Which Burke pointed out was a good thing. No prying eyes upon them from afar.

They took their time walking back to the house. The windows glowed yellow from the lights burning inside. To Quinn it felt like being in a children's book illustration, everything was just so perfect.

She was shown to her room upstairs—a small rectangle next to Burke's larger room. Both were furnished with antiques in such perfect condition that Quinn was afraid to touch them for fear of accidentally nicking something.

Quinn brushed her teeth and put on her nightgown and headed back to her room while Burke went into the bathroom.

Frank came out of his room at that moment and almost ran into her in the hall. "Oh, sorry," he said awkwardly, but he didn't move.

Quinn took a step back and around him. "That's okay. Good night, Frank. See you in the morning."

"Wait."

She stopped.

"Do you— do you need anything?" he asked.

See? Nice guy. She didn't know what Burke was talking about. He was probably just jealous of her saying something nice about another guy. Especially his brother. There always was a certain sense of competition between the two of them.

"No, I'm good," she said to him. "But thanks." She went on into her room and closed the door behind her.

It was very quiet. Old houses tend to have that weird quality of shutting out the whole world, and this one was no exception.

Quinn climbed between the cool clean sheets and reached over to turn the light out.

Pitch-black.

Suddenly she felt very alone.

Even though it had been a joke, designed to lead up to the startling end, Quinn started thinking about the ghost story Burke's grandfather had told and wondered if there was any truth to it. It was all too easy to imagine the restless spirits of Confederate soldiers milling around outside, especially now that she was alone in the guest room.

Quinn got out of bed and looked out the window. She could swear that she could see filmy movements below, like faded sheets blowing in the wind.

Her heart quickened and she went to the shared wall between the two bedrooms and tapped on it.

Almost immediately he tapped back.

She knocked again, frantically, her own Morse code for, *Get in here quick!*

Her door creaked open a moment later. "What's wrong?" Burke looked concerned.

"I think it's haunted here."

His shoulders relaxed and his expression eased. "It's not. That was just a joke."

"I know, but look outside!" she whispered. "I think there are . . . *things* out there. Seriously, look."

He shook his head and went to the open window. "What am I looking for?"

She joined him, her breath mingling with his. The wind blew the fabric of her thin homemade nightgown. "There!" She pointed to a place in the distant woods where she thought she saw a billowy white form. "Did you see that?"

He laughed outright. "No."

"Look *closely.*"

He did. He looked like he really tried. But then he looked back at her like she was crazy. "That's just the wind moving the leaves."

"Yeah, and ghosts."

"I don't think so."

She frowned. How could he not see what she was seeing? "You're just not sensitive."

"Hm." He looked out again. "You think?"

She nodded. "I'm scared."

He looked to the door, considered, then looked back at her. "You're being a dumbass."

"I am not!"

"Shhh. Quiet. They'll hear. Just lie down and go to sleep. Stop being a baby."

"Fine." She went back to the bed and pulled back the crocheted bedspread, then climbed between the sheets again.

"Good girl." He laughed, then sat down on the edge of the bed with a creak.

She turned to face him. "You're a jerk," she said, reaching for his hand and twining her fingers with his.

"Why are you always surprised by that?" He rested his other hand heavily on her hip, the solid weight lending comfort and warmth.

Suddenly she was tired. The steak, the fresh air, the sugar low after eating the snowball that afternoon and about a dozen chocolate chip cookies after dinner all got to her at once, and she could barely keep her eyes open.

"You should be nicer," she said, closing her eyes and breathing in the scent of clean sheets and old house.

"I try."

The wind lifted outside and whispered across her hair. "Try harder."

They fell into silence then, and he left the room without a word.

Finally, the ghosts forgotten in the face of sheer exhaustion, she drifted off to sleep.

Chapter 9

Present

Dottie called that afternoon and wanted me to come right away, urgent urgent urgent, as she was *most* concerned about making sure I had everything I needed to make sure her dress was as perfect as she knew only I could make it, and now she was worried that she'd fouled everything up by getting hurt so that she couldn't come in for her fittings, so even though she knew it was more trouble than I had planned on having to go to, would I mind . . . ?

"When I saw him this morning, I told Frank to tell you not to worry," I said, certain he *had* given her that reassurance.

"Well, that's just very easy for a man to say, isn't it?" she returned. And, honestly, she did have a point. "I couldn't believe *him*, I needed to hear it from you!"

"Well, now you are worried," I said, trying to calm her. "No need. We'll get it done."

"So you'll come?"

A tremor of apprehension skittered across my chest but I tried to ignore it. Always bad policy, by the way. "Yes, I'll be there in a couple of hours."

"And plan to stay for supper," she added. "I'm having some folks over. Just casual, of course. Nice beginning-of-summer party."

I knew she loved those. "That's really nice, Dottie, but I don't want to interrupt your party. I can take the measurements very quickly and get out of your way."

"Out of my way, are you kidding, child? We could use a little infusion of your bubbly energy in the mix!"

It was clear I wasn't going to be able to get out of this gracefully, so even though I would rather have gone home and started cutting the material and watching Bravo, I asked, "Is there anything I can bring, then?"

"Just your sweet self, Quinn."

I had to laugh. "Okay, but at least let me contribute something to the feast." I'd been to her Golden Cup beginning-of-summer parties and they were always huge festivals of cookout foods. Of course, those events were usually catered, as there were hundreds of guests, but I knew what summer meant to Dottie. It was sun, and fun, and picnic tables, and beer.

So I'd bring my mom's "famous" macaroni salad. Everyone who ever had it liked it, and it was generic enough to go with hot dogs, hamburgers, bratwurst, whatever.

Macaroni salad is always appropriate, right?

"Honey, you can do whatever you like, but you just get yourself on over here, I can't wait to get started!"

So with that invitation, I ran home, threw some elbow noodles into a pot of boiling salted water, and mixed up the mayo, sour cream, dry mustard, tomatoes, and several other ingredients typical of any sixties back-of-the-box recipe, and let it chill while I took a quick shower.

I figured Frank would be there, as I'd only run into him a few hours earlier, but I didn't have time to get dolled up for him, nor the inclination, given that he'd seen me looking pretty rough at the grocery store. Besides, it was going to take me at least forty minutes to drive there and I wanted to make my appearance, get the measurements, and go, so I just threw on a sundress, brushed my wet hair into a part, and ran, carrying my flip-flops in hand.

I drove down U.S. 15 with more than a little trepidation. I had certainly been on this road a few times in the past ten years, but not very many. And, for reasons I couldn't quite articulate, every vista along the way—none of which had changed much, by the way—was etched in my mind as belonging to *him*. And to *that time*.

Which I guess explains why I hadn't made this drive much. I didn't have much call to head south, for one thing, but the temptation had certainly struck, more than once, to take a melancholy trip into the past. Sometimes it was a sunny fall day when the mood struck me; other times it was a muggy, rainy, gray summer day. Always it was a trick of the mind to travel back in time and invariably end up feeling weird and sad.

Because, like I said, I had really seen myself ending up there someday. The crazy fact that it looked like my childhood play set just seemed like *fate* to teenage me.

Thirty-one-year-old me wasn't quite sure what to do with it.

Anyway, perhaps if I had business outside of town and this drive had, for any reason, become a regular thing for me, I might have gotten used to it and grown to associate the landmarks along the way with other things. Ordinary things. A hair appointment, a cranky bride, taking my car in for detailing, or driving to a mall or favorite Thai restaurant.

But none of that stuff was down this way. The only thing here was a long gray ribbon of road, stretched like tape stuck by a toddler onto a rolling carpet of green hills under a huge arch of blue sky. This is Virginia. My Virginia, anyway.

The landscape narrowed some as I went through The Plains and into Fauquier County, and the tight little band of roads that led to the farm. I had to stop and take a breath before turning onto the old familiar dirt road.

It looked exactly the same. I guess that's not entirely surprising. There were only two houses on the road and the owners of each were older now, had been there forever, and wouldn't be very motivated to pay whatever it would cost to pave a mile of dirt. The oak trees that flanked the road had been there for so long that a mere ten years wouldn't have made an appreciable difference, so the entire effect was as if time had stood still in this few square miles.

And, in a way, I guess it had. Dottie hadn't been motivated to change anything. She'd said a million times, "You know how I am: old dog, no new tricks." Which was one of the reasons it was so astonishing that she was getting married.

That was a new trick.

Anyway, it was with great apprehension that I drove past the now-abandoned bakery and turned down the bumpy dirt road to the farm. I felt a sense of fear straight down through my core, and I couldn't really say why. There was nothing to be *afraid* of except my own mind—the places my memory would take me upon seeing the place again, and the way I'd feel when it did—but this wasn't time travel and I knew it. This was today, not ten years ago, and I was going to see Dottie, whom I'd seen hundreds of times in the ensuing years, and a group of her older friends, many of whom I'd probably recognize from town.

I parked the car and grabbed my purse and Tupperware and went to the door of the main house. I'd spent more time in the tenant house, of course, Burke and I stealing away in there and doing all kinds of unholy things by candlelight, but the main house, I knew, would remind me of what I had always anticipated my life would *become*. Dignified. Dark polished woods, antiques, elegance . . . always with the tenant house right there to sneak off to for fun.

The paddocks, which used to be full of horses, were now empty, save for one closest to the house. There was an old chestnut gelding I recognized immediately as Rogue. His coat was shaggy from the end of winter and lack of grooming, but I would have recognized the star on his forehead and the three white socks anywhere.

There was something both touching and reassuring about seeing him there, but I couldn't help but wonder what would happen to him when the farm was sold. Someone was almost certainly lined up to take him. Most of the people who came here and would be familiar with him had farms of their own.

I made my way up to the large stone main house.

Dottie opened the door before I touched the bell. She was leaning on a crutch, her ankle wrapped but visibly swollen. "There you are!" She beamed. "I'm so happy you've come!"

"Thanks for inviting me," I said, and looked around. The place seemed empty. Apparently no one was here yet, which meant my escape plan would be put off indefinitely.

"What have you got there?" she asked, indicating the Tupperware. It was an old piece, very early eighties, kind of a strange turquoise green that seemed to get brighter with the years, rather than the opposite. "Isn't that a pretty container!"

"Oh. I just made some macaroni salad." Just standing there on the threshold to such austere elegance, to me the plastic felt impossibly cheap and lowbrow. "I'm not sure it goes with what you had in mind so maybe I should just—"

"Nonsense, macaroni goes with *everything*." She took the bowl from me with her free hand and said, "Let me take this into the kitchen and you go on into the parlor and wait for Frank and Burke."

I stopped literally midstep. As in, foot in the air, and for a moment I really and truly had to fight the impulse to turn on my heel and run. Ask no questions, just get the hell out of there.

Because Burke was there. This wasn't some outdoor picnicky cookout with the old folks from town, this was a setup. She wanted whatever was *wrong* with Burke, Frank, and me to be *right*. Maybe it was part of the housekeeping involved in selling the whole place, marrying someone new, and moving away. I didn't know her well enough to be sure what her motives were, or could be, but I knew her well enough to know she had something in mind and she'd had it there ever since watching me react to the news of Burke coming back to clear out the farm.

I didn't know what to do. Just straight up didn't know what to do. I wanted desperately to not be there. To be almost anywhere but there. In line at the department of motor vehicles. At the gym. Standing in the sweltering heat of August at an amusement park with no water. I was panicked to leave but too polite to do anything but stay.

"Dottie," I began.

She met my eyes. "Trust me, you need this. You need to face your demons and move on."

"I already *did.*"

She pressed her lips together and shook her head. "I don't think so."

I took a steadying breath and reached for the bowl. "At least let me take that into the kitchen for you, it's crazy for you to try and carry that while you're hobbling around with a crutch."

"Not a problem," she insisted. "I've got to learn to fend for myself, don't I?"

Oh, she could fend for herself very well, thank you.

It was the rest of us who had something to learn.

"You go on into the parlor, missy. I'll meet you in there for the measurements and a nice little sip of something, how's that?"

"Fine." I think I sounded sulky. I was afraid I did. But this was really not what I'd signed up for. First, I hadn't wanted to come back here at all. These were not memories I had to revisit. These were not demons I had to fight. This was not my life anymore.

And I was going to tell her that. As soon as she came into the parlor, I was going to tell her, like a grown-up person (which I obviously was, but sure didn't feel like!), that I was uncomfortable with this whole thing and I just wanted to do what I'd come to do and go back to work, and I'd apologize for the inconvenience if she'd been planning on me for dinner, but I thought it would be best for everyone involved if I just went on my way.

I was thinking all of that with absolute conviction as I entered the parlor and beheld the completely unchanged arrangement of mahogany and chintz. I wouldn't have realized it until I heard it but even the loud ticking of the mantel clock was familiar, and the framed display of old pistols on the wall, like something from the Wild West. Assuming you didn't look too closely at the date of the Sunday *Post* on the desk, this was *exactly* the same as it had been ten years ago. It was like walking into an old oil painting by an unknown artist.

"I didn't think you'd come."

This time there was no doubt as to whose voice I was hearing. There wasn't even any need for thought, my body just *reacted*. A Scud missile, crashing through the roof and exploding in the middle of our table couldn't have sent a bigger jolt of adrenaline through me.

So obviously I wasn't going to get away with my escape plan. It was time to face the music, even if it was an old song that made me cry every time.

I turned to face him and heard myself say his name. "Burke."

So many emotions rushed through me. Anger and happiness and hate and lust. I don't want to say love. I didn't love what that man did to me. I couldn't love a man who had done that to me. Or, at least, I couldn't *keep loving* a man who had done that to me.

I'd buried that deep inside a long time ago.

So it was crazy that I should have to *remind* myself of that now. But looking at him . . . well, like I said, it wasn't *only* the anger that came back to me.

It wasn't that he looked exactly the same. There's a difference between twenty-three and thirty-three for everyone. But of course I would have known him anywhere. If anything, he was hotter now, and that was some feat, given that, at least to the outside world, that had always been his *thing*—he was gorgeous. A very, very good-looking man.

His hair was the same gleaming dark of the ebony bookshelves that lined the back wall, and framed his face in the same unruly waves he'd had since he was a kid on the playground at school. Though it was shorter than it was when he was younger, it was the kind of hair that couldn't really be tamed. His eyes were exactly the same. Sweet. I know that word doesn't connote "hot," but, trust me, given the granite strength of the rest of his features, it worked.

But it was his mouth that always got to me the most—impossible to describe, really, except something about the curve of it was nothing short of adorable when he smiled, yet was as sensuous as any sultry movie star photo.

It's not everyone who can pull off cute *and* hot.

"I didn't think you'd fall for Dottie's trick."

I shrugged, making an effort to seem casual. Like my heart *wasn't* pounding out of my chest. "Hook, line, and sinker."

"Old Quinn was more suspicious of people."

My chest tightened. "There was certainly a point at which that became true."

He gave a single nod.

"Anyway, you haven't even met the real Quinn."

He tilted his head and assessed me. "No, I guess I haven't. Or I never knew her. Depending how you look at it." He looked me over with those blue eyes, almost detached but with just the smallest *hint* of a heat I recognized deep in his expression.

Suddenly I was very aware I was still going commando.

And I really wished I weren't.

"You know, I really don't want to do this," I said, a sharper edge to my voice than I would have wished. It gave too much away. He'd know I *felt* things, and I didn't want him to know that. "You and I don't need to have a contentious exchange here. We don't need to have an exchange of any sort. I'm just here to help your grandmother. I'll do what I need to do and go, okay?"

He splayed his arms, a pantomime of concession that he clearly didn't mean at all. "Absolutely. I'm not here to stop you." Could I read the edge to his voice as emotion, as I feared he'd read the same in me? Or was he just impatient with me? I couldn't say. I knew the boy, once. I didn't know the man.

"Good heavens, there is tension in here you could cut with a dull butter knife." Dottie hobbled in, her face knit into an expression of fret. "Burke, are you giving Quinn trouble?"

He smiled at her and, wow, what that did to my insides. That beautiful, rakish smile. He could have charmed anyone.

Maybe even me.

I wasn't going to let that happen.

"Of course not, Dottie," he said.

Her brow dropped. "Well, you'd best not be. Run along and wash your hands for supper. Quinn and I have some lady business to do in here alone and then we'll meet you in the dining room."

He gave a nod, glanced at me as he passed, and said, "Yes, ma'am, Grandmama, ma'am," in a singsongy voice. He'd always been playful with her, and even though part of me wanted to punch him in the face, another part was touched at how cute he always was and apparently always would be with her.

"Find your brother and have him do the same," she called after him, her brow still furrowed as she watched him leave.

"Yes, ma'am" came from the hall, like he was still singing the same song.

She looked at me. "Forget the Eskimos, he could sell ice right on back to God, couldn't he?"

Yes, ma'am.

"I'm sure he'd try, if he thought it would benefit him." Ooh. That was too snotty. So I added, "Or those he loved. It's very nice that he and Frank are here to get you ready for your new life."

She nodded. "I'm so very lucky to have them."

"They were always lucky to have you too, Dottie. What with their mother being gone so much and all." Their mother hadn't only been gone "so much," she'd been gone virtually all the time. After their father died when they were young—something Dottie had always blamed their mother, Adrienne, for on some level— she had spent most of her time gallivanting with various D-list foreign royalty. Dottie's contention was that she wanted to officially become the princess she always thought she should be—this was still in Princess Diana's heyday—but instead she ended up basically disappearing into foreign skies.

I'd always wondered if the truth was something closer to heartbreak than detachment, but I didn't know the woman—whom I'd heard was on her own pseudo-spiritual journey through the best hotels in the Far East—so I guess I was really only hoping the mother of these boys I'd loved hadn't been heartless enough to simply jump ship on them.

Whatever the reasons, Burke and Frank had been lucky to be raised by their grandparents from an early age. It was sad when their grandfather died, but thank goodness that hadn't sent them back to their mother. They stayed with Dottie alone from the ages of seventeen and eighteen on, which meant they were basically raised by then but had to take on the more manly role of "protector" earlier than most.

I had to admire them for it, albeit somewhat reluctantly at times.

"Don't even *mention* that woman." Dottie made a show of shuddering. "I hope she never darkens my door again."

"Guess she's not invited to the wedding, huh?" I gave a laugh, then immediately regretted making light of it. This was a big issue in the family. *Huge*.

"Heavens, no."

I wasn't sure what to say. "We want this to be the happiest day of your life." I thought of her first husband. Suddenly everything I was saying sounded wrong. "Or *one* of them!"

That seemed to do. "Amen!"

"So let's get started." I got my bag and took out some of the cuts of fabric I'd started for her dress and held them up to her, making marks. It only took a few minutes, but it was important.

But for those few minutes, I was going to have to endure the rest of whatever this evening was to bring.

Chapter 10

Dinner was a catastrophe, of course.

I was seated right between Burke and Frank.

Of course.

No one sat on the opposite side of the table. Just like a sitcom, only on a sitcom it's done for filming purposes and you don't usually notice that everyone is sitting on one side of the table in a row, like three weird children in time-out together, but in this case there only seemed to be one possible explanation.

Dottie was trying to get one of us, or all of us, to "confront your demons and move on." Having heard her state, more than once, that this was her big philosophy in life, it wasn't impossible to imagine that was what she had in mind, though it was hard to imagine how she might have thought this could possibly go well.

There *had* to be easier ways to throw us all into the deep end.

In fact, taking us all out on a boat and *literally* throwing us all into the middle of the Atlantic Ocean would have been easier than this torture of weird silences and seemingly loud sipping. We all had ice water, and there were wineglasses at each of our places as well, along with red and white wine on the table.

Burke had half a beer, the label torn halfway off, though I recognized it as the same brand he drank all those years ago.

"So do you all know each other?" Lyle asked, looking bright-eyed and seemingly guileless in our direction. His handsome face was the very picture of innocence. It had been about five minutes since I'd met him, but something about him made me feel like I already knew him. Not that there was a lot to know, it seemed, but then again he might have figured the same about me, idly asking how Burke and I knew each other.

I thought at first I had to have misheard him. Did we *know* each other? He didn't know all about his fiancé's diabolical plan to *heal* us? Was that even *possible*?

Frank reached for the bottle of red wine, possibly because it was closest to him—he'd hated wine last time I'd seen him—and filled his wineglass, then raised it to me as an offering, but I shook my head, thinking of the drive home and how I hoped it would come very, very soon.

A silent moment passed and, as is always the case, my politeness kicked in and I filled it. "Yes, we've all known each other for a while," I said, nodding and looking at my empty plate, suddenly wishing it were filled with something—anything—I could shove into my mouth and point to as an excuse for not being able to answer anything else.

"How?" he asked, looking—I swear this is true—genuinely interested, as if he had no clue.

Was he an actor? That had been my first thought when I'd seen his picture, that he looked like a cheap old TV actor. Maybe this was part of Dottie's plan. To have him play dumb to get us to talk.

But she wasn't even paying attention to him at the moment, she was issuing instructions to one of her staff members, I guess a maid, in hushed tones.

"We met in high school," I said.

"Were you high school sweethearts?" Lyle persisted. "Not all three of you, of course, that would be odd. But did you date either of these handsome guys, Quinn?"

"I—I—" I was drowning. This was awful. How could he be asking such pointed questions if he didn't damn well know the answers?

Frank shot a look at his brother. It was a look I recognized, his exasperation that Burke wasn't doing what Frank thought he should be doing. "I'm sure Burke can explain it best."

I felt, rather than saw, Burke's hostility shoot over my head and back at Frank. Then he said, "Quinn and I used to be engaged—"

"Is that right?" Lyle asked, and he looked so completely surprised that I honestly don't think even Robert De Niro could have done a more convincing job. "You two?" He swished his index finger at Burke and me and raised a questioning brow.

"That's right," Dottie said.

"A long time ago," I said weakly.

"We made it all the way to the altar," Burke said, then gave a dry, humorless spike of laughter. "Well, *I* made it all the way to the altar. Quinn got a little hung up outside with Frank."

"Hey, wasn't *my* fault," Frank said. "You're the one who messed up there."

"Everything would have been fine if you hadn't stepped in."

"I don't think—" I began.

But I got run over by Frank, whose anger pulsated across me toward Burke, even though his voice remained even. "Sure, if Quinn had wanted to live a lie. Call me crazy, but I thought maybe she should make this huge life decision based on *the truth.*"

"*Your* version of it."

"Facts, Burke. There were no *versions.*"

"Stop it, both of you!" I said.

Lyle's smile didn't dim, but something in his eyes did. "I don't follow. What happened? Did you get married?"

Burke shook his head. "She ended up missing the wedding altogether."

My face grew hot.

"That's not quite an accurate characterization," Frank said sharply. He wasn't about to back down. "Is it, Burke?" It was strangely protective and even more strange that I liked it. I was too old to need a boy to protect me, and it wasn't a particularly proud moment, but I liked it anyway. Maybe that was because Burke made me feel so vulnerable.

"I don't know, brother, that's how I remember it." Burke took a generous swig of his beer and set it down hard on the table, making Dottie jump slightly. "I never did get a straight story about what happened out there. How many versions of *that* story are there?"

Two that I knew of. My truth and my obfuscation.

"I notice you didn't come to find out at the time," Frank returned hard.

"I didn't know where you were. I was waiting for *my bride* at *the altar*, which was where we had originally agreed to meet at that particular time." He shifted his narrowed eyes to me, only for a second, then back to Frank. "Though I was definitely expecting to see my best man"—he let the words die in the air for a split second—"in there too."

I shrank in my seat. Did you ever see that episode of *The Flintstones* where every time Fred gets embarrassed he literally shrinks until he's, like, two inches tall? That's how I felt. Like a tiny cartoon Fred Flintstone, between two angry giant cartoon men having an overblown cartoon conversation.

Meanwhile, Dottie just watched right along with Lyle, not offering a word to the conversation. She'd thrown a match on the gasoline and now was just letting it flame. Though, to be fair, how much could she say? Despite the fact that everyone's tone seemed civil and no one made a physical move, there was a certain violence in the air that no sane person would want to get into the middle of.

"I think it's Quinn who never got the straight story," Frank countered blithely, lifting his wine to his lips. He wasn't easily rattled. "At least not the whole one. Wasn't that the problem, Quinn?"

I wished I'd gotten wine. God knew the water wasn't doing squat to ease my nerves.

"It was so long ago. . . ." I looked at Lyle. Despite the fact that he'd started all of this—wittingly or unwittingly—he was the only focus I was comfortable with at this moment. Suddenly *he*, this stranger, was my only driftwood in the water.

"I think the *problem*," Burke said, "was that she listened to a bunch of b.s. from someone with ulterior motives and instead of talking to me, she hauled her ass out of there vowing to, if I'm not mistaken, *cut my balls off* if I ever tried to contact her again in what she prayed would be my painfully short life." He looked back at me. "Have I got that wording right?"

I cleared my throat. "That does sound familiar, but—"

At that moment, thank goodness, the swinging door from the kitchen opened, and I allowed myself to be interrupted by the maid Dottie had been talking to earlier, who entered the room along with a whip-thin man of perhaps forty-five or so, who looked like an old movie caricature of The Butler. Each held a silver platter.

They came directly to me first and stood on either side of me, lifting the lids of their respective platters to reveal the kind of gorgeous gourmet food normally reserved for a special occasion at a AAA four-diamond restaurant.

It was a weird dichotomy that Dottie did things this way. She was so relaxed and easy to be around, yet dinner service was always so elegant. I'd asked Burke about it once, years ago, and he said it was because this had been the one tradition Dottie's mom had apparently instilled in her before she passed away when Dottie was still a teenager, and it was the way Joss had liked things once they got married. Ever since then, Dottie had maintained it, even under the most seemingly absurd circumstances.

"Filet mignon with *sauce béarnaise* or demi-glace reduction with port wine," the maid said to me, indicating the choices.

"I— either. I'll just— béarnaise," I concluded lamely. I couldn't ask her to decide. That *wasn't done* in surroundings like this. At Ruby Tuesday, yes, maybe I could have let the waiter choose which sauce he thought I'd like for my boneless Buffalo tenders, but in Middleburg's finest homes, a guest was expected to behave and be treated like (or *almost* like) the lady of the manor.

It was going to be a long night.

It already was.

"So, Lyle," Burke said, and the edge to his voice caught my attention. "Have you been married before?"

"Nope," Lyle said.

Burke looked at him in silence for just a little longer than was comfortable. "Why is that?"

Lyle shrugged. "Never found the right girl, I guess."

"Mm." Burke nodded in a way that said, *Bullshit*, louder than words could have. What was he thinking?

"Well, you have now," I said, sounding more chirpy than I meant to. "You hit the jackpot with Dottie."

"Exactly," Burke murmured.

Apparently Lyle didn't hear that. "I sure do love her," he said.

"Ooh, go on." Dottie giggled.

"I think you guys will be really happy together," I said, feeling Burke bristle beside me. He was clearly against this marriage. "In fact—"

I was interrupted, thank goodness, by the surprisingly high, reedy voice of the butler. "Asparagus amandine, roasted baby beets, and scalloped truffle potatoes—which would the lady like?"

Under normal circumstances? All of them.

Tonight? A nice hemlock salad would have really hit the spot.

A little cyanide dressing on the side. Just in case.

"Potatoes, please," I said, thinking they would be the easiest to dish out quickly, so he could move on and the Spotlight of Service could move off me.

They had a much easier time with everyone else, and it seemed to take the same amount of time to serve the other four collectively as it had to get me to dither my way through a choice.

I was relieved when they left the room, only to have the rebounding horror of seeing them return with more platters.

"Salad of microgreens, arugula, caramelized shallots, and roasted rainbow carrot, topped with champagne vinaigrette?" she offered in a practiced voice.

"Sure." Wouldn't want to insult anyone. "Just a touch, though, thanks." I watched her scoop a pile onto a salad plate I hadn't previously noticed.

Then, of course, the pièce de résistance.

As if in schlocky slow motion, he lifted the lid of his platter to reveal my grandmother's obnoxiously colorful Tupperware bowl, with a gleaming silver serving spoon poking out of it like found treasure buried under an old tree.

Talk about cartoons! The plastic somehow looked even more *plastic*, brighter than a special-edition crayon, when perched on a gleaming antique silver platter.

"Macaroni salad?" he asked, somehow with a straight face, though I swear there was a smirk in his voice.

I can't honestly ever remember being so embarrassed in my life. "You know, I don't think that really *goes* with the rest of this. I was under the impression that this was"—I looked at Dottie pointedly—"a kind of picnic or something *very informal*."

"Well, honey, this *is* informal," she said, then gestured acknowledgment at the servers. "Oh, I know this all seems very stuffy, but look who's here, it's just us. We're *family*. What would be more comfortable and casual than this?"

A firing squad?

"I can think of a few things," Burke murmured.

"What's that, honey?" Dottie asked, straining in his direction.

"*Casual* and *comfortable* aren't the first words that come to mind as far as describing this meal," he said to her. "Now, you know that, Dottie."

"Nice, Burke," Frank said. "Make everyone feel awkward. By the way, I tried the macaroni salad in the kitchen, it's really good." He looked at me with utter sincerity. "Seriously, it's really good. I love that stuff."

Burke just scoffed. Didn't even bother to dignify it with an answer. I remembered when he'd figured out that technique with Frank.

It drove Frank crazy.

Obviously it wasn't fair to make like *Burke* was the reason everyone might be feeling awkward right now, but I didn't know what to say to ease the situation. If anything, I was the spark in this powder keg, and the quieter I remained, the better.

The servers made their way around the table and, to my utter humiliation, everyone politely took a splat or two of macaroni salad on their plates next to the elegant entrées.

"I *love* macaroni salad," Lyle even said, tucking in and looking for all the world like he really meant it. "My dad made the best, believe it or not. He'd add bacon or ham hocks." He took a bite and kept talking. "He was a barbecue man, and all summer long he'd do all the cooking. He wouldn't even let my mother do the dishes, he'd just rinse them off with a hose and send me and my brother in to scrub them. The ones that weren't paper, that is. We'd just throw the paper ones away. Isn't that convenient? Just"—he made a throwing gesture—"threw 'em away."

"Paper plates are *very* convenient," Dottie agreed.

And the conversation went on like that. Paper plates, and a particularly long detour into doilies, which Lyle had quite a lot of feelings about, surprisingly.

So I had no warning that the conversation was going to take such a bad turn until it was upon me. We were discussing the sale of the farm, that Dottie felt ready since that chapter of her life was over and that Frank felt ambivalent about it since he didn't have the time to be a part-time farmer on the weekends.

Burke said nothing, but I felt his unhappiness pulsating from beside me.

"If there were children who could inherit it, I might think twice about it," Dottie said, and I felt a little pinch of sadness because of course I had once expected to have the very children she was referencing.

"Well, I'm not looking at marriage and kids anytime soon," Frank said, "and of course with Burke's first marriage," then he amended, "*only* marriage, I mean. That didn't turn out so good, so it's not like we've got any real expectation of impending heirs."

I kind of heard the whole sentence, but, honestly, I really lost my focus after the first seven words or so. *Marriage.* It was a shock every time I thought about it. I looked at him and he must have seen the question in my eyes.

"It was brief," he said . . . briefly.

It was as if everyone else in the room faded into the background. "Care to elaborate?" I asked quietly.

He very deliberately took a bite of macaroni salad and shook his head. "Nope."

I resisted an urge to jab him with my elbow.

Some habits die hard.

Okay, so at this point, I will admit the tension around the table was getting a little thick. Clearly no one wanted to interrupt— even when people are being rude, if they're marching forward with a strong agenda, it's hard to jump in front of them and say, *Hey, let's just have some more macaroni salad and get along.*

Got it.

But at the same time, there was no stopping this boulder from rolling through the maze in this cave, just like something from Indiana Jones. The truth had been unleashed and, while I didn't want to be knocked over by it, I had to know it in its entirety before I could take an easy breath again.

I didn't taste anything else I ate.

When the meal was finally over, after what seemed like hours, and everyone had gotten up from the table, I told Dottie I had to leave.

Her expression dropped. "Are you sure, honey? I was hoping maybe you'd stay to play cards!"

She meant it. She actually thought the trauma had passed, that things were better, and that we could all sit down and play a nice game of cards together. I wished I could. I wished it was that easy for me. It should have been. It had been a long time and there was no need for me to feel weird about something that had no more relevance to my day-to-day life than an old episode of *Full House*.

"I've got a lot of stuff to do," I said, and smiled in what I hoped was a firm but inarguable way. "Thank you so much for dinner." I started to leave but was stopped by Burke.

"I'll walk you out to your car," he said.

I met his eyes and felt that same stupid shiver of pleasure I always felt when I met his eyes. It was immediately replaced by memory, and then resolve. "That's really not necessary."

"I believe you mean *thank you*."

"No, I mean *no*."

"There are bears out there," he said with a hint of a smile.

"And wolves in here," I said, unable to keep from smiling back. Arrrgh! Why was it so easy for him to disarm me? "I'd rather take my chances with the bears." Carrying a picnic basket and wearing a dress made of salami and Snickers bars.

"I think you'll fare all right. You'll make it all the way into your car without incident, I guarantee it." He put a hand to my elbow and guided me toward the door. My skin felt warm under his touch.

"Good night!" Dottie said, and I heard the subtle excitement in her voice.

"Good to meet you," Lyle added, and there was nothing more to his tone than that.

I didn't know where Frank was at that point, but I was glad not to be in the middle of a round two between him and Burke.

As soon as Burke and I got out into the cool night air, I shifted my arm to lose his grip. "So it's interesting that you did get married after all," I said, not too sharply—I was making an effort—but I was afraid my possessiveness came through in my voice.

"Jealous?"

Obviously. "Just surprised."

"It was short-lived. But it's not like you didn't have a chance first."

The gravel of the driveway crunched under our steps.

"Actually it's a lot like I didn't have a chance," I said, wishing to God I were alone. There was no way this conversation could possibly end well. No way. "When it was all said and done I felt like I'd *never* stood a chance with you."

"Ridiculous."

I stopped and looked at him under the dim drive lights. "What's the story?"

"Does it matter?"

Dread threaded through me. "Tell me."

There was a moment of cicadas and crickets before, "You really want to hear it?"

Trepidation built in my chest like a big pile of Jenga blocks, ready to crash down unexpectedly at any moment, given one wrong move. "I'm sure I don't."

"Then I won't."

"Do."

He shrugged. "It was ill-advised."

I took an uneven breath. "All your marriages seem to be."

"Lucky for my brother."

"What is *that* supposed to mean?"

"He scored big-time, didn't he? Got to run off with the girl he'd always had the hots for, *and* screw me over at the same time. You played right into his hand."

"Are you saying he wasn't telling me the truth?" I asked, and at that moment I could have believed whatever he said to me.

"I don't even *know* exactly what he said to you. All I know is that he stopped the wedding and told you something that ended seven years of you and me together. Then you guys got in a car together and drove off to California."

Wow, he didn't even know where we'd gone.

Those two really *didn't* talk.

If Facebook had been around at the time, I would have been checking in all over town, probably, drunkenly trying to stick it to Burke in whatever lame way I could. But it wasn't and I hadn't, so apparently this secret remained buried.

And I saw no reason to resurrect it.

"I notice you're avoiding the question of your *marriage*," I obfuscated. "Who was it?" I was sure he was going to say Sarah Lynn. Absolutely sure. As if somehow Burke Morrison and Sarah Lynn had gotten married and all of the town had missed it or failed to talk about it, even though other tidbits, like Jennifer Kearny's gall bladder removal had practically made it to the front page of the local *Gazette.*

If he said Sarah Lynn, or any name I knew, I would have to go get one of the ceremonial pistols off the wall of the library and hope to god it had a bullet in it, or at least enough gunpowder residue to make some sort of impact. Was that even possible? Probably not. In all likelihood, Burke would report something surprising and upsetting and I'd go into the library, take a pistol down, hold it to my temple and pull the trigger for an anticlimactic click, and then have to simply clock myself with it and wake up on the sofa with a bag of Dottie's frozen peas on my head.

At the very least, I could give myself credit for thinking ahead and bracing myself, as strongly as possible, for whatever he was going to say.

"No one you know," he said.

"So she has no name?" I couldn't help being snarky. None of this was my *right* to know, so I didn't know why I was being so ugly about it, but I couldn't shut up. "Or is that her name? Was she foreign? *Nooneyouknow.* I don't know—that's not Italian, right?" I didn't wait for an answer. "So who was it?"

Now I needed to know. This was out there, it existed whether I wanted it to or not, and I couldn't make it not true simply by not thinking about it. At this point, I couldn't imagine going home with only the memory of his *no one you know* to comfort me. Technically he could have said that about Sarah Lynn, because I didn't really even know *her*, I just disliked her on sight and on principle.

So this could well be someone I was familiar with—whether anyone else would characterize that as *knowing* her or not—thus, the potential for further anguish was alive and well as far as I was concerned.

Though, to be honest, the potential for anguish was *always* alive and well where Burke was concerned, which was why I'd worked so damn hard to get him out of my head for so long.

Now I couldn't let it go. I was a dog on a meaty bone.

"Perry Watkins."

"I'm sorry?"

"Perry Watkins."

"I don't know who that is."

He laughed. "I told you that."

"You married someone named *Perry*? Are you serious? Isn't that a guy's name?"

He shook his head. "Not in this case, no."

"Where did you meet her? How long did you know her? How long were you married?"

I saw his smile flash. "I thought you didn't care."

"I don't," I lied. "What did she look like?"

"Small, dark-haired, dark-eyed. You'd say she looked like Audrey Hepburn and I'd disagree and we'd probably have an argument about it, but there's your point of reference."

I almost laughed. We *never* agreed on celebrity look-alikes. That was a weird thing about us. We would be able to knock heads over whether or not someone looked like Jon Bon Jovi or Dave Chappelle. But I was both touched and saddened by the fact that he knew me well enough to know who I'd think she looked like.

On the other hand, I didn't like that she was an adorable little bright-eyed pixie with a waist the circumference of string cheese and a big white smile, which was how I was picturing her now.

But this was all crazy. It wasn't my right to care about this at all. "Well, you've always had good taste."

"If bad sense."

"Maybe."

"It's not a mistake I'll be making again," he said, hooking his thumbs on his belt loops. "Getting married, I mean."

And, yes, I had left him at the altar. Yes, I had rejected him. Yes, the choice had been mine and I'd chosen not to be with him.

I knew all of that.

So why did it bug me to hear him say that?

It had to be some strange, leftover impulse deep inside. Some part of me that hadn't gotten the news that the relationship had run its course and long since passed.

"That's what you say now," I said anyway, I suppose trying to goose him into some openness.

"Nope. I'm a lone wolf. A pack of one." He was always quoting movies, I think because he knew it drove me crazy. "I don't need anyone else."

And there it was again, that pang of hurt that he didn't want me, even though I'd been the one to end it.

"Whatever," I said. Childish.

He laughed. "Why does that bug you?"

"It doesn't. I have no stake in what you do."

"That's right. Someday you'll find a decent guy and go with him."

"I don't want *any*one," I said, parroting him even though I hadn't set out to. "I'm a lone wolf too."

"You're no wolf." He put his hands on my shoulders and pulled me close. He hesitated only for a split second before kissing me. Mouth open, tongue warm and familiar against mine. Funny how something like that comes back to you. We'd done this a million times in our lifetimes and it never, ever got old. For all the times I might have been annoyed with him or straight-up livid with him or tired or sick, there had never been one time I didn't feel like kissing him. There had never been a time when his mouth on mine didn't send a thrill straight from my heart right down to my core.

Immediately I wanted him. I wanted more. I wanted everything. And I mean *immediately*. There was no stopping to think, to assess, to consider the pros and cons. It was probably *all* cons, but in this moment I didn't care because that's what his kiss did to me.

It was a chemical reaction.

I cupped his face with my hands, skidding my thumbs across his high cheekbones, like I'd done countless times before. The shadow of his beard was a little rough against my skin. I could remember coming home, red-faced and raw and happy after making out with him for hours in the back of his old Chevy.

Everything about this was wonderfully familiar, like a favorite dessert, even while everything in my head was screaming for me to stop. It was madness, this complete lack of control. Before tonight, the last time I'd seen him was, literally, stomping out of the church in a filthy wedding dress with gum on my ass. That had been his last view of me.

Now, after a couple of hours of sniping back and forth like

children, over issues we either should have solved years ago or never revisited at all, I was wrapped up in his arms, lips locked, standing on the driveway to a property I'd once thought I would never see again.

In a way it was like time travel.

He slid his hand down my back and dipped his fingertips under the waistband of my jeans. I felt him smile against my mouth.

"Going commando?"

"As a matter of fact, yes." I tilted my head and kissed his cheek, his jawline, and tangled my fingers in his hair.

"Since when?"

"Yesterday."

"This isn't like you."

"That's the idea."

His mouth found mine again and I opened to him eagerly, but said, "We shouldn't be doing this."

"That's for sure."

"Why are we doing this?"

"I don't know." He ran his hands up my back again and pulled me closer. Not that *closer* was really possible. Tighter.

And I felt so *safe*. For just a moment, here in the arms of the wolf himself, I felt completely safe.

But I forced myself to draw back. "I've got to go."

He looked at me for a moment, then took a step back. "Probably a good idea."

"Is this the part where I say it was good to see you again and then I spend the rest of the night kicking myself for saying something so small and ridiculous?"

He nodded. "That's exactly where we are in the script."

"Okay, then. It was good to see you again. And kind of bad. Actually kind of awful."

That smile. "Ditto."

"This"—I gestured vaguely between us—"what just happened cannot happen again. Nothing good can come of that."

"I hear you."

"You need to do more than hear me, Burke, you need to *agree* with me and make sure it doesn't happen again."

He sucked air in through his teeth. "I don't know, if you come at me, I'm not sure I'll be able to stop you."

I rolled my eyes but had to smile. "Somehow you'll just have to find a way to fight me off."

"And if it's the opposite, if I approach you, you have my full permission to beat me off as well."

"Very funny."

"Thanks."

"Look, we've always had this chemical attraction. *Apparently* that still exists even though there are many, *many* reasons, we both know, that we are a bad combination."

He shrugged.

What did *that* mean?

Wait, it didn't matter what it meant. I didn't want to care what it meant. There was no room in my heart or my head to revisit Burke Morrison.

"So I'm going to go now," I said. "And that's not going to happen again. Agreed?"

He paused, then nodded. "Agreed."

"Good. So. Good night."

And with that, I left. And with every foot, every yard, every mile that subsequently fell between us, I—or maybe some deep gut instinct—tried to tell myself to stay away, stay away, stay away . . .

Stay *away* from Burke Morrison.

Chapter 11

Late July, Fifteen Years Ago

Quinn knew she shouldn't have tried pot.

She had always been completely straight and narrow. When people started lighting up at a party, she'd go to another room, or go home, or whatever, it just wasn't her *thing*.

But it was midsummer before her senior year and she was supposed to be having the time of her life, and instead Burke had upset her by saying . . . something, she actually couldn't remember *exactly* what his wording was, but it was to the effect that he was going to "keep my options open" when he started college in the fall.

As soon as she'd gotten upset, he'd taken it back, of course, but by then he'd already said it. He couldn't *un*say it.

So she went with Karen and Rami to a party at Rami's friend's house down some endless dirt road, way outside of town. No parents, no close neighbors, the music was throbbing, the keg was spilling over, and after about five beers when a cute guy asked

Quinn if she wanted to get stoned, she thought, *Fuck Burke*, and went into a darkened back den of the house with the guy. He lit a bong, took a hit, and handed it to her.

She had no idea how to use it.

So he laughed and told her, and for about fifteen minutes they passed it back and forth. At first she felt nothing, beyond the harsh rush of smoke in her lungs, but she kind of enjoyed the process of passing it back and forth, like they were playing a game.

She'd always heard that you don't really get high the first time you smoke. That the chemical needs to build up in your brain or something, so it might mellow you out a little, or make you hungry, but it wouldn't blast you.

So she was completely unprepared for the room to start spinning.

"Good stuff, huh?" the guy—she thought he said his name was *Nard*—said.

"I . . . don't . . ." She swallowed and blinked hard. "Yeah," she said, suddenly aware that she needed to get out of the smoky room and into fresh air. Alone. "Thanks." She got up unsteadily and made her way to the door, feeling like she was in a spinning room in a carnival funhouse.

Except there was *nothing* fun about it.

Why did people do this?

She went outside and made her way to Rami. Even in her state, she could tell that Rami, who had driven that night, was hammered.

"We're going to stay here, okay?" Rami slurred. "Can't drive. If something happened, my parents would *kill* me."

Quinn made an effort to focus on her. She was disappointed

that they weren't leaving, but there was no way she wanted to get in a crash on the way home. That had happened to too many people they knew.

"I think I'm going to try to get home," Quinn told her. "Another way."

"Huh?"

"I'm calling Burke."

"That *asshole*. Screw him! Just stay here. I think Nard likes you! Go with him instead!"

Just the mention of his name gave Quinn a surge of nausea.

"What's wrong?" Rami looked concerned, though she herself was teetering. "Are you okay?"

There was no way she could admit to Rami what she'd done. She couldn't admit it to anyone. The thought of telling Burke the truth was terrifying, he would be so mad. But what if she needed to go to the hospital or something? What if the pot had been laced with something? This wasn't a reaction she'd ever heard of, so *something* else seemed to be going on.

"Fine," Quinn muttered, "just going to go find a phone." She went back into the house, hoping she wouldn't run into Nard. (Was that *really* his name?) She found a phone on the wall in the kitchen, glanced at the digital clock on the stove, which seemed to say it was 11:41 P.M. though the 1's and 4's kind of blurred together. As bad as it was to have to call Burke's house phone so late, she hoped it wasn't 4:00 A.M. instead of 11:00 P.M.

She dialed and leaned against the wall, holding the phone to her ear. *Please don't let Dottie answer, please don't let Dottie answer, please don't let Dottie answer. . . .*

"Hello?"

Oh, thank *god*. "Burke, I need you to come get me. I'm at a party and I'm sick and Rami drank too much to drive, and . . ." She started to cry, like a kid who'd fallen and skinned her knee. "I just want to go home."

"This is Frank. Burke's not here. But where are you? I'll come get you."

"Burke's not there?" The tears burned.

"No, but don't worry, I will leave now, just tell me where you are."

"I don't know!" She felt frantic, like a caged animal. "I don't." She shook her head even though he couldn't see her.

"Have you been drinking?"

She grimaced. "Yes."

"Okay, are you in someone's house?"

"Yes."

"Can you ask someone the address?"

It was too pitiful to say, *I don't know anyone here*, so she said, "Hold on," and started to put the phone down to begin the humiliating task of asking someone where she was. Then she noticed a pile of mail on the counter by the oven. "Wait. There's mail. I'm at . . ." She squinted and tried to read the printing on the catalog addressed to *Clark or Resident*. She read it off, then looked at another piece of mail and read it again to make sure she was consistent.

"Got it," Frank said. "I'll be there in about thirty minutes."

"I'm going down to the end of the driveway," she said, hoping the walk would do her good and knowing that being away from the people would. "Don't run me over," she added with a lame laugh.

"I won't," he said, but his voice remained gentle.

She made her way down the drive. It seemed to take forever. Even alone, she was embarrassed to be so wobbly. She took big gulps of air, willing the freshness in and the toxin out, but everything was still spinning and once she even had to stop and be sick into the bushes. It was horrible. What a mistake.

She'd always been anti-drug, so it figured the one time she went against her own principles something like this would happen. *Lesson learned*, she thought. *Let it end now.*

She sat down on a brick wall by the end of the driveway and held on with her hands, gripping the rough surface hard so she wouldn't fall.

After what seemed like forever, headlights appeared in the distance and a car came slowly down the road, drawing to a halt in front of her. He flicked his lights and she got off the wall and went to the passenger door.

"Thank you," she said, climbing in. "I don't know how to thank you enough."

"Don't worry about it. Seriously."

"I didn't wake your grandparents up by calling, did I?"

He gave a laugh. "An earthquake wouldn't wake them up."

There was that small mercy at least.

He started to drive and she felt her stomach lurch.

"Maybe you should get sick," he said. "Get rid of whatever might be in your stomach waiting to go into your bloodstream."

"I already did." She started to cry again. "Frank . . ."

"What's wrong?"

"I didn't just drink."

He stopped the car and turned to face her in the mostly dark. "Okay . . . ? What did you do?"

"Swear you won't tell anyone."

He paused. "If you need medical attention, we're going to *have* to tell the truth."

"I don't think I do. Swear you won't tell Burke."

"Okay."

"*Swear* it. You'll *never* tell him."

"I swear I'll never tell Burke," he said. "What am I not telling?"

"I smoked pot."

Even in the dim light, she could see his features relax. "Quinn, that's not *that* big a deal—"

"I think it was laced with something."

His gaze shot back to her eyes. "What?"

"I'm not sure. It's just that I've never done it before and it made me really, really dizzy and I'm seeing vapor trails and it's been like, I don't know how long, and it doesn't seem to be getting any better, and"—a wave of nausea came over her—"I don't know if it's *supposed* to be like this or what. I've never done it before."

"Who gave it to you?" His voice was hard. He was ready to kick ass on her behalf, it was clear. And she appreciated that.

"I don't even know," she admitted. "Nard or something."

He thought. "Bernard Wolfe?"

She shrugged and swallowed hard.

"Tall, skinny, black hair?"

She nodded. "Maybe."

"Motherfucker."

"You know him?"

"Barely. He's a dealer. He probably hoped you'd like whatever the hell this is so you'd buy more."

Great. So the supposedly cute guy hadn't even liked her for herself, he just wanted her to be a new customer. Maybe she deserved that.

"So you don't think it's dangerous?"

He glanced at her, then pushed the gas to resume driving. "Probably not. I'll stay with you till you feel better and if we need to go to the ER, we will. I can kill Bernard later."

She wanted to thank him, to express how this wasn't like her and she didn't normally do anything crazy and would never, ever do it again, but she was afraid if she didn't stay very still she was going to puke.

So instead she leaned back against the seat and closed her eyes.

She didn't think she was tired but she fell asleep anyway, and the next time she opened her eyes, she was lying across the front bench seat of Frank's Chevy Impala and the sun was just beginning to rise over the horizon.

He was sitting on the front hood of the car, watching it.

She sat up and put a hand to her head, still woozy. The world wasn't spinning anymore, but it wasn't exactly "normal" either.

She opened the car door and got out into the fresh, warm air of another perfect summer morning.

"Hey," she said.

"Oh, hey." He turned, surprised, and got off the hood. "I was just thinking I should wake you up so we could go before your parents get up."

"Yeah." She rubbed her eyes. "Thanks." She met his eyes. "Seriously, thank you."

He smiled. His eyes crinkled at the corners and his whole face softened. "Get in the car."

She did, and as they started toward her house, only a few blocks away, she said, "I know you really went out of your way to help me last night and I really appreciate that. I also know I don't have any right to ask you any sort of favor on top of it, but, like I said last night, I *really* don't want Burke to know about this. It's . . . it's just really embarrassing."

"He's not going to hear it from me."

"Do you mean it?"

He glanced at her. "Quinn, I think you've been through enough hell from last night. Why would I add to that? What could I possibly gain from it?"

She felt her face grow warm. "Thank you."

They finished the drive in silence.

When he pulled up in front of her house, she took a steadying breath, then looked at him one more time. "Thanks again."

"I'm glad you're okay."

They looked at each other for just a fraction of a moment too long, and Quinn felt a tremor go through her. Embarrassment, she rationalized. He'd seen her at her worst.

How could she ever face him again?

It wasn't until later in the afternoon that the most obvious thing occurred to her: Where had *Burke* been in the middle of the night when she called?

It wasn't the last time she'd wonder something just like that.

Chapter 12

Present

Speed dating. Tonight. I already signed you up.

Glenn had used a bigger envelope this time so he could fit a pamphlet in for Short Stops Speed Dating. Tonight's meeting was in a good restaurant in a bad strip mall twenty-some miles away, in Leesburg.

"Oh, good, you got it," Glenn said, coming through the front door of the shop.

"Like you weren't standing in the window watching."

"I was," he admitted immediately. "I had to rush in and quell the objection I *know* you're going to make."

"Not necessarily." But probably. He was probably right.

"Listen," he said. "I went to a few of these when I lived in Savannah and they were really fun, though, admittedly, a different crowd. Each round is just a few minutes, then you're off the hook.

Honestly, this should have been a Day One activity, and I tried, but they sell out for women so fast, this was the soonest I could get."

"Which means there will be, like, three men there?"

He hesitated. "There *do* tend to be more women than men," he acknowledged. "Especially in the big metropolitan areas. That's what everyone says."

"Great. So it'll be like musical chairs. Some people sitting and chatting, while everyone else stands around awkwardly, trying to figure out what to do with their hands." I hated that feeling, the self-conscious posture that came with knowing there was no way to look cool in a given situation. Like inhaling on a doctor's command, or waiting for a ball you may or may not have to dodge.

"But you are *superior* to most women. Besides, nothing ventured, nothing gained."

I rolled my eyes. "You're not expecting me to get a boyfriend out of this, right?"

"Tonight? No. It would be *nice*, but the main objective of you doing this tonight is to get you mingling with people who don't live within two miles of you. Consider it mere practice for a later assignment."

"That sounds daunting."

He raised an eyebrow. "Let's just stick to the task at hand, okay? This is going to be totally refreshing. Think about it—how often do you get to meet new people and *not be allowed* to talk to them for more than six minutes?"

I nodded. "I have to admit, there is some appeal there."

"And if you find a guy to keep your mind off the Morrisons?"

I thought about it. "There is *definitely* some appeal *there*."

"So you'll do it?"

This one actually made sense as far as breaking my routine. "Sure. Why not?"

Kate Newton was one of the sweetest people I'd ever met. Seriously. Everything about her just emanated *kindness*.

She'd come to me in March with an outdated pink bridesmaid dress in hand. "Can you make this into a wedding dress somehow?" she'd asked. "It's the most formal thing I have and we don't have a lot of money to waste on something we'll only use one day."

I'd half expected her to go on to tell me they didn't have *time* either, that she needed the dress for a shotgun wedding—not that there's anything wrong with that—but it turned out she was a teacher and he was a truck driver and they were saving their money for a house someday, so everything to do with the wedding had to be on the cheap.

It made sense, really, and even though I was in the business of making quality, and most often *costly*, gowns, I was more impressed with her attitude than that of many of my clients.

So I wanted to help in any way possible.

The dress was a challenge, I'm not going to blow sunshine on that one. It looked like something from the eighties, slick satin cut into an asymmetrical hem, higher in the front, ankle-length in the back. I imagined there was probably some sort of uniform flower or hair band for the bridesmaids, and shoes dyed to match.

Fortunately, Kate wanted her gown cocktail-length, which

eliminated the hassle of trying to blend a different fabric in to make a long gown that didn't look like patchwork, which it would be.

So, with some work, and a few nice bolts of fabric I'd had left over from other projects, I'd managed to make her bridesmaid dress into one of the prettiest, if simplest, gowns I'd ever made.

Now it was her final fitting and the first time she saw herself as the bride she was about to be.

The dress was actually pink, but so pale with time and the wide weave of the fabric that it actually looked more like an elegant ivory. Gone was the bi-level hem—the Farrah Fawcett hair of dresses—and it was now a swingy (but not hip-exploding) cocktail length, tight in the bodice and up to a straight neckline that could *only* be flattering on someone as modestly endowed as Kate. But on her it was perfect, creating the illusion of an ample breast and narrow waist, neither of which she would have probably attributed to herself naked in front of the bathroom mirror.

Yet she came out of the dressing room slowly, her eyes gleaming. "I can't believe you did this."

"Come on," I said, ushering her in front of the three-way mirror. "You've got to see all the angles."

She stepped up and, even in bare feet, looked so much like a doll on a music box that I could have cried myself.

It was perfect for her.

She looked for a long time, shyly checking the side views and the back, then turned to me and ran her hands along her forearms. "It gives me goose bumps," she said. "Is that really me?"

"Of course!"

"Charlie is going to be so surprised. He saw the dress the way it used to be. He's no seamstress, but even he could tell that it was horrible."

I laughed. "It wasn't *horrible*." It was, though. "But I'm glad you like it now."

"I love it." She looked at me evenly. "I will be so proud to wear this now. I will never, ever have another wedding, and even though we couldn't afford to make it into the social event of the season, it is going to be the most special day of my life." Tears began to roll down her cheeks then. "I didn't want to look like a clown."

And then I was verging on tearful too. "You never could. You would have looked beautiful no matter what. No one as happy and in love as you are could look anything less than that."

She smiled. "Well . . . the hem . . ."

"Yeah." I wrinkled my nose. "There was that hem."

"Thank you," she said, sobering. "From the bottom of my heart."

"You're welcome. From the bottom of mine. You want any adjustments before you take it?"

"Nope. No point in messing with perfection."

She went back into the dressing room to change and I felt a pang of jealousy. It was an ugly feeling to inject into such a nice exchange, but it was hard not to. Love seems like such a simple thing to ask for. Such a basic right. It takes no skill, no experience, no money, no education, nothing—it can happen to anyone.

But it doesn't happen to everyone.

Even though everyone, deep down, wants it.

Anyway, I do.

. . .

It was still light out when I left the shop at seven to go to the Short Stops meeting. As I stepped onto the sidewalk, I noticed a guy tacking a FOR SALE sign onto the building across the street. It used to be a bar, but they'd lost their liquor license and it had been vacant for almost a year, which had made for blissful silence at night. When I saw the sign going up, up went my guard.

This was just more evidence that the rest of the world was moving on while I was not. Or at least while I was resisting. Despite the fact that I felt somewhat disheartened by this knowledge, it did reinforce my determination to take tonight as an opportunity to get out of my head.

I was really sick of being in my head.

I was even more sick of *Burke* being in my head.

For a moment I entertained the crazy idea of getting Frank to go with me. He'd always had that protector thing going and this was not a situation I was comfortable walking into alone. But I didn't think it was appropriate to bring a date to a dating service, so, of course, I opted against that.

Half an hour later, I parked in the freshly painted parking lot of the Golden Mile strip mall and headed for the bar. With every step, I felt more and more apprehensive. According to the rules, I'd spend six minutes each with ten men, then write down those I was interested in seeing again. If any of the ones I put down also put my name down, Short Stops would get us in touch with each other.

But I'd been raised to be polite to a fault—no, seriously, to a *fault*, my life was *full* of unnecessary guilt because of it—and since I was pretty sure I wasn't going to be interested in anyone, I was already worried about hurting people's feelings.

Not that I was assuming everyone was going to want me. But what if even just one did? How insulting it would be to find that I hadn't written him down as well.

Of course, the alternative was to write everyone's name down and end up hearing way too much from people I thought way too little of.

Maybe this was a bad idea.

Don't you dare wimp out, I heard Glenn's voice saying in my head. *You're just looking for a convenient excuse to stay in your tiny world and die alone except for a bunch of cats.*

That was true. True, true, true.

My original objective was still sound. I was getting out of town for a bit. In a couple of hours I would be on my way back to the familiar safety of my own home. No harm, no foul.

This was a good thing.

Fortified with new optimism, I took long, confident strides to the door and pulled it open.

Hello, everyone! I'm here!

As soon as I walked into the dingy room, my optimism seeped out like water from a half-filled broken glass. There were a lot of women there. A lot of women. And about three men, none of whom looked, how shall I say it, like candidates.

Not even *possible* candidates.

"Name?"

I jerked my attention to a pert little blonde who was wearing a pert little mock-baseball outfit, with shorts so tiny that I could almost see her uterus.

"Quinn Barton."

She looked down at the clipboard she was holding, mouthing the names as she went along, until she got to mine and checked it off. Then she took a whistle from around her neck and blew a shrill note right through my brain. Then she shouted my name to the room, like it was a debutante ball, and said to me, in a normal tone, "You can take a seat at table four." She pointed to a table across the room with a piece of printer paper that had a 4 on it. It was flanked, unsurprisingly, by tables 3 and 5.

With a heavy heart, I went and sat down, feeling like a nervous third-grader on the first day of school.

At exactly eight o'clock the blonde blew her whistle for the hundred and fourth time and pranced into the middle of the room. "Hello, everybody!" she trilled. "I'm Judy. Welcome to Short Stops!"

There was an awkward muttering of vague responses from around the room, but she didn't seem to notice.

"All of you gentlemen picked a number from my hat on your way in." She tipped her baseball cap. "Next time I blow this whistle, you will go to the lady seated at the table with your number on it. You will have six minutes to chat before I blow the whistle again and you move on to the next number. Any questions?"

There was dead silence.

"Good!" She blew the whistle and we were off.

A guy named Al lumbered over to me first. That is, I think his name was Al. It could have been Lv, but it was more likely that his name tag was just upside down.

"Hi," I said, too brightly. I was determined to give this a chance, or at least to be able to report to Glenn that I had. It wasn't fair to judge on first appearances. Maybe, with a little exercise and electric shock therapy, Al/Lv could be Ryan Reynolds.

He sat down and the wooden chair squeaked under his weight.

"Yeah, hey." He waved my outstretched hand away. "What's your name?"

"Quinn. And you're—"

"My ex-wife's sister's name is Gwen." He patted his greasy-looking Fred Flintstone black hair into place. "She was a hot number. Part of what got me into trouble."

What could I say to that?

What could I *possibly* say to that?

"So let's cut to the chase," Al/Lv said. "I'm looking for someone who'd like to get together and have a little fun in the afternoons. Sound like something you could handle?" He leaned back and I noticed a gold necklace so tight around his neck that it was cutting into his doughy flesh.

"No." I had to be open-minded and give people a chance, but this was ridiculous.

I was ready to give him a helpful and comprehensive list of the things about him that made his suggestion distasteful, but he didn't give me a chance.

"Okay." He stood up and lumbered away, over to the bar, where he made a big show of dipping his meaty paw into the peanuts and then s-l-o-w-l-y chewing, while looking at the next tables.

Humiliation burned in my cheeks. What must people think when they saw this guy wasn't even able to speak to me for six minutes? At least I had been willing to make small talk before he moved on to the next woman.

Judy's whistle trilled after what felt like an hour of me sitting there alone, and another man made his way to my table.

This one was nice-looking, in an innocuous sort of way. Sandy-blond hair. Grayish eyes. He was a little thin for my tastes, but after Al/Lv, that was less of a liability than it might normally have been.

He put out his hand. "Hi, how are you? I'm Gerard."

"Hi, Gerard, I'm Quinn."

"That guy's a jerk," he said, sitting down. "He comes to a lot of these things."

So must you, I thought, *if you know he does.* He'd tipped his hand, which broke rule number one of hypocrisy. But I tried not to let that prejudice me.

"So tell me what you're looking for in a man," Gerard said, looking directly into my eyes. That was good, he got points for eye contact.

Somehow it hadn't occurred to me to be prepared with answers, and suddenly my mind went blank. I thought back to my college biology unit on attraction. What did women look for in a mate? "Well, first of all, I'm looking for someone in very good health."

He nodded, understanding. "I've been tested."

"Tested?" What, SATs? Driver's license?

"You know, for . . . disease."

Realization dawned. "Oh, no, that's not what I meant. Although that's a good point." Ugh, I sounded interested. "I just meant someone who's generally healthy. Strong." I was floundering. I was going to lose another one prematurely because I couldn't think of a few small things that could constitute "health" in a prospective mate. "No heart disease, no addictions. No alcoholism."

He looked thoughtful for a moment. "I only drink socially."

"Good," I said eagerly, ready to leap on any topic of conversation that would keep him from marching away from me to the bar peanuts. "Do you exercise as well?"

"Can't you tell?"

No, I couldn't tell. My guess would have been no, but the fact that he asked made me believe the answer must have been some variation of yes. Badminton? Ping-Pong?

Burke's muscular physique came to mind.

I dismissed it.

"Obviously?" It came out like a question, but he didn't seem to notice. I guess it was the right answer. "What about school?" I asked quickly. Move on, move on. "Did you go to college?"

He looked uneasy. "I didn't like school much as a kid. Don't get me wrong, I did okay. But does that really matter now?"

This was quickly becoming torturous. "No, probably not." How long had it been? Weren't six minutes up yet? It felt like it had been sixty. "So what are your hobbies?"

At last, the pained expression left his face. Actually, he even puffed up a bit. "I like to fly airplanes on the weekends."

"Oh! Really?"

He gave a cocky nod. "Absolutely."

I wouldn't have taken him for a pilot. That required intelligence, didn't it? Maybe Gerard, whom I would never ever go on a date with, was a cosmic reminder that sometimes people had unexpected talents or depth. "I've never really understood aeronautics myself. Every time I'm in a plane I wonder how it's staying up."

He nodded, but in way that almost seemed bored to me. "It's important to understand that in order to fly them, that's for sure."

Well, I hadn't said I wanted to *fly* them. "So what do you fly, like the little twin-engine things, or bigger commercial aircraft?"

"Rubber band."

I laughed. I had to hand that one to him, one point for sense of humor.

Except he didn't laugh. "I belong to the Tri-State Model Airplane Club. We meet every Saturday afternoon over in Penstock."

"You're serious?"

Clearly he took umbrage. "You think it's a joke?"

"No! It's just . . . that's interesting." Maybe it took intelligence to make model airplanes too. I mean, it was an achievement to get anything to fly, wasn't it?

I can't really remember the rest of the conversation, since it went on in about the same direction until Judy blew her whistle. It might have been my imagination, but I could swear Gerard looked relieved as he moved on to table five.

The few guys after were so generic that I cannot even remember enough detail to describe them. Suffice it to say, not only were they not *attractive*, they weren't even as interesting as Al/Lv and Gerard. They were so ceaselessly monotone and dull that my mind ran a steady movie of Burke. Burke when I first met him. Burke when he first kissed me. Burke in bed. Burke throwing hay.

Burke Burke Burke, to the point where I just wanted to get up and leave so I could put on the radio in my car and think about the road signs I was passing instead of obscuring these dull faces with memories of Burke Morrison's.

When Aaron came to my table, I wondered how I'd missed him before, since I felt like I'd spent more time looking around the room than gazing into the eyes of the man in front of me. But I hadn't noticed Aaron before. He was tall, with dark hair and warm brown eyes. Very nice-looking.

My inner Glenn shifted with curiosity.

In retrospect, that was my first warning.

"Hi," he said, sort of shyly.

"Hey."

He waited for a moment until I indicated he should sit down.

Points for politeness.

"Are you enjoying yourself?" I asked, in the winking manner of one sharing the same horrible experience.

His eyes met mine. "Honestly?"

We laughed.

A couple minutes of conversation flowed effortlessly and we laughed about the difficulty of putting yourself out there for people to judge. I was vaguely aware that I was laughing a little too loud, but I wanted everyone—not just the men there, but everyone—to know that I was more charming than Al/Lv and Gerard might have them believe.

"So. What are you looking for in a woman?" I asked, after we commiserated for a few minutes. That might have sounded like more interest than I wanted to convey, but it seemed like an appropriate question, given the circumstances.

Besides, I wanted to know the answer. Just out of curiosity.

"I guess I'm looking for—" He stopped and let out a breath, like he'd been holding it. "Quinn, can I tell you the truth?"

"Of course!"

"I'm here to try to find a date for my family reunion in two weeks."

The turning wheels on the train of thought in my head started to slow down. Something weird was coming, I just knew it. Were there no normal guys left at all? Anywhere? "Why do you need a date for your family reunion?" I asked.

He put his face in his hands for a moment, then looked me square in the eye. "Because my grandmother's going to be there and she doesn't know about me."

I waited for him to continue with what I knew was coming.

"She doesn't know I'm gay."

Judy blew the whistle.

By the end of the night, I had decided to become a nun. But thinking about the other women there, and how so many faces had gone from nervous hope to discouragement, I figured their best prospects were Mark, who referred to himself as "Marko" and who had a little bit of toothpaste in the corner of his mouth, but who otherwise appeared to be sane; and Aaron, who was gay but who might be persuaded to hang out some in exchange for a date to his family reunion.

I left the blank index card Judy gave me—shaped like a big baseball—by the door when I left.

Maybe they could use it for the next event.

. . .

"I'm never going to have sex again," I complained to Glenn after work the next night. "There are no really attractive men out there. None. Your plan *totally* backfired. I'm ready to hide in my room and never come out again."

"Maybe you're not giving them enough of a chance," he said.

I gave him a look. "Have you heard what I've been saying about Short Stops for the last half hour? Did *any* of those guys sound appealing to you?"

"Aaron sounded interesting," he said with a smile.

"Exactly. One in ten guys is gay, if not more. Lucky for you. One in ten is a probably married creep, looking to have sex with a woman two decades younger than him." I reiterated the stories I'd just told him, concluding, "And one has a case of the hiccups that he can't get rid of. And so on." I sighed miserably. "The odds are really against all the single women out here."

"The point was to get out there and eyeball some different scenery. Think about something other than Burke and Frank and the whole Morrison clan. As far as I'm concerned, this is mission accomplished."

"Burke." I sighed and slumped back in my seat. "He marched through my head so many times last night you'd have thought he had one of those big high school band drums."

"Oh, no."

"Oh, *yes.*"

"Keep reminding yourself that's just sexual attraction. It's not real. It's not the most important thing."

"Are you sure?" I challenged. "Because at the moment it feels a lot like the most important thing."

"So Frank is forgotten?"

"Frank?"

He nodded. "You said he was hot. You can't totally ignore that in your whole Morrison-fest here. Let's not play games. You've been in bed with both of them."

"Okay, fine. Yes. And, yes, that was one thing Frank was *very* good at."

"Worth keeping in mind."

No, it wasn't. Yet, my heart beat faster just thinking about those two brief encounters we'd had. Young as he'd been—at least from my perspective now—Frank was gifted. Now that I had a fairly extensive list of comparisons, I knew it was true.

"Quinn?" Glenn snapped his fingers in front of my face. "You with me?"

"No, leave me alone. I'm basking in the memory. This may be my only chance to have sex again."

"Stop it. You *will* have sex again."

"With who? Some big fat idiot who can't put his name tag on right side up but still has the confidence to think he can do better than me? A paper airplane engineer? A failed cartoonist who hiccups his way through a seemingly endless description of his main character while his eyes wander the room looking at other women? I'd rather just settle down with a vibrator and a Costco pack of batteries."

Glenn laughed. "I know what you mean. I went through a long period of time where I was just stuck with *this* asshole." He held up his right hand.

It took me a minute to understand, then I laughed. "Too bad you're gay, huh?"

He shrugged. "Too bad you're a woman."

"Touché."

"Is Frank really that great?" Glenn asked after a moment. "Or do you think maybe you're romanticizing the past some here?"

I looked him in the eye. "There were things he did that no one else *ever* did. And the way our bodies fit together . . ." I actually sighed, remembering. "I can't even describe it."

"I'm not sure that's as rare as you think it is."

"Then I'm not sure I'm talking about what you think I'm talking about. In my experience, it's rare. The perfect storm of physical chemistry and emotional combustion."

Glenn nodded thoughtfully and, after a long moment, said, "That sucks."

And after that, there was really nothing left to be said about it.

Chapter 13

"This was a complete waste of money." I put ten lottery tickets in the drawer under the cash register. It was Buy Ten Lottery Tickets! Day, which Glenn had considered soft after Go Commando Day and Speed Dating Night, but he was right, I never bought lottery tickets. They were always a waste of money, but never more than on a day like this. "Money I can't *afford* to lose right now, by the way."

"Then there's no gentle way to bring this up." He took out a copy of *Washingtonian* and opened it to a page he'd marked. Society weddings. Markham-Beasley.

"So what?" I asked, too sharply, I knew.

"Look what it says." He pointed. "*The bride wore an Augusta Jones original. . . .*"

I looked at the picture. "That is *not* an Augusta Jones! For one thing, Elizabeth Markham was in here a few months ago pricing gowns and she thought *I* was too expensive."

"That's because you work for more than six bucks an hour," Glenn said, then nodded toward the front window.

"No!" The Sneaky Seamstress struck again?

"Taney," he said. "I'm sure of it."

"Well, shit" was all I could say. "One more thing to worry about."

"Honey, I think your livelihood should be the *main* thing you're worried about. Forget the boys, that stuff will work itself out if you give it a little time."

I doubted that. It had been ten years and apparently it hadn't *worked itself out* so far. "I am so completely filled with horrible black energy right now, there is no way I could *win* anything. Except maybe a bet that not one of the numbers on these ten tickets will come up. Not one." I raised an eyebrow. "Care to wager?"

Glenn put his hands up, the sign of surrender. "No way, sista. I'm not taking you on right now."

"Wise," I said, and shut the drawer. "Very wise." I sat down and sank my head into my hands. "Oh, my *god*, he was *married*!"

"So?"

I had been all ready to dissolve into self-pitying tears, so this answer wasn't exactly what I was going for. "What do you mean, *so*?"

"What was he supposed to do? Sit around and mourn over you forever?"

"That"—I jabbed a finger in Glenn's direction—"would have been *excellent*."

"When was the last time you got laid?"

I looked at him blankly. "I beg your pardon, sir?"

"It's been months, right?"

"I have a perfectly healthy sex life."

"Maybe I'm not remembering this right," he said, in a way that suggested he was about to reenact something I'd done or said with such crystal clarity that I wasn't going to be sure if he was him or me, "but I *believe* you had a very hot relationship with a certain Arlington bank president for several months earlier this year."

"It was very casual."

"If you do that kind of thing casually . . ."

"Good grief, Glenn, what are you getting at?"

"I'm just wondering if you were thinking about Burke while you were doing that."

"Probably not."

"So you actually"—he gestured like he was searching for the words—"*went on with your life.*"

"Okay, okay, yes, I get your point. I'm not saying he wasn't within his rights, Glenn, I'm saying it makes me feel like total shit. Can't you see that? He loved someone else enough to *marry* her!"

"Yet when he was going to marry you—first, I might add—and you rejected him, you contended that you did that because he didn't love you. He, who was going to *marry* you."

"My head hurts."

"It should. You're not being fair to him."

"Maybe." I groaned. "It's just that he kissed someone else, had sex with someone else—oh, my god, what if it was better than it was with me? Is that possible?"

He splayed his arms. "I have not had sex with you."

"We're not talking *skill* here, Glenn, it's about *passion*. If there's one thing we had together, it was *passion*. I mean, even the night of Dottie's dinner party . . ."

"What?"

I remembered the kiss and felt slightly twitchy at the memory. My heart pounded. "He kissed me. I kissed him. Whatever. We kissed. It was searing hot. And then I *hated* myself afterwards."

"What? *Why?*"

"Because that's not what I want. *He* is not what I want. In fact"—I meant this—"I'd even go so far as to say he is *exactly* what I *don't* want. I don't have the emotional cash to spend on that man again."

Glenn assessed me. "I think there may be a certain wisdom in that, Quinn."

"You do?"

He nodded. "I don't know, but maybe—*maybe*—Burke represents, more than anything else, a past you are clinging to so hard that you cannot have anything new in the present or, worse, anything fresh in the future."

"You're right," I said, the full impact of the misery hitting me. The very fact that I felt so melancholy about Dottie selling the farm, as if with it went all of my dreams of the future, was proof of that. That future hadn't even been a *possibility* for me in ten years. "You're right about everything. I've been stuck in this weird rut that allowed me to sleep through day after day after day until what happened ten years ago could have happened two years ago or yesterday. Nothing ever changed, didn't get better, but it didn't get worse, and I think that was the imaginary safety zone I was trapped in. Not getting worse."

"Has it been good?" Glenn asked, without judgment. "That is, honestly, on balance would you say it's been mostly good?"

I thought about that. Really thought about it. Because it was easy to say "okay" was "good" because it wasn't *bad*, but those were three distinctly different states of being. Three.

And I'd only been living in one of them.

"I'm afraid of bad," I confessed, worried about sounding like a basket case even though this was my best friend I was talking to. "I've been to bad before, I don't want to go back."

"What do you define as *bad*? What do you mean when you say you've been to bad before?"

I met his eyes. He hadn't been there in my *bad period*. I didn't have a more creative, artistic term for it than that, it was just a depression. Maybe not much different than anyone else ever had. "I went through a couple of months once where I just didn't want to be alive," I said. "Not in the bored teenager sort of way, but in the way that I had to remind myself that in a hundred years nothing I was doing or seeing was going to matter anymore. That was the only way I could get through it."

He looked thoughtful. "So you're talking clinical depression. Not just the blues. Or the mean reds."

I would have laughed at the Audrey Hepburn *Breakfast at Tiffany's* reference, had it not brought a vivid picture of Burke's weirdly named wife to mind. But I wasn't going to broach that subject with Glenn because it would start him on a tear about how lovely Audrey Hepburn was—it was one of his favorite topics—and that would just keep her in my head and it would all be one big mindfuck for me.

"Yes," I said. "This was way beyond the *mean reds*. I felt like I was inside a car all the time, looking out at the world but not feeling the sun or the wind or the rain or anything. Just observing it from inside some transparent shell."

"Was this after Burke, I assume?"

"Directly."

He smiled kindly. It was sympathy. "How did I know?"

"You have a very keen sense of the obvious."

He tipped an imaginary hat. "Thank you very much."

A moment of silence passed, not uncomfortably.

"You know what I'd think about sometimes?" I asked at last. "Princess Diana."

He frowned. "What did I miss? Are we in a different movie suddenly?"

"I mean, think about it. She was a regular person, given this great opportunity, or *seemingly* great opportunity, when she was just nineteen. Married the future King of England. Was supposed to be the future Queen of England. And I think she was in love with him, I really do."

He screwed up his face. "Come on."

"No, seriously, I used to get my hair done in Georgetown by the same woman who did Diana when she was in town. A Brazilian woman who did the ambassador's wife, so I think she actually knew her pretty well. And she said Diana really loved Charles right up to the end."

"So she was nuts, is what you're saying."

"Maybe. But whatever the reason, I think she really just wanted love. The simplest thing in the world, or at least the most basic.

Think about all the stories that came out later. That she liked hanging out in her lover's mom's cottage in some obscure coastal town, or that she was in love with that doctor who didn't give a shit how famous or beloved she was, he was your classic hard-to-get guy anyway." I'd actually given this more thought than I probably should have, except that I thought it was a perfect example of how it didn't matter what it looked like you *should* be grateful for: if you had a voice, you had a void. "I just think that all the worship was nice, and she enjoyed it, and she probably would have been blown away by the adoration around her funeral, but I also bet she would have given it all up to be a happy housewife in Dover."

"Your point being that you don't want to be the Queen of England either?"

"That is exactly my point." I leveled a gaze on him. "I also don't want to be queen."

He smiled. "Your point," he said slowly, "is that you don't care about the glory, you don't want the proverbial *big life*, you just want the simplicity of love, and happiness, and peace, and *that* is why you've stayed in this little life here without venturing too far away."

"Right. Because I already know all that glitters is not gold."

"You think that you're in this rut because you know what's out there and you know that's not what you want, you want exactly what you already have here and now, so there's no point in venturing out of the cave."

It was times like this when I was so grateful to have a friend who really and truly understood me right through to the core. "Exactly."

"Because that glitter might just be pyrite."

"Exactly." This validation felt good.

Until he said, "But, baby, *nothing's* glittering here."

Something in me deflated. What if he was right?

"So that's not really what this is about," he went on.

"Why not? Why can't it just be simple? Why can't I just be *right*?"

"Because you're not happy. You have shut down whole huge parts of your emotional life, just boarded up the windows, and you're hiding inside. You yourself just said love is one of the most elemental wants or needs we have, but you *refuse* to experience it because of the experience you had with *that* guy, in *this* town."

Maybe. "If you're right . . . *if* . . . what do I do?"

He tipped his head and considered me. "I wish I knew exactly what you need and could say it, so you can have that forehead-slapping moment of realization, but I honestly don't know. I don't believe you want to be alone forever."

I smiled. "This is the part where I'm supposed to argue that I'm perfectly fine and self-sufficient and don't need a man or anyone else to complete me, but"—I shook my head—"you're right, I don't want to be alone forever. Over all these years, a small part of my brain has been entirely devoted to these echoey watercolor memories of my time with Burke, and I don't think anyone else could have had a chance of pushing that out of my brain even if I'd let them try."

"But you don't *know* that." Glenn looked at me intently. "You don't *know* that because you never let anyone anywhere near. You *have* to get out of your head, you *have* to get out of this fantasy world that's composed of bits and pieces of the past, real and imagined, and you have to *live*. Meet new people. Have new experiences. You're basing everything that you think you want on an ideal you formed when you were fifteen, and there could be so much more to your life than that."

I heard him. I honestly did. There absolutely was wisdom in what he was saying, but my heart kept saying that what I needed was right here at home. That I didn't need to be the girl who went out and traveled the world and had adventures with many men. I'd been born into this small part of the world and this was where I was supposed to be.

But that argument wouldn't hold water with Glenn, and if he'd lobbed it at me, I would have rejected it as well. I would want better for my friend, just like he did.

Why didn't I want better for myself?

Leave it to Glenn to take a potentially decent plan—his "do something every day that takes you out of your comfort zone" plan, which had *pretty much* gone well so far—and make it into something straight-up undoable so, basically, the entire thing was blown.

Like a diet foiled by Girl Scouts Thin Mints cookies.

The instruction paper lay on the counter of my shop next to its little red envelope:

Have a one-night stand.

"This was a Partridge Family song, right?" I asked, not bothering to say hello before launching in when he answered my call. "You're telling me to listen to a song, right? Because I *know* you're not telling me to have random sex with someone just one night."

"Of course I'm not!"

I sat down. "Thank God."

"Not just *one night*, that's way too random. You don't have that sort of time. No, I meant *tonight*. I happen to know you don't already have plans, because tonight is like *every other night* for you."

"There's no way I'm doing this."

"You have to. You agreed to my terms."

"Show me where I signed off on this, devil."

"It was an oral agreement," he said. "That is just as binding in a court of law."

"And you're going to sue me if I don't get laid tonight?"

He made a noise of sarcastic derision. "People have sued for dumber things than that."

I closed my eyes. "You're ruining this whole thirty-day plan of yours. You know that, right?"

"No, Quinn, no joke, this is important. I think it's going to really help you."

"Not gonna happen," I said, with absolute conviction. Even if I *wanted* to—which I totally did not—it wasn't like I was going to go man-hunting in the D.C. metro area with an eye toward activity that at the worst could give me a disease and at the very best could make me feel weird about myself.

Well, okay, I guess "at the very best" could, arguably, be that it did what Glenn thought and took me further out of my cocoon. But I couldn't see that happening. Lone girl in the big city, looking for a man? I was likely to find too much more than that.

And I most definitely wasn't going to find someone suitable sticking around in this tired old town.

Uh-oh. There it was. The proof of Glenn's point.

I was glad I hadn't said it out loud.

"Think about it!" he implored, his voice rising with his vehemence. "What a shake-up that would be!"

"I'll say."

"From an energy standpoint, you would be shifting everything! This could be spiritual Drano for you!"

Spiritual Drano? Where did he come up with this stuff? "That is too wildly inappropriate for me to even answer, Glenn."

He laughed uproariously. "Okay, so it was a pun-laden example. But I mean it!"

"Sorry, can't hear you!" I scratched my nails across the tiny microphone area of my phone. "The connection's breaking up. I've got to go!"

"Quinn Barton, don't you dare hang up on—"

I pushed the button. It didn't have the same old-fashioned pleasure as slamming a receiver down, but he got the point.

A one-night stand.

Who did he think I was?

The only time I'd come close to doing that was, in fact, the *two*-night stand with Frank. And that was *Frank*, not some stranger who could land me in some weird place physically, emotionally, or, god knows, *geographically*.

Then again, Las Vegas wasn't my usual stomping ground geographically.

I took a moment to think about that. It really had been fun, truth be told. It was *sinful*, in a way. Not my usual way of life, not the way I was raised, not something I'd generally say was the mark of a dignified woman, but, damn, it *had* been fun. We'd driven something like seventeen hours a day for two days, stayed in Vegas one night, then turned and came back.

It wasn't the destination, it was the journey. I'd hoped to shake off all the vestiges of Burke along the old and new highways of America. And, yeah, wherever you go, you still have your own head to contend with and obviously I couldn't just completely forget the man I was in love with, who had hurt me so badly, but there had been some genuinely cool moments out there on that long ribbon of highway.

I remembered stopping at a weird little diner near Albuquerque. The waitress was strangely beautiful, but her makeup was too heavy and I just knew she'd never get out of that small town and learn that she could have looked like—no, she probably could have *been*—a serious movie star. Anyway, everyone else in the diner had been old, and everyone was fond of her, no one was making moves on her, and Frank and I talked later about how if she didn't have a boyfriend already her chances of meeting someone and being swept off her pretty feet looked slim.

There was a raccoon in the bathroom of a rest stop near Memphis. That was the first time I used the men's room without caring if someone walked in—there were no locks on the doors—as long as they were human.

Texas had been hot and so humid, even at night, that I felt like I'd been slapped in the face with a wet washcloth when I got out of the car to get a Coke from a Texaco food mart.

And the lights of Vegas had been more dazzling than I had ever even imagined. Honestly, everywhere we went there, I felt like I was on the set of a Miss America show. If my conscience had allowed me to stay longer, I wonder how much farther away from this briar patch of Burke I could have gotten.

Chapter 14

It was pretty safe to say that Dottie was trying to set Burke and me up at this point.

Whether she imagined there was some great reconciliation in the future or she was just trying to "heal" us, I couldn't say. Her attempts were pretty ham-fisted, but there was nothing I could do about it easily. To refuse her requests to come do her fittings when she was physically up to it would have felt petty.

Unfortunately, when I arrived on the afternoon of One-Night Stand Day, she wasn't there.

No one was.

I tried her cell phone number, but there was no answer.

Huh.

What was I supposed to do now?

I could have left, of course. If this was just an ordinary client who wasn't there when I showed, I'd leave and let them come to me next time, but, for one thing, it was Dottie. And for another thing, it was Injured Dottie. She might have been hobbling as fast as she could to her car in the parking lot of the Safeway, fretting about the time and too deaf to hear her phone. Or maybe she was stuck in a doctor's office, and had the ringer off. Or who knows? I'd left Becca in charge of the shop, so there wasn't any reason I couldn't wait around at least a little while.

I wandered over to the paddock and old Rogue came over to the fence where I stood. I touched his silky muzzle, then patted his forehead and ran my fingers down his rough mane.

"Where's your mistress?" I asked him. "Did she lure me here to make me think about the past?"

I turned my face toward the sun, which was setting, predictably, in the west corner of the property. Amber light slanted through the trees, casting lengthening shadows across the perfect stretches of green grass. It looked almost like a golf course, the fields were so immaculate.

It was easy to remember why I'd loved it so much here. Why I'd thought this was going to be *It* for me, forever and ever. It was a beautiful place. Not everyone's cup of tea, I guess. Lisa Douglas, from *Green Acres,* probably still would have preferred New York, but I doubt she'd have been as miserable here as she was in Hooterville.

This was definitely not Hooterville.

To me, it was heaven. And that fact would never leave me, so it hurt to be standing here knowing that before long it would belong to someone else and I wouldn't be able to even visit anymore.

I took my phone out and tried Dottie again.

Again, she didn't answer.

So I walked across the gravel drive and on toward the tenant house. Part of me wanted to resist. But most of me had to go, had to see, had to face it. Maybe it would be cathartic. Maybe I would surprise myself by not feeling what I thought I'd feel.

It was like that when my grandfather had died. I'd been so upset to begin with, and, on top of that, so afraid to go to the funeral because Michaela Whitney, who was a bitch even in second grade, had told me they would have his dead body lying out for everyone to see. Of course, she'd said it in even more graphic, Halloweeny detail.

And she was right, though it wasn't quite like the picture she'd had me imagining. In the end, I'd even managed to go to him and whisper good-bye, even touching that familiar thatch of gray hair. After that, I was less afraid of death.

Maybe facing the past would make me less daunted by it.

I walked across a sweep of newly cut grass to the tenant house and to the front stoop. The wood thudded dully beneath my footsteps. Then, following an impulse I probably should have ignored, I pulled open the screen door, and gave a sad smile at the still-familiar creak of it. This wasn't a place where anyone had ever spent much time, except for Burke and me, so it didn't surprise me that no one had bothered to replace the old door. If things were still the way they used to be, once every other week Dottie's maids came down and did a cursory dusting so it didn't become a Disney-like haunted house, but other than that, no one came here unless it was to get the Christmas decorations out of the storeroom, or to put them back in.

I tried the main door and was surprised it was unlocked. Not that that gave me a license to walk on in like a thief. This was still trespassing, but I knew Dottie wouldn't mind.

The floorboards groaned beneath my weight. That was something else that had always been true, even at my high school weight. In a way it sounded like an old song to me, played a million times so that I knew every subtlety of every instrument.

The thing that I didn't realize I'd recognize was the smell. But it made sense. Ten years didn't put that much age on antiques. They'd had that smell of old wood and furniture polish for decades, why would that be any different now? It was just something I'd never thought about back then, probably because we were always so eager to run inside and tear each other's clothes off. The smell never registered on a conscious level.

For a moment I just stood there, breathing it in.

I used to imagine living here, once upon a time. I'd pictured myself passing birthdays and holidays here. Open windows with wind lifting lace curtains in the summer, a woodsy fire in the stone fireplace in the fall and winter, and a symphony of azaleas coming into bloom out front soon after the first crocus of spring.

This place felt like "home" to me in a way no other place ever had.

Why had he ruined that? He'd wanted it as much as I had, I was *sure* of it. Why would he ever have done anything that he knew could risk our future together? Had he imagined he could just insert someone else into my role if I didn't work out?

Maybe he hadn't thought at all. Maybe he'd taken me so thoroughly for granted that the intricacies of right and wrong, cause and effect, abuse and consequences, never even entered his mind.

I'd probably never know for sure. How could I ever believe him, no matter what he said?

All I knew was that we probably could have had a wonderful life together. We could have spent our whole lives living toward those wonderful words Robert Browning had written: *Grow old along with me! / The best is yet to be, / The last of life, for which the first was made . . .*

Had he once felt that way about *Perry?*

Could I ever feel it about someone else?

Was it *necessarily* Burke in my visions of living in this house? In the most obvious sense, yes. But having grown up an only child, heavily reliant on my imagination, I think most of my imaginings were of me cooking dinner in the kitchen, me waking up to the expanding green outside the window, me on the porch in the summer with the fireflies and toasted marshmallows. . . . Certainly I'd loved Burke. Enough to marry him. And I would have been a good wife. But I think maybe a big part of my heartbreak after the breakup was the whole imagined life I'd lost, not just the man.

I sat heavily on the old wing chair by the stairs and spent a good few minutes reveling in my own pity party. This was the perfect place for it. No other environment could have made so much emotion bubble up in me so fast.

In a way I was glad the place had remained abandoned, though I recognized that was selfish of me. But it just would have been too weird, too sad, to think of someone else here, some stranger, living the life I'd thought I'd have.

Interesting how garbled and confusing the past becomes under the anesthesia of time. You try to count the years and make some sense of them, but almost immediately they blur and become one big thing.

The past.

I stood up and walked through the little rooms, remembering stories I'd heard about some of the things on the walls and tables. Knickknacks and tchotchkes collected around the world during Burke's grandparents' younger and more adventurous days. There were a lot of pieces from Ireland in particular, as Burke and Frank's grandfather had believed Irish Thoroughbreds to be superior and infused his stock with plenty of Irish blood.

I paused at the door to the little bedroom we used to sneak off to. It took a minute to gather myself enough to look. When I did, it was like looking at a snapshot. Like everything else in the house, the bedroom remained unchanged. That might have seemed more strange had it been a high school bedroom in a generic house in suburbia, but here it seemed right, in this room with its four-poster bed topped with a hand-sewn Pennsylvania Dutch bedspread and a thick warm duvet from Germany.

I remembered what it felt like snuggling up under the sheets on cold winter nights. In my mind's eye, I could see Burke's forearm, strong with prominent veins, pulling it up and over us. It felt protective. Funny how safe I'd felt in those days, how completely carefree, when my adult self realized I should have been terrified my parents might have found out I wasn't really sleeping over at my girlfriends' houses.

Or, worse, Burke's grandparents could have come out and discovered us. That had the potential to be tremendously embarrassing. In so many different ways.

But, like I said, no one paid much attention to the little house on the edge of the property.

"Enjoy yourself while you can," I said to the ghost of the younger me. Or, rather, to the empty bed. Even though it all still looked frozen in time, I was deeply aware that it was not. Time had passed. So many things outside these walls had changed. "Relish every moment, because, like every sorry old song will tell you, you don't have forever."

I felt tears threaten and chastised myself for being able to work up angst about this so long after the fact.

Glenn was right, there was nothing healthy about being imprisoned by the past. Every layer of my consciousness, right down to the deepest subregions, knew that even though a lot of things *looked* the same, they weren't. It was so easy not to notice you were getting older when every single day was pretty much the same as the last or the next. Before you knew it, you'd aged, but who could say at one point it had happened? It happened at no point, and at every point.

I didn't want to feel like this.

More accurately, I couldn't afford to feel like this. If I'd been given a million emotional dollars at birth, I'd already spent 999,099 of them.

The screen door banged, startling me out of my melancholy thoughts, and giving my heart the jolt of touching a live wire.

I whirled around to see Frank coming in, which repeated the whole adrenaline-jolt thing.

He must have seen the shock on my face. "The door was open," he said, as if he owed *me* an explanation for coming in to find me stalking on his family's private property.

"I know, I—" I what? I found it that way myself? That would set off false alarms. Better to just tell the truth, or at least enough of it to explain the inexcusable. "I'm supposed to meet Dottie, but she's not here, so I thought I'd kill some time, and . . ." There was no way I could let him know what a basket case I was. I had to, at least, make the effort to sound detached, so I added, "I wondered if it was the same in here, so I couldn't resist coming in to take a look."

He took slow deliberate steps toward me. "Exactly the same, huh?" He looked around, and I thought I could see, in his expression, the same tender sadness I'd felt looking at it.

"I know you think I'm impervious to it, but I hate to see it go too."

"Do you come here a lot?"

"Not in ages. I don't even know how long." He shook his head. "I think I put a few things in storage a few years ago, but I can't remember what, or when. Just in and out. I didn't stop and look around."

I swallowed. My history here had always been inside of me, a feeling remembered, even if there weren't descriptions attached to it anymore. "I kind of wish I hadn't. It's kind of sad."

He tilted his head ever so slightly and looked at me. "I remember when you used to come as a kid. Seeing you in here like this is kind of like seeing a ghost."

My face grew warm under his gaze and I shook my head. "Ghosts don't age."

"Seems like you don't either."

"That's not true."

"It is." He stopped a few feet away, far enough to take me in entirely, and I felt him do exactly that as certainly as if he'd touched me. "When I first saw you the other night. Whew." He paused, looked lost in thought, then met my eyes again. "I loved you once, you know."

"*What?*" It wasn't quite the needle scratching across the record, but the effect was the same. "You loved *me?*"

He narrowed his eyes. *Come on.*

I waited.

"Perhaps you've forgotten our own history, short as it was?" he said, lifting an eyebrow. He was defensive too. Maybe not *as* defensive as I was, but certainly on alert.

"Bad subject," I amended, hoping to close it before it got even more uncomfortable. "Bad time in general."

He gave a hollow laugh. "Yeah, that'll make it go away."

"There's no reason to revisit it."

"Nope, you're probably right." He took another step toward me and I felt it as surely as if he'd touched me.

More disturbingly, I felt like I *wanted* him to touch me.

A flush spread over me. What was *with* me? Not only feeling everything, but showing everything I felt. Suddenly the most reliable thing in my life was my body's betrayal of me.

Was my need for "revenge" against Burke still so great that I had an internal instinct to do this?

Or was it just the prospect of comfort, the *relief,* of letting go of control and letting someone else—someone capable—handle things that was appealing to me?

The one thing I knew for sure was I was *not* interested in Frank Morrison. It was just too much to have serious relationships with two different brothers.

"Where is Dottie?" I asked, my voice sounding a little high and fast, even to my own ears. I took out the phone and hit redial, all but tapping my toe and chanting, *Answer answer answer please, Dottie, answer.*

She did not.

"I think she had a doctor's appointment," he said, and he really seemed unaware of the rising turmoil inside of me. "Maybe it was a lawyer. Some sort of appointment."

"Well, who knows how long she'll be, then?" I swallowed hard and tried to take a step backward, but I couldn't force myself to move. "Maybe you could just tell her I came by but I had to get back to the shop?"

"Do you?" With one final step he closed the distance between us. Now he was directly in front of me, looking down into my eyes. I could feel the heat of his body. Smell him, his clothes, his skin, his hair.

It was like *safety* was within reach, but that was crazy.

No, I told myself. Just, *No. Wrong guy.*

But I wasn't a good listener. "Do I what?" I asked.

He reached out and touched my cheek, idly brushing his thumb along my skin. "Have to get back to the shop?"

"Yes." My voice was barely a whisper.

He cupped his other hand on my rib cage and trailed it down a few inches before pulling me against him. "Now?" He moved his mouth next to mine. I could feel his breath on my skin.

I nodded. Mute. And made an effort to step back but couldn't. My phone rang.

I jumped and put a hand to my chest, lifting it to my ear. "Hello?"

"Quinn, dear, it's Dottie. I am so sorry to do this to you, but I am stuck in Middleburg and I don't think I can be there inside of an hour. Could be even longer. Can we reschedule?"

"Sure." My breath was still uneven. "Call me when you know what works best for you."

"I will. I will do that. And, honey, I am so sorry. This is very poor manners. I assure you I know your time is worth more than this."

"It's all right," I said, probably not convincingly, and we hung up.

"Dottie?" he asked.

I nodded. "She's not coming."

"That's a shame." He put his hands on my shoulders. Braced them, warm against my skin, but light. But if I'd wanted to move, and he wanted to stop me, there was no question who would have won. I'd have been Lot's wife, frozen into a pillar of salt.

But I didn't want to move. "Is it?"

Then he smiled, unexpectedly. Rakishly. "Yeah, it is. I've got an appointment I've got to get to even though I'd rather"—he tilted his head so slightly I almost missed it—"try and figure you out." He took a step back, still regarding me.

"Not much to figure out."

"That's definitely not true. Never was." He shrugged and looked at his watch, then back at me. "Good to see you again, Quinn. I'd like to . . ." He hesitated and, for the first time, I saw an uncharacteristic uncertainty cross his expression. "See you later."

And with that he left, and I wondered if he meant he'd like to see me later or if he was only throwing the standard good-bye at me.

And I wondered why I wondered.

Chapter 15

"Have you ever been to Las Vegas?"

Ironic timing for that question, given how much Vegas had been on my mind, and trotted through my fantasies, lately.

The bride-to-be was in her mid-forties, lived in Maryland, but had come down to the shop after a friend had told her about me.

"I was there once," I said. Then gave the kind of shrug I knew she'd interpret as, *I basically lived my own version of* The Hangover, and added, "Can't say I recall much."

She laughed. "I'm hearing that a lot. Would you believe I've *never* been there? Forty-six years old and I've never been to Las Vegas. In fact, the only time I went out West I was twelve and with my parents. We went to Disneyland. I hear that's kind of what Vegas is like. Only with drinks."

"Lots of drinks."

"Only champagne for me! This is going to be a real big celebration weekend for us! We both vowed we'd never get married again, but here we are, going for it."

"So you've both been married before?"

"Just the one time. To each other."

"Ooooh, it's a *reunion* wedding!" I liked that. "I don't get many of those."

"Most people don't." She laughed. "Most people are smart enough to remember they ended it for a reason in the first place, but not us. What can I say? We love each other."

I smiled. "Pretty good reason to get married."

"I hope so." She nodded. "No toaster was wasted on us after all. I'll grant you it's been twenty years since the first wedding, but . . . I do still have the KitchenAid my aunt gave me. Hopefully I'll have time to use it to make my husband something this time!"

"That's the attitude!"

"What can I say?"

"It's all good. So what do you have in mind to wear?"

"Oh! That's the best part. I hope this will be fun for you. I just want the tackiest, most sequined thing you can possible conjure. I mean, I want it sexy, maybe to about here"—she karate-chopped her mid-thigh—"and low-cut, because when you've got big boobs like I do, the lower the neck, the skinnier you look. I'm sure you know that."

She meant because of my sewing expertise, not because of my obviously lacking cleavage. "True. Colors?"

"Red. Red, red, red. If you're gonna go, go big, right?"

"Huge!" I could already picture it. She was clearly a firecracker to begin with.

My job was to make her totally look like one.

We went over some designs and did some measurements and talked so much that when she finally had to go, the place felt deflated without her energy in it.

So I turned the CLOSED sign twelve minutes early—sue me—and went next door to Glenn's.

"Maytag blue," I said. "Stat."

He laughed and cut a slice of cheese and threw it unceremoniously onto one of the sample plates along with some crostini. "Here. What's up?"

"I'm miserable."

"Then I guess I should have asked, *What's new?*"

"Very funny."

"Only not very funny. What happened?"

"Nothing." I ate some of the cheese. It was tangy and creamy and wonderful, and I could totally understand how people gained loads of weight when depressed. A night of cheese, perhaps followed by chocolate fondue, and I would have been okay for *hours.* "I've just had so many happy, excited brides in lately."

"That's good, right? Taney's not taking away all your business."

"I've got business," I said, but my defenses were low. "It's not even about that, though."

"What, you're jealous of the happy brides?"

"No!" I thought for a fraction of a second. "I mean, yes. *Yes.* Of *course!* Who isn't jealous of people stupidly, blindly, blissfully in love? Everything looks like sunshine to them. Ughhh. It makes me ill, but I want it."

He nodded ruefully. "I want it too."

I was surprised. "You do?"

"Everyone does, dummy. Who's going to sincerely say, *No thanks, no happiness for me?*"

"Yup. I see your point."

"Question is, what are you going to do about it?"

"Short Stops, obviously." I flashed him A Look. "That's where the best prospects seemed to be."

"Okay, okay, and short of Short Stops? Are you seriously regretting not being married to Burke?"

"I'm regretting not being happily married to Burke, yes. Absolutely."

"Right, and I'm regretting not being the Queen of England. Or Warren Buffett. Or a bunch of other things I'm not. Are you sorry you're not married to Burke *for better or worse?*"

He was asking, of course, about *worse*. And the answer to that alone was easy. It was the rest of it that wasn't so clear.

"Okay, got it," I said. "No, I don't think I made the wrong decision back then." *I just hope he's different now*, my mind pressed on. *I hope he regrets losing me forever and would do anything to try to win me back.* "But you've got to see where the temptation to get him in bed is . . . considerable."

"No! That's *not* what I meant by a one-night stand! And you know it! The whole point of raising the idea was to break you open, not to embed you more fully, like a dragonfly in amber. Would it give you any sense of closure?"

No. No, it probably wouldn't. It would probably raise more questions than it answered and leave me wanting more desperately. One more kiss. One more touch.

One more night.

Then *one more night* quickly became *and more and more and more*. I was very well familiar with the sense of longing this man gave me, the feeling of infinity that mingled with fear that I could never really have *it*.

Despite the years that had passed, I fell so easily back into the habit of wanting him, of feeling like I was crazy in love with him. Whatever strength I'd built the day I'd left him, and maintained in all the time that lay between, had been lost in my attraction to him.

This was what he'd *always* been able to do to me.

"I don't think I'm ever going to have closure," I told him, saying out loud the thing I really hadn't wanted to admit in any solid way. Because it wasn't just Burke, it was also Frank. And all the reminders around town of both of them, but it was, elementally, Burke and Frank. It had always been Burke and Frank.

Or rather Burke versus Frank.

A thousand years ago I'd started something with Frank that we both later just agreed to call a *mistake*, but when I allowed myself even a moment to think about it, the rest of the family wasn't in my head until I put them there. Frank was his own man and he held his own lure.

It was my head that told me it was crazy to take that seriously.

"Never," I reiterated. No closure for me. I give up.

Glenn sighed. "Not with that attitude, you're not."

"I *want* it."

"I'm not even sure I believe that."

He was right. And I didn't have it in me to defend myself against his truths right now. This conversation could only result in me looking too closely at things in myself that I didn't want to see.

Time, I told myself. All I needed was a little bit of time to regain my distance and detachment. This, what I was feeling, was an illusion. A temporary psychological trick.

"I've got to run," I said, "but come on by after work tomorrow. We can talk then if you want."

"Or I could just go on in there and try and shake some sense into you."

"Either-or." I groaned. "I hate this."

"I know the feeling."

"Make it go away."

"I'll try. But I can't. Only you can."

I closed my eyes. "I'm trying. Come by if you can. I have a feeling I'm going to be pretty desperate to get out of my head."

"Will do. Hang on, kiddo. This is a process. It feels like you've turned around and found yourself in the middle of something sticky again, but actually you're approaching the other side."

"Do you really believe that?" I asked, with a certain skeptical hope.

"Don't ask."

My hope deflated.

If only he *could* shake some sense into me. If only *anyone* could. I'd welcome it at this point.

Chapter 16

"Our wedding is in New York on June fifth," the bride, Sigma, told me, while her always-silent partner, Chris, stood by like a bodyguard.

I had never heard Chris speak.

Though this was only the third time they'd been in, and the first two times had probably totaled seven minutes or so, so it wasn't surprising that we hadn't had a very deep conversation. Even tonight, Sigma—whip-thin and pixie-like, with her short cropped hair and wide Audrey Hepburn eyes—had slipped all but silently through the door and waited wordlessly while I wrote up a sales slip on six garters for a Vegas wedding, then opened with her wedding date, as if answering a question I'd just asked.

Although Sigma herself always seemed sweet and soft-spoken, I knew I had to be careful not to push her buttons, because usually when one of the affianced doesn't say much it's because they're afraid to say the wrong thing.

Thank God for my job, I thought. *Thank God I'm forced to interact with people and think about something else.* I'd been in this business for so long that the customer service habit was deeply ingrained. That was always a blessing but never more so than it was right now.

"That's plenty of time for the dress to be ready," I said to her. There was barely any work to be done on it at this point. "Don't give it a second thought."

She gave a soft laugh. "That's the problem, Chris keeps giving it a second thought. Dress or suit? White or blue? I'll tell you, I'm just ready to have this over with so we don't spend the rest of our lives talking about whether or not it was right." She looked affectionately at Chris, who stood ramrod-straight and—with tawny skin, cropped hair, and narrow eyes that could only be described as *beige*—all but blended into the walls.

My gaze was more expectant.

Neither of us was rewarded with a word.

Sigma didn't seem surprised. She casually brushed a wisp of pale blond hair out of her eyes and said, "Anyway, I absolutely *love* the dress I commissioned and I'm *definitely* not changing my mind, so . . . onward and upward, right?"

"Right."

"Hellooo!" Glenn called, hurrying in the door with an apologetic grimace. "Hate to interrupt, but do you have an Internet connection?"

"I— I *guess* so. Why?"

"My stupid connection is out *again*. My fault. Left the router by the window and left the window open in the rain. Fried." He went behind my counter and started punching the keys on my computer, then paused, looked at Sigma and Chris, and said, "God, I'm rude. Hi. Sorry to interrupt, I was just in the middle of something"—he shifted his focus to the screen but kept talking—"and everything went out and just . . ." He raised his hands and shook his head for a moment, then returned to the keyboard. "I hate that. Don't you?"

"I hate that," Sigma agreed.

"I don't feel strongly about that," I said.

Glenn glanced at me, a little impatient. "You would if you were me. Oh, here we go. Here . . . we . . . go . . ." *Click click click.* We were all suddenly silent, everyone's attention fixed on him as if there were suddenly a fire in the middle of the room. "Carry on, sorry to interrupt, just do whatever you were doing."

I looked back at Sigma. "So the dress should be ready by the end of next week, beginning of the next at the latest. We only have one more fitting before I sew on the lace, and that'll be it."

"Oh, wonderful." She sighed and looked dreamy. "You are going to make this my dream wedding, Quinn, you really are. You and Chris, that is. It may not be what everyone expected, but I don't care, I'm the happiest girl in the world."

I could see why people didn't expect that. Frankly, Chris was kind of glum and personality-free, to my eye, but, whatever, it wasn't my wedding. Sometimes people had unexpected depths and I had to believe—or at least assume—that might be the case here.

The truth was, seeing Sigma's enthusiasm was inspiring. It wasn't fair for me to make a judgment on their personal relationship. I didn't really know anything about it, and it felt like bad juju for me to be guessing at the odds of their marriage working out, so it was better for me not to think about it at all. Just to do my job.

"All right, then how about you come back Monday afternoon and we'll fit the corset, and then your part is done?" I smiled in what I hoped was a reassuring manner. "Well, your part of getting the dress. Obviously you're still going to have to do the wedding."

"Can't wait!" Sigma squealed.

She really was so sweet. Maybe I just wasn't used to unidimensional people. Maybe there wasn't a dark side at all.

Then again, there was always a dark side, wasn't there? To just about everyone.

"Okay, okay, okay," Glenn murmured to himself a few feet away.

"Do you have family in New York?" I asked, looking from Sigma to Chris and back.

She shook her head. "Nope. Just, you know, that was *the place* to do it."

Ooooh, yes. I'd heard this one before. Probably yet another *Sex and the City* knockoff wedding at the public library, I surmised. Sigma had a distinct Charlotte vibe to her. And yes, I know it was Carrie who planned the wedding at the library, but I figured if she *was* a fan, the idea probably appealed no matter which character appealed to her.

And why not? It was a lovely idea.

"I'm sure it will be wonderful, Sigma," I said to her.

Sigma took Chris's hand, and, to be fair, I did notice she was rewarded with a little squeeze. Acknowledgment. "It will be," she said dreamily.

"Got it!" Glenn cried, startling all of us. He put his hand to his heart and patted his chest. "That was *way* too close for comfort."

"Okay, I'll bite. Tell us. What are you *talking* about?" I asked, a little embarrassed that he'd come in and acted so weird in front of clients.

He met my eyes and I could tell he immediately realized what he'd been doing. "I am so sorry." He looked at Sigma and Chris. "Truly, I am so sorry to interrupt your moment like this. It's just that I was in the middle of a final countdown on eBay when, *poof,* my connection disappeared. And the timing of sniping is just so . . ." He snapped his fingers.

"Precise," Chris offered with a surprisingly commiserative nod.

Leave it to Glenn to draw just about anyone out of their shell.

"*Exactly,*" Glenn said, pointing like the first word in his game of charades had been guessed correctly. "It's *so* precise. Grammys-LoveBug nearly got it out from under me. So close. *So* close. Man."

"What did you get?" Sigma asked with interest.

Glenn's face lit up like he was about to admit he'd gotten a treasure map that led directly to an early retirement in Bora Bora. "A Barry Manilow lunch box! Vintage, of course, from the late eighties."

My jaw dropped. "They *made* Barry Manilow lunch boxes?"

He nodded happily. "You bet!"

This was incomprehensible. I pictured a metal lunch box with Barry—suited up somewhere between Liberace, Elvis, and Wayne

Newton—holding a long phallic microphone, singing about making it through the rain.

"But—why? *Who* on earth would want one? Surely there couldn't have been a sufficient market to manufacture them in bulk! I mean," I sputtered, "especially back then, lunch boxes were mostly a kid thing, and what weirdo kid would want a *Barry Manilow* lunch box?" I tried to picture that thing sitting on the big pull-down lunch tables at my elementary school, next to the *Star Wars* ones shaped like R2-D2 and the Barbie lunch and thermos set that I'd had.

He looked hurt. "*I* had one."

I gasped. I couldn't help it. "You did?" I looked at Sigma and Chris, probably for some bewildered expressions that showed they thought it was as weird as I did, but they just looked at Glenn and blinked. I think Chris even looked sympathetic, albeit in the smallest, most infinitesimal way imaginable.

"I love that song 'Could It Be Magic,'" Sigma said. "And 'I Made It Through the Rain.'" Of course. Of course she did. "When I came out, that was a very inspiring song for me. For *us*." She smiled at Chris. "Barry's great."

Wow. I just wasn't going to win this one at all. And, really, I didn't need to be the jerk who tried. "Well, way to go, then, Glenn. I had no idea. But you really need to get your router fixed. Don't want it going out when you're in the middle of a hot bidding war for a *Torkelsons* tea set or something."

For one split second, his eyes lit up. "If only."

If I had the time and inclination to search things out and resell them on eBay, I could have made so much money off Glenn.

"Should I make an appointment for Monday?" Sigma asked, me. "Or is it okay just to come midafternoon sometime?"

I returned my attention to her. "That should be fine," I said. "If you want to call and confirm on your way in, that might be better still, just to make sure you don't have to wait."

"Okeydoke!" She looked me in the eye. "Thank you so much." Then she hooked her arm through Chris's.

"You're welcome."

They started to walk toward the door and she waved, fluttering her fingers. "Thanks a bunch! See you then!"

I smiled. "Yup, see you then!"

They left, the door thudded closed behind them, and I turned to Glenn. "Are you *insane?*"

He didn't blush, but he *should* have. "I know, I know, it was just *really* important. This might even be the very one, *the very one,* I had myself as a kid. It's got a dent in the exact same place in Barry's nose. This could be *mine.*"

That was too easy. I wasn't going to take it. "I bet there was a bully in every single school some hapless kid was willing to take a Barry Manilow lunch box to, who was willing—no, *eager*—to dent Barry's nose. I seriously doubt your old lunch box has been traveling around from one person to another until you could finally reclaim it."

"You never know."

"See? This is how ridiculously romantic you are when it comes to stories that are not my own. You can even make up a fated story about a lunch box. This," I said, then leaned toward him for emphasis, "*this* is exactly what's wrong with love."

"Is it?"

"It is."

He frowned. "Having a bad day?"

I shook my head. "Nope. My day is fine. I'm just being realistic, that's all."

He looked dubious. "Did you follow my instructions from this morning?"

"I tried."

"And?"

"No luck. I don't think the water pressure in my shower is good enough."

"You tried to use the *shower* for that?"

"It was all I had!"

"You don't have a rabbit or something?"

"No!"

For a moment he looked surprised by my outburst, then he cracked up. "I'd say you protest too much, but I believe you. Honey, you need a rabbit. The shower will never do. Otherwise you're stuck with"—he grabbed my hand and held it up between us—"this asshole. And you can do better than that."

I felt my face grow warm. Every time I thought I was used to what Glenn could dish out, he'd come up with something new and even more awkward. "Can we not talk about this?"

"Sure. What do you want to talk about instead? The lesbians?"

I rolled my eyes. Obviously he was on a theme and he wasn't going to let go easily. So I bit. "What lesbians?"

"The ones that just left." He gestured at the door.

"There were no lesbians in here. Has eBay addled your mind?"

He gaped at me. "There were no lesbians in here."

"None."

"You didn't just have a lesbian couple here."

I looked him dead in the eye, trying to find some sign of either kidding or sudden onset dementia. "No, Glenn, I didn't. What, have you suddenly gone straight and started having *Girls Gone Wild* fantasies?"

He looked at me the way I *knew* I had just looked at him. "Sigma and what's her name, the ones that just left."

"*His* name is Chris," I said incredulously. Maybe he wasn't crazy. Maybe it was just his eyesight. After all, Chris had said exactly one word and his voice was neither high nor low, so I guess if you were looking at a blurred figure, his slight frame might have passed for female.

"You're kidding, right?" Glenn asked.

This was crazy. "No, are you?"

"You're being completely serious."

"I can't do this all day, Glenn."

"That was two *women*, Quinn." He was looking at me as if he still wasn't sure if I was pulling his leg. "Please, God, tell me you didn't refer to one of them as *him* or *he* or *sir* or anything like that."

Was it possible he was serious?

Was it even *slightly* possible he was right?

I tried to think. *Had* I? Could Chris be a woman? Could I be that wrong? Was that even possible?

He didn't wait for my answer, just continued his tear. "They even said they're getting married in New York, didn't they?"

"So?"

"*Duh!* It's legal there, remember?"

What was? Pot? What was he talking about? "Legal?" I repeated like an idiot.

"Gay marriage, dumbass!"

My complete reorganization of thoughts was interrupted by the bells on the door, then completely erased by the sight of Burke striding in. I met his eyes, and his mouth flickered into the briefest hint of a smile, then back. "Dottie instructed me to bring you this." He held up a coin.

"What is it?" I asked, taking it. "Oh, sixpence."

"She owed you sixpence?" Burke asked with a spontaneous laugh. "What year is this? Wait, what *country* is this?"

"Sixpence is supposed to be lucky on your wedding day," I explained, then handed it back to him, a little too aware of the still-lingering irony. "But tell her she's supposed to put it in her shoe."

"She said you'd know what to do with it."

"I do. Tell her to put it in her shoe."

"But she told me to give it to you."

"So you can't give it back?"

He smiled. I loved it. "You know how she gets."

"Fine." I held out my hand. "*I'll* tell her to put it in her shoe when I see her."

He drew back. "Well, hang on, I don't want you to lose it if you're not *sewing* it into something."

"It's a *coin*! What could I be sewing it into?"

"You know . . . ," Glenn said. I'd forgotten he was there and felt a moment of intrusion, as if he'd walked in on a private moment, until he added, "I think I'm just going to meander on out of here."

Go go go.

"Oh, hey, man." Burke stopped him and held out his hand. "I'm sorry. We were . . . Good to see you, Glenn, how've you been?"

"Great." Glenn's voice was a bit butcher than usual. Suddenly the room had more testosterone in it. Believe me, that almost never happened. "Yourself?"

"Can't complain."

I took a moment to actually feel bad that Burke "couldn't complain" about his life.

I was really a ghoul.

"I'm trying to think when the last time I saw you was," Burke said, and his face assumed the position of *thoughtful*, one of many expressions of his I knew and remembered all too well. "All I can picture is you on the football field, but I know we've seen each other since then. I just can't think where it was."

"Don Hoffman's funeral."

"*That's* right. Man, that was, what, six years ago or something now. Sad day."

"Enviable turnout, though."

Burke tipped his hand from side to side. "Yeah, if you don't mind going six feet under afterwards."

They laughed.

It was a moment of ease, the likes of which I hadn't shared with Burke in a very long time.

And now I was managing to somehow feel betrayed that two people who *owed* me nothing, certainly no explanations or accounts of their activities, had done something I hadn't known about in which they'd seen each other.

That it was a funeral showed just how selfish this situation had turned me. Or maybe I was to begin with. I mean, seriously, only a monster gets jealous of the guest of honor at a funeral.

They made small talk for a moment, then Glenn—perhaps feeling the heat of my gaze on him—bowed out. "I've got to get back to the shop. Candy's in there alone and she's a numbskull. Still doesn't know Maytag from Gorgonzola Dolce." He shook his head like this was a problem everyone could relate to.

Cheese idiots.

"Good to see you, man," Burke said, and they did a manly high-five sort of thing I'd never witnessed Glenn doing before.

I guess old habits, even those of hiding who you really are, die hard.

"Good to see you, Burke," he said, then, to me, "*Ciao, bella.*" He lifted a brow, the subtle equivalent of a wink, then went out the door, leaving Burke and me alone.

Chapter 17

And that left us alone *together*.

Again.

It was my mind that had a problem with that, of course, not my heart or the visceral reactions of my body. I *knew* I shouldn't want to be alone with him. Hell, I knew it would have been wise to stop Glenn from leaving or to even call him back, but the sad fact was being around him was like a drug.

Maybe he was an addiction.

Maybe he always had been.

"What brings you here?" I asked, hoping he couldn't actually hear or, worse, *see* my heart pounding like an alien trying to burst out from under my shirt.

I had to admit, he looked more than a little self-conscious this time himself. Already we'd had too many "coincidental" encounters, we both knew it. We were being set up, but we were allowing it.

Was it *attraction* that kept drawing us together, or the need for genuine closure? I suppose either could have brought peace of mind, and that's what I really needed.

He reached into his pocket and pulled out a piece of paper. "Dottie did her own measurements and thought I should bring them to you. She said to tell you again how sorry she is for the inconvenience of having you come all the way out for nothing." For a moment it looked like he might add to that, but he didn't.

I took the paper and looked at it. Then frowned. "These don't make sense. Are they . . . centimeters? But, no, that wouldn't translate either. I'm not sure what—"

"I'm pretty sure it was a ruse," he said, stopping me from too much unnecessary puzzling. "She's not a very good liar, so when she told me you needed to get these measurements or she'd have no wedding dress and it would be all my fault for being a *selfish boy*, I was pretty sure she was up to something." He gave a laugh.

"Ah." I nodded. "And this way I'll have to go back out to the farm and measure, almost certainly when you're there."

"That'd be my guess."

"So what does she think is going to happen now?" I asked tentatively. I knew what *should* happen now. I should thank him for the fake measurements and send him on his way, foiling Dottie's interference and hopefully keeping myself sane in the process.

But I didn't. I waited to see what his move would be.

I'd just listen to what he had to say. Make a decision from there. Obviously I'd been pretty vehement about this when talking to Glenn, and myself, for that matter, but I was willing to try to be flexible. Maybe that was the cosmic good in my going to that miserable Short Stops meeting. It gave me a clear picture of what was out there if I really went all out and tried to date. Match .com, eHarmony, Short Stops, all of those organized matchmakers would be the go-tos, at least to start, and the prospect was daunting.

"Do you want to sit down?" I asked Burke, indicating the fussy white chairs I had set up in front of the dressing room.

"No, that's okay. I won't take much of your time."

This wasn't beginning the way I expected.

"Look, Quinn, I'm really sorry about what happened the other night. When I kissed you."

Sorry?

"Sorry?"

He gave a quick smile. Just a lightning flash of that smile I loved so much, but it was enough to take my breath away. "Okay, not entirely sorry. Obviously I enjoyed it. But . . ."

I frowned. My face felt frozen. Suddenly I wasn't sure what to do with my mouth. My expression. My hands. I was suspended in a weird limbo. "But . . . ?"

"Well, you know." He fixed his eyes on me. Eyes I'd never forgotten. Eyes I'd hoped I'd never see again. "You and I have always had a draw to each other. When I saw you at my grandmother's, it was kind of like all the time that had passed disappeared."

I nodded, mute.

"So when I walked out to your car with you," he went on, and I could tell by the way he shifted his weight from one side to the other that he was getting uncomfortable, "I didn't even think before kissing you."

"There wasn't a lot of thought on my part either."

"Until you pointed out we shouldn't be doing it."

Had I? I guess I had. "It was all so unexpected," I said, which could have meant anything. And didn't mean anything. I didn't know *what* to say. All I knew was that standing there like a wide-eyed plastic doll wasn't going to buy me anything but an indelible memory in his brain of me looking like an idiot.

He laughed softly. "I wasn't expecting to see you there at all."

"I wasn't either." Suddenly I felt like I had to defend myself, to make it clear that I hadn't been in on anything.

"Oh, yeah, that was very clear from the expression on your face."

I was relieved. "I was never very good at hiding my feelings."

"Especially not when you were feeling abject horror."

"Well, *that's* an overstatement."

He tilted his head.

"Okay," I corrected, and tried to figure out what to do with my hands, finally settling on simply crossing my arms in front of me. Which undoubtedly looked schoolmarmish. "Maybe there was some *shock* there. You and I had a pretty emotionally volatile relationship at the best of times. Obviously the last time we saw each other, it wasn't as strangers at a community yard sale, so, yes, I think a lot of emotions came to the surface when I saw you."

"For me too," he said, and I was glad to hear it.

"And I tried to stop it because I thought it could be dangerous to dive into free-floating emotion like that."

He gave a nod. "I agree. At that moment, I didn't, I wasn't listening to my head." He shrugged. "I couldn't resist."

"Me neither." I never could. I wouldn't be able to right now if he came to me.

"That was always our pattern."

"Undeniably."

"But there's a reason we're not together anymore, obviously. Our patterns didn't really work out for us. So it's foolish to give in to a physical impulse like that when there is the potential for so much damage when the house of cards falls down."

All at once I hated this conversation. This relationship was no longer up to me. It hadn't been since I'd nixed it ten years ago. I'd blathered on and on to Glenn about it as if it were *my* choice and *I* didn't know what to do. . . . How arrogant of me.

This was more evidence of how out of touch I had become. My rut expanded to include memory as well, in that I had *forgotten* that someone who had been out of my life for ten years might have moved on in ways that left zero room for me.

I'd *forgotten* that people who weren't looking at the same old scenery day after day might not be living in the same old past-is-present-is-future day after day.

I had *forgotten* that someone whom I remembered so well might have all but forgotten me.

In fact, in this me-me-me pool I'd been swimming in, it hadn't even occurred to me—until this very moment—that maybe Burke had not only had other relationships in the ensuing years since our breakup (having slept with his brother, I couldn't criticize him for that!), but maybe he had one right now.

That was probably it. He had a girlfriend. Or someone he was interested in. Or something that made this more "complicated" for him than it was for me.

Or—please, no—maybe he knew about Frank and me. It had only been the two nights, but that didn't make it go away. Worse, there was still *tension* between Frank and me, maybe Burke felt that. And how could I argue with it if he did?

Then again, maybe he hadn't noticed anything. Maybe this was all about him just wanting to get away from me and from the mistake of an impulsive kiss.

I wanted to ask, but couldn't bring myself to. I knew that leaping to conclusions was always Bad Policy, but there was no sense in cranking open a few cans of worms.

And I knew this feeling, this disconcerted things-aren't-quite-right feeling that, so many times, had preceded an unwinnable argument between us. Granted, it had been a long time, but I knew this feeling as well as if I'd had it yesterday. I'd get pouty, wishing for reassurance, but there was an armor of self-protection that would prevent any progress from being made, no matter what anyone said.

In short, if we talked about this now, he couldn't say anything to make me feel better, but I could say a lot of things to make myself feel worse. It was preferable for me to sleep on it, give it some time, figure out exactly what I wanted and then how to say it, and then—*maybe*—he and I could have a discussion.

"We definitely don't want to find ourselves under a house of cards," I said, hoping to sound agreeable. Mature, even. "Look, Burke, we're both adults now. We don't need to talk this to death. We have a history, we can't deny it, but we've both moved on. Nothing more to it than that, really, is there?"

"Nope. Doesn't need to be anything more to it than that." Was it my imagination, or did he look relieved?

Fortified by the fear that he did, I went on. "We're bound to run into each other more in the time leading up to, and including, the wedding—"

He scoffed. "If there is one."

"What do you mean? Of course there's going to be a wedding. Why wouldn't there be? They're so happy!"

"Just because two people are happily anticipating a wedding, that doesn't mean it's necessarily going to happen." He looked at me significantly for a moment, but before I could say anything—and what could I say?—he went on. "There's something about that guy I don't trust. We'll see if he's really in this to marry Gran."

I was flummoxed. "I can't believe you even wonder that. He adores her."

"I hope so. But I'm afraid he adores her money even more."

Of course my first thoughts, when Dottie had shown me Lyle's picture, were along the same lines. He was younger than she was and pretty good-looking by any standards. That was the kind of guy who always came out of central casting as *opportunist* for just about any Sherwood Schwartz show. But I didn't want to admit that to Burke and add fuel to his fire.

Instead I just said, "I think you could hand that guy a hundred-dollar bill and he wouldn't know what to do with the change from McDonald's."

"Meaning . . . ?"

"He doesn't have grandiose tastes. And I don't mean that in the insulting way it's coming out. I think he's just simple. Happy.

He likes to have fun and Dottie is such a spitfire they have fun together. I don't think there's more to the story than that."

"There's *always* more to the story. And it always comes out in the end."

I appreciated that he was being protective of his grandmother, but at the same time I didn't recognize this cynical person as Burke. When had that happened? Was his divorce more bitter than I had been led to believe?

"Anyway," I said pointedly. "You and I are bound to run into each other some more, so let's just agree right here and now that we don't need to feel weird about it, okay? Dottie may be trying to matchmake—or shit-stir, I don't know—but we have our own lives. Right?" I got too brisk at the end there. Sounded like I was protesting too much.

"Right."

I couldn't tell from his response if he thought I was being as weird as I felt or not, so, possibly making things worse, I added, "Sorry, I don't mean to sound impatient, I'm just in kind of a hurry. I've got . . ." What? What? *What?* "A . . . thing." I gestured like it was just too complicated to try and explain right now.

"Yeah, okay, sorry, I didn't mean to keep you from anything. I just thought, you know, we should talk this over before it got weird or anything." He started walking toward the door.

"I appreciate that."

He paused at the door and turned back. "So I'll see you around."

I smiled. "Probably more than either of us expects, if Dottie has anything to say about it."

He laughed. "Right." Then he nodded to himself and, with a final glance toward me that could have melted my heart right then and there, he walked out into the night.

I watched him go, glad I had abbreviated what would surely have otherwise been a long and pointlessly circular conversation that made us both feel worse.

What I'd done was mature.

Maybe I was making progress after all.

The next day at lunch, I was walking over to Mom's Apple Pie—where they actually have a really good light turkey sandwich with cranberry jelly instead of mayo—when I spotted Burke on the corner of East Market and Newley.

That itself wouldn't have been so noticeably weird if he hadn't been peering around the corner like a bad actor on *Get Smart*.

"What are you doing, Burke?" I asked.

"I was on my way into the courthouse to get copies of some documents, and"—he frowned—"I'm pretty sure I just saw Lyle with some woman."

"Lyle?" I echoed, then looked in the direction he'd been looking and saw nothing but a strip of shops and the post office. "Where?"

"They went in Calloway's."

"Oh." I narrowed my eyes and tried to see inside the windows of the jewelry store but couldn't. And even if I could, what would I have seen?

"Why does that matter?"

"Hopefully it doesn't, but . . . why would he be going to a jewelry store with some other woman?"

Interesting that Burke's mind went straight to cheating. "I don't know, why don't you just go in and ask him?"

"Because if he *is* up to something, he'll have some quick, pat excuse and dismiss it, and then he'll be warned I'm onto him and he'll be that much more careful." He shook his head. "I'm really afraid he's using my grandmother."

This again.

"Look, Burke, this doesn't ring true to me. Does she really have that much gold to dig?"

He looked at me like I'd just kicked him in the shins. "Do you have any idea what that property is worth?"

"She hasn't sold it, so at the moment it's not worth much to a gold digger. It's a hypothetical asset. In a terrible real estate market, to boot. That's really not worth chasing down, is it? Surely there are more certain things out there."

"Quinn." He leveled his gaze on me. "If she sold that property for *half* what it's worth, his efforts would be well remunerated."

I crinkled my nose. "I don't want to believe that. He really didn't strike me that way."

He looked in the direction of the jewelry store. "I don't either. . . ." In the silence hung the question of why he'd be with another woman in a jewelry store, though.

And I didn't have the answer to that.

"Did he strike you as being in love with my grandmother?"

I thought about it. "There's *something* there. Definitely affection.

Maybe it's more of a"—I searched for the word—"*Svengali* kind of relationship, but I think it's genuine."

He gave a short laugh. "You see Dottie as a Svengali?"

That wasn't quite right. "Not as much as I see Lyle as a kind of . . . protégé. I don't want to say she's *maternal* toward him, because that isn't it and that sounds oogie, but, honestly, I think she kind of likes taking care of him."

Burke nodded. "I'm not sure it's so great if he likes *being taken care of.*"

"No, that's not what I mean. I think it's more like he's a pet she adores." Wow, that sounded even worse. But more accurate. "And he's kind of looking at her from that point of view too. He's not trying to *take* her, he wants to be taken."

I thought I'd nailed it perfectly, but Burke looked at me like I was crazy.

"He has almost nothing in his bank account," he said. "It's not even interest-bearing. His IRA has eight hundred and fifty-eight dollars in it, from an initial deposit of twelve hundred that he made *eighteen years ago.* He has one credit card, I'll give him that, with a limit of seven thousand bucks, but it's practically maxed. Other than that, he's got nothing."

"Doesn't he have a job?"

"He sells furniture at Rolfe's."

"Actually, I've heard those guys can make a lot of money." I didn't add that I'd dated a guy who sold furniture at Macy's Home Store and who had enough to take me to nicer dinners and dates than, I don't know, *Burke* had, for instance.

"Negligible."

"Define *negligible*."

He laughed. "You're impossible. Okay, I don't know *exactly* what he makes, it's based on commission and his taxes have varied pretty wildly over the past few years."

I was aghast. "You checked his *taxes*?"

He looked at me. Silent.

"Isn't that illegal?"

"You're missing the point."

"Or *you* are."

"We're talking about *character* here."

"What kind of character does it take to dig into someone else's private business to try to get dirt on them that may or may not be an accurate picture?"

He shook his head, rejecting my argument. "The kind that would do anything to protect someone he loved," he said, with genuine emotion. "And I will do anything to protect her."

Something in me softened. There was something noble in that, for sure. "Okay, I get that."

"I'm not condemning him. Not calling the police or the hit men. Just keeping an eye on the situation. What kind of person would I be if I didn't?"

More like me, maybe. Maybe *too* cautious. Too afraid what people thought. "I don't know" was all I could say.

He looked at me for a hard moment, then said, "I've got to get back to work here." He glanced over my shoulder in the direction of the jewelry store. "I'm not going to have a pointless confrontation with the guy here and now. But . . ." He didn't finish. He didn't need to.

We said our good-byes and I stood there for a moment, trying to remember what I had been doing and trying to figure out why I felt so weird about the conversation we'd just had.

Then I turned and saw Lyle walking right toward me.

I smiled.

He smiled back. Then he said, "Excuse me, do you know where—" He stopped, and I watched his face morph into surprise, like watching a stop-motion film of a flower blooming. "Quinn!"

"Hey, Lyle! What are you doing here?"

"I'm just coming from—" He gestured, and I wondered if he was going to lie. That's how quickly paranoia like Burke's can get to you. "That jewelry store," he concluded.

"Calloway's?"

He snapped and pointed at me. "*That's* it. Calloway's."

"What were you doing there? Looking for something pretty to get for Dottie?"

"Actually, I was looking at watches."

"For *Dottie*?" She didn't seem like a watch kind of person.

"Nah, for me."

Oh, dear. Red flags were being raised on their staffs in my mind. "For you."

He nodded. "Dottie is *insisting* on getting me a watch."

"Okay . . . ?"

"And she wants to spend an absolute *fortune*."

At this point, what he'd said could have gone either way, but it was beginning to seem likely it was going in Burke's "user" column.

"I've never really understood the point of expensive watches," I said carefully, watching him for signs of cunning. Perhaps a sharp glance, a momentary look in the eye that told me all of this was calculated. But instead he just looked as guileless as ever.

"Me neither," he said. "So when I ran into the salesgirl from there in the coffee shop I asked if she'd take me in and help me figure out which watch was the least expensive without being so cheap that she'd have me figured out."

"You wanted the *cheapest* watch?" I clarified. This was *not* what I'd been expecting to hear.

He nodded enthusiastically. "The cheapest one I could get her to believe I want. I don't really want a watch at all. I hardly ever wonder what time it is."

"You need to know when it's time to get off work, don't you?" I said it like I was joking, but, again, Burke had gotten to me and I found myself testing poor Lyle.

"There are clocks *everywhere* there. Every living room display, every bedroom display, plus you can always ask someone what time it is, since everyone *else* has a watch."

"That makes sense." And it did.

"Plus I work until the work is done," he added. Extra points. "If I don't close the sale, I might as well have not come in."

"That makes *total* sense." I couldn't wait to tell Burke this. "So what did you find, watch-wise?"

He sighed. "They're all so expensive. I'd rather just have a nice dinner. That one we had when you were there was good. I sure did like your macaroni salad."

My face grew hot at the memory. "Thanks."

"Do you know what time it is?"

I glanced down. "Four-ten."

"See?" He pointed a finger gun at me. "You can always find out what time it is from someone else if you want to."

I had to laugh. "You got me."

"No, I really wanted to know what time it was. But you also proved my other point." Only then did he look pleased with himself. "I've got to go. Do you know where the Newley Street parking garage is? My meter's going to run down."

I was tempted to ask at what time, but that would have belabored the point and been starkly unfunny. "We're on Newley," I said, and pointed north. "You just want to go that way about two blocks. It's across from the library."

"I know, I'm in one of the library spaces," he said. "That's why I have to hurry, I need to go check out a book because those spaces are reserved for library patrons only."

Okay, there was a certain *extra* level of honesty there. I made a mental note of it. I couldn't wait to tell Burke. "It was good to see you, Lyle," I said. "Tell Dottie I said hello."

"I can't do that," he said. "I don't want her to know what I was up to."

"Oh, right. Then I'll just tell her myself next time I see her."

"Perfect!" He said it like I'd hatched the ultimate plan.

As I watched him go, it occurred to me that there are all kinds of reasons for people to couple up. I'd never thought about it before because it seemed so singular to me. I had always wanted the big happily ever after. Didn't everyone?

But happily ever after depended on what you thought would make you happy. In my case, maybe it was love and romance and all the fairy-tale accoutrements. Yet maybe in someone else's case, like Dottie's, it was the sweet, earnest companionship of a guy like Lyle. Maybe his slight dopiness lent to the charm for her. Who knew?

All I knew was that it wasn't for me to judge. I hoped she'd get her happily ever after no matter what it was.

Chapter 18

It was as if the dry cleaner's were suddenly the first Pinkberry to come to the East Coast. At least to my eye it was. People were coming and going—a large percentage of them women, by the way—all day long. Often leaving with long garment bags.

"I wonder if she can do a replica of Audrey Hepburn's *Breakfast at Tiffany's* dress," Becca stage-whispered, looking at the front window next to me.

I looked at her. "*I* could. I just *haven't* because it's Givenchy, and it's dirty pool to do a knockoff."

"Wow, I never even thought of that!"

I nodded.

"You could really copy it?"

"Becca! Anyone competent can copy a design, it's just not *right*."

She shrugged and looked back at what might as well have been a line forming outside the dry cleaner's. "I think the prices for those designer clothes are outrageous sometimes, so I'm all for the knockoffs."

I could kind of see her point. But if I were Vera Wang I knew I'd be a lot more hesitant to agree. "I don't know . . ."

"Okay, but right or wrong, it's what people are obviously interested in. I've seen them showing fakes on *The Today Show* a million times, so it must not be illegal."

"Not if it's 'inspired by,' rather than a total rip-off."

"Okay, then maybe you should be *inspired by* a few famous designs, up your business, and put those people"—she gestured—"out of work."

I really didn't want to admit it, but that was a good idea. I mean, I *like* good ideas, but I didn't want to admit I could boost business by going trendy instead of trying to stick to my own style. But when I made that dress for Nicole, inspired by Grace Kelly's wedding dress, was that so different from what Becca was suggesting?

I was about to ask her when her phone rang. She answered in the same stage whisper she'd been using with me, then immediately, in her regular sharp voice, asked, "He put *what* in his ear?"

And right then I knew she was going to have to cut out early again. This was the problem with Becca as an employee—she had three little kids and they each did about ten bad and/or dangerous things a day, so she was constantly having to leave on a moment's notice.

She'd been working with me for three years, since her youngest—Teddy—was a baby. She did great needlework and was at ease with the register, computer, and customers, so she was the perfect part-time employee . . . except for the fact that her times weren't always the ones I was planning on.

But she was a friend too, so I wasn't going to fire her. Yet I couldn't afford to hire someone else for the same number of hours Becca was hired for. And there wasn't anyone out there who would be willing to sit around and wait for a Matchbox-car-tire-in-the-nose emergency to work maybe a few hours a week.

Becca said into the phone, "Hang on, hang on," then put her hand over the bottom, as if that would do anything, and said to me, "I've got to go, Craigie has a green bean in his ear. Will you be okay?"

I smiled. A green bean in his ear. Good lord. "Yes, of course, go, go!"

"I'm *really* sorry!"

"It's fine. Business is slow, as you know." I gestured limply toward the street outside.

"I'll make it up to you!"

"*Go!*"

"Man, I am *worn out*—I have got *no* energy for this." She went back to her urgent instructions on the phone, saying things like, *Do* not *use a Q-tip, do you understand me?* as she went.

Six uneventful and customer-free hours later, I was thirty-five miles away and I was seventeen all over again. Which was bad, because when I was seventeen, I had a lot of thirteen-year-old moments.

This was one of those.

So much for maturity and making decisions that were regret-proof by the light of day.

It was eleven at night and Glenn and I were huddled in his Toyota convertible across the street from Burke's house—or what every indication we could find on Spokeo and Switchboard was Burke's house in Northern Virginia—watching for . . . I don't even know what. Some sort of clue about his life. It was a cool, drizzly night, matching my mood, but Glenn had brought what he called "stalking provisions," including seedless red grapes as sweet as candy; sandwiches of thin white bread, Brie, sweet mustard, and roasted red peppers; and tiny little plastic flutes of chocolate mousse.

So far, so good, in that we hadn't seen any clear indication that he had a woman there.

However, we also hadn't had any clear indication that he was there either.

"How long are we going to sit here?" I whispered.

"Until we know something," he whispered back.

We could have spoken in full voice, it wasn't as if anyone was around to hear us, but something about peering through someone's windows shrouded only by the dark of night, and hopefully by the anonymity of someone else's car, made it feel necessary to stay as quiet and still as possible.

"We don't even know if anyone's in there," I said, narrowing my eyes and trying to draw some sort of conclusion from the sage-colored walls of what looked like might be the kitchen, based on the brass lamp that I thought was hanging from the ceiling but couldn't swear to it, thanks to partially closed blinds.

"So that's one thing we need to find out. It should become evident."

"It's only going to become evident if we see someone. If we don't, we still won't know if that means no one's there or they're just asleep."

"Stop borrowing trouble. And did you hear what you just did there? You said *they*. I, myself, am almost positive there's no *they*, only a *he*. Furthermore, I have a feeling we're going to catch at least some sort of glimpse of him."

"*Almost* positive?"

"Okay, positive."

"Too little, too late."

"Sh!" He pointed toward the window. "Did you see something?"

Nothing had changed. Not one light in one window of the house we'd been staring at for almost an hour now. "No."

We fell silent. Rain ticked, thin and sharp, on the soft convertible top that was a delight to have down on a sunny day but more depressing than a Siberian winter to sit under in bad weather.

"I can't be this person," I said after a bit.

"This is exactly you."

"No, this is exactly who I *don't* want to be."

"Consider this a bonus round in our game. Another thing you're uncomfortable with—facing the truth."

"What if I don't *like* the truth?"

He steeled his gaze on me in the mostly dark car and said, "Make no mistake. You *can* handle the truth. It will set you free.

That's why we're here, to exorcize the demon Burke from your mind once and for all."

"You're mixing up your references there."

"Sue me."

"Anyway, what if you're wrong? What if we see something really upsetting and then I have to live with that? What if the suspicion becomes a visual certainty that I can never unsee?" Panic at the idea built in me. "I can't do this. I can't. We have to go."

"*Face it!*" His whisper became a fierce stage whisper. "Conquer this!"

"No!"

"No?"

"No."

"Yes."

This was asinine. "What do you mean, *yes*? You can't just *yes* my *no* and think it's over. Your yes doesn't trump my no, and you don't trump me."

"Oh, yes, I do." He gave a slow, purposely maniacal chuckle. "I'm the one driving."

I reached for the door handle.

Glenn must have read my mind, because he clicked the automatic lock button before I could touch it. One tug at the door handle told me he'd pressed the child safety lock too.

"Good thing you locked the doors," I cautioned. "This isn't the best neighborhood. I hope no one comes along with a blunt instrument and smashes the windows."

"You don't scare me, little one. There isn't a house in this neighborhood priced at under five hundred grand. This isn't exactly Thugville."

"Thugs don't hang out in Thugville, they go to wealthy neighborhoods to steal."

He flashed me a wordless look.

"He's not there," I said after a few minutes. "No one is. This is stupid." But the thought made me feel curiously bereft. I'd been ready to see him. Ready to glimpse him. Eager, I guess, to glimpse him.

"He's there," Glenn said, suddenly serious. "Look. Top left window."

My eyes were not what they used to be, but I stared hard until I saw the flicker of someone walking past a distant light.

"Oh!" I felt the familiar cocktail of excitement and fear at the prospect of seeing him.

"Careful, Quinn." I felt Glenn's hand on my shoulder. "Someone's liable to think you care."

"At this point, we've been looking at this house for so long that *anything* is going to make me feel like a lion pouncing its prey."

Rain drizzled against the window, forming teary rivulets against the glass. It was a perfect metaphor for the way I felt, sitting outside this house feeling emotions that hadn't changed one iota since I'd been with him, even though our lives had changed immeasurably.

Or Burke's had anyway.

We sat in the stillness for a long time, watching the darkened house, waiting for some follow-up. The distant light was extinguished and I waited with bated breath for a light to click on in the bedroom, like a movie flickering onto a big screen, but it didn't happen.

Then Glenn's voice broke the silence. "What would you do," he said slowly, "if he swung past the window right now, buck-naked, on a trapeze?"

The image was so unexpected I cracked up. "Okay, that's it. I've had it. This was a dumb idea, albeit a good dinner."

"Wait!" He pointed silently. A shadow form appeared in the window upstairs.

"That's *him!*" There was a strange gratification, even while panic filled every inch of me.

"He looks alone."

"Maybe. But what does that prove? We've got to go, Glenn. Please. *Please.* I have a bad feeling. It would be so humiliating to be caught out here."

"Calm down, we'll go." He reached for the ignition, then glanced at the house and said, "Oh, shit."

I looked. Burke was coming out the front door, heading straight for the car.

"Why?" I asked. "How did he know we were here?" I looked around frantically, and that's when I noticed the red glow illuminating the street, the trees, the cars behind us. "Oh, my *god*, Glenn, have you had your foot on the fucking brake *this whole time?*"

Immediately he lifted his foot and the red light went out.

Oh. My. God. The brakes had provided a beacon of light through the misty night, much like a lighthouse three hundred yards off the coast.

"I'm so sorry," Glenn said, uncharacteristically humble. "It's habit. If you're sitting behind the wheel, unmoving, you keep the brake on. I'm so sorry, Quinn, really."

I couldn't speak. It was too late.

Burke was approaching the driver's window.

Chapter 19

"H ide!" Glenn rasped.

"*Where?*" I returned frantically. "Gun it! Get out of here! Maybe he hasn't recognized us yet!"

"He's *here*. Turn your face to the window," he said through his teeth. "And don't look back for *anything*. Act like you're asleep."

I tried to scoop my hair to the side, and turned so I was completely facing the window. One good thing about the dark little convertible I had just been complaining about having the top up on is that when the top *is* up, it makes the inside that much smaller and cramped and dark. It was possible that Burke, at six feet tall, could stand at the driver's window talking to Glenn and never see anything higher than my ass.

Which he would probably recognize.

Also, who *else* would be here with Glenn? Or, better question, why would *Glenn* be here at all?

This was all so obvious.

"Go," I barely whispered. "Drive, drive, drive. I don't care what he thinks he's seen, he can't be sure—"

"*Sh!* I've got this covered." This was followed by the sound of his window slowly lowering, then, "Hey, man, what the hell are you doing here?"

"That's my house," I heard Burke's voice say.

"No kidding!" Glenn sounded genuinely surprised. I made a mental note of his ability to lie convincingly. "We were just at a party at the Barcowskis'."

"Yeah? The Barcowskis'? Right across the street from me?"

Glenn gave a casual laugh. "Small world, huh?" He started the car.

"Who are you with?"

Another laugh from Glenn, who shifted his voice to something just above a whisper. "She's beat, I think she's sleeping. Anyway, it was good to see you, I'm sure I'll see you around the ol' hometown."

"No doubt. Or if you come back to the Barcowskis' house."

"Whew! They're going to be cleaning up for a while, I'll tell you. We had a ball." I felt the car shift into gear. "See ya!"

"Night."

And then, finally, *mercifully*, the car started to move. When I felt him round the corner, I turned around and looked at him. "The Barcowskis'? How did you come up with *that*?"

"What, you think this is the first time I've stalked someone?"

I looked at him, the streetlights illuminating his face like a strobe light as we passed. "I'm gathering it's not?"

"Oh, hell, no!" He returned his attention to the street in front of him and adjusted his grip on the wheel. "First rule of stalking someone who thinks you shouldn't know where they live is look up the people around where they live. Get some names, other streets nearby. So, depending on the circumstance, on who catches you, you can either say you were here but at someone else's house, or ask for directions to a nearby place. That way it's understandable that you're a few streets off." He glanced at me and I could see the smugness in his expression.

And I had to hand it to him, I was impressed. These details would never have occurred to me, but maybe he was right, maybe it had saved us this once.

"Do you think he knew it was me in the passenger seat?"

"Naaah." But something in his expression allowed for doubt. There was an unspoken *I hope not.*

By both of us.

I leaned back in my seat and made myself take a few deep breaths. "He hasn't been around," I rationalized, more to myself than to him. "He doesn't necessarily know how close we are. I mean, sure, he saw you in my shop that one time, but that doesn't mean I'd be with you at some party. In his neighborhood. On a Wednesday night." My own words were deflating me quickly. "Oh, I am so screwed. He totally knows."

"No, he doesn't!"

"If he doesn't know it was me here, he at the very least thinks I sent you here. Which is probably worse, come to think of it." I covered my face with my hands. "Oh, my god, he thinks I sent you to spy on him!"

"Now, wait a minute," Glenn said, as I felt him accelerate onto 15. "You just agreed that kissing him was a mistake and that you don't want to get back together. Why would he think you were spying on him after that?"

"Because everything he needed to know about how I feel about him was *very* clearly communicated in that kiss, *believe* me."

"Slut."

I laughed. "That's me!"

He was laughing as well. "That doesn't give him X-ray vision, though. He's too tall to have seen you in that seat when he was standing right next to my door. Trust me."

"I *did* trust you! Look where it got me!"

"Tell you what, I'll give you a day's credit for this, even though it was a miss. Stalking was definitely outside your wheelhouse, so it was still a worthwhile assignment. You're done for the day."

"Thank goodness. Does that mean tomorrow will be something easy, like Wear a Red Shirt Day?"

"No." He looked thoughtful. "But I'll definitely come up with something that'll make you feel better after this." He nodded slowly. "Actually . . . yes. I've got it. Tomorrow will be fun." He glanced at me. "I promise."

Yeah. I'd heard his promises before. We'd have to see.

At least there would probably be cheese involved.

Suffice it to say, Improv Class Day was every bit as bad as you might think it would be.

After two hours of instruction from a community theater actor who himself couldn't act like anything less than a caricature of an *actor*—to say nothing of the simple happiness of the other students (obviously I was the only one who had been forced there by a friend on a mission to crack their shell)—I was feeling like a little black rain cloud.

No, a *big* black rain cloud.

At another time, under different circumstances, I might have gotten a kick out if it. I'd never want to be an actress, I'd never be comfortable on a stage, I had no illusions about that, but the enthusiasm of most of the people there was the kind of thing that's normally infectious.

Not tonight.

When it had finally ended—late, of course, because people had questions and apparently the Groupon had only been for one class—I'd driven home alone, feeling more and more melancholy by the minute.

It's funny how heartache can take up residence in you and live on and on and on, even if it's not fed for years. It whispers in your mind, insisting things weren't as bad as you remembered, as sharp as you remembered, as *whatever painful thing* as you remembered.

Obviously I hadn't gone for ten years without ever thinking of Burke. It wasn't as if I'd flipped a switch, turned the feelings off, and never thought about him again until he was right in front of me. If it were that easy, I would, at least, have been encouraged that maybe I could flip the switch again when he was gone and this turmoil would pack all its questions into a bag that was never to be opened again and would lock away all my tangled feelings with it.

But as I sat on the stoop outside my house looking at the

waxing moon and starry sky, it was small random moments that came to me and pinched at my soul. A sunny day when Burke and I were meeting in the afternoon but he'd missed lunch so I'd stopped by Puccio's Deli and picked up a steak-and-cheese sub for him. Swiss cheese, lettuce, tomato, onions, sweet peppers, Italian dressing. I'd placed the order and waited in the little dining room at a Formica table, completely content with every single thing in my life. I was in love, I was so lucky—I truly thought this at the time—to have never had to go through the heartbreak most people did. It wasn't a remarkable day, I honestly don't even remember what he and I were doing when we met up that afternoon, I just remember the small ordinary moment of picking up lunch. The way the sun felt on me when I got out of the car, the way the deli smelled when I walked in, the cold of the refrigerator case when I reached in and picked up a bottle of Coke for him. . . .

Silly, right? A totally unremarkable event on an otherwise unmemorable day. Puccio's is still there. I can't even imagine how many carryout orders they fill per day, but I bet more than one went to a girlfriend picking up for a boyfriend on a day she'd never imagine would stand out as remarkable.

For a long time after we broke up, those were the kinds of memories that haunted me. The wedding dress was easily dismissed—too big, too obvious. It was almost sarcastic in its sadness. Likewise any recollection of sewing it, of picking bridesmaid dresses, wedding rings, and so on. It wasn't even that I avoided those thoughts, it was that they were just too big to take in and wholly redigest.

But cleaning out a closet and coming across a bag containing an old nightshirt and a Ziploc bag of little hotel toiletries I'd packed to take on an overnight at the farm could reduce me to sobs.

A cheap aluminum spoon I'd taken from a restaurant after we'd had lobster bisque and a crabby waitress made grief well up in me and spill over my body, bringing physical discomfort to what was otherwise just emotional distress.

Dredging up those memories now led, necessarily, to the memory of the end and the long ellipsis it had left in my life where I would have preferred a period. Or an exclamation point.

Instead it was like opening a can of flat soda, there was just a soft, fizzy sigh and then . . . nothing. I was heavy with the knowledge that I had to deal with all the things that had been woken up in me. Sad things. Ugly things I didn't want to look at. Hard things I didn't want to know.

Things I probably should have confronted at the time. No, not *probably*, things I *definitely* should have confronted at the time. Somehow I'd thought if I didn't look at them they'd go away. I think on some level I even believed in fate, and trusted that if Burke wasn't the right guy, then someone even better—someone unimaginably wonderful (I certainly couldn't imagine him)— would come along.

Fairy tales die hard in the minds and hearts of some girls.

I wish I were cooler than that, but I'm not. Deep inside, I'm Cinderella. I still hope the shoe fits. Unlike the conclusion I'd drawn about Dottie, my standards for happily ever after were decidedly romantic.

So, sitting there looking at the sky, I felt very aware of how familiar this heartache was. I had looked at this same sky years ago, wishing on the first star I saw that something would happen in my life and make me forget all of this pain.

I don't recall the exact date, or what had happened during the day or week that might have ratcheted up my loneliness for Burke, but I remember it was more than a year after we broke up because I felt I didn't have anyone to talk to about it. Friends who had been patient and supportive at first had, understandably, begun to look or sound distracted if I broached the subject. Sometimes there was a tiny snap to the responses, which always struck me like a blow, and I would back off quickly, trying to assert that I hadn't meant I was still really thinking about *him* or, god forbid, *missing* him. Of course not! We all knew he was El Diablo, I'd have to be a complete idiot to waste one more tear on him.

Etc., etc., etc.

So it was a peculiar feeling to look back on that memory as a moment of some sort of warmth. At that time it had felt very cold, but with all the distance of time wedged between then and now, it almost felt quaint compared to how reality had shaken down.

Ten years later and here I was, alone. Sad. Thinking about kissing him, touching him. Thinking about getting him a sandwich. Thinking about holding hands while walking across the parking lot to a restaurant under a lipstick smear of sunset in a sky that could have been April or November. I can't even recall.

When you find yourself looking back on *previous* melancholy with melancholy, you've got some crap to deal with.

I went inside to my computer and, calling on that fate that I had only a tenuous belief in—and some anger at, if it *did* exist and had abandoned me—I opened my e-mail and typed his old address into the "to" box. It might not be his anymore. It probably wasn't; now that he'd moved and opened his own business, he probably had a different account. In which case he'd never get this and maybe I'd be relieved.

Nevertheless, I typed:

You don't owe me anything and I know it but I'm thinking about our past and I think it would help me to talk to you.

I added my cell number and hit send.

And regretted it *immediately.* I'd just handed him all my vulnerability. He might well look at that and think I was crazy for resurrecting something that he may have deleted 90 percent of from his mental hard drive. He might not answer, pretending never to have received it, thereby letting me off the proverbial hook while both of us knew the truth and could never, then, *un*know the truth.

I still cared, I'd revealed it too many ways, and maybe he didn't.

So when the phone rang, maybe forty-five minutes after I'd hit send, my heart nearly stopped. I hoped it was him and I hoped it *wasn't* him. But mostly I hoped it was.

And it was. "Where are you?" he asked.

"At my house."

"Where's that?"

I'd forgotten he'd never been here. I'd only just gotten the house about five years ago. Perhaps that was the one big thing that had happened in my otherwise stagnant life.

I told him where the house was, and he asked, "Is it okay if I come by?"

Reflexively my hand flew to my ponytailed unwashed hair. "When?"

"Tonight. Now. I'm still at the farm and was about to leave. I could swing by there first."

"Sure." My breath was tight. "I'll be up for a while anyway."

The moment we hung up, I hit the shower. It felt like I was moving in slow motion even while I felt frantic to get cleaned up and dressed so, even if the conversation went badly, he wouldn't leave with the satisfaction of thinking I was an unkempt pig. Not that he'd have such an uncharitable thought. I'd never known him to be that way.

But I sure didn't want him to start tonight.

As it turned out, I was ready well in advance, which gave me time to wander the house, wondering what to do with myself. And wondering why I was so nervous about seeing Burke and having this talk that probably any psychologist in the world would say was long overdue.

I guess if you avoid something for long enough, as uncomfortable as it is to have it unresolved, in some ways it can be more uncomfortable to take it out and examine it.

Then again, maybe the problem was just my premonition that it was going to go badly.

Fortunately, before I had time to drive myself well and truly insane speculating about it, there was a knock at the door.

I took a steadying breath and then walked over, not hurrying. Didn't want to appear breathless or eager when I opened the door.

Chapter 20

When I saw him standing there on my front stoop, his dark hair gleaming under the light of the porch sconces, it very nearly did take my breath away.

He was a very good-looking man no matter how you sliced it, but his bone structure was such that shadows and light invariably upped his hotness infinitely. He looked like a movie star, he really did. He always had, but somewhere back when he and I were a couple I had gotten used to that and wasn't daunted by it. But perhaps nothing could have prepared me for the attractiveness of this older Burke.

"Hey," he said, when I didn't say anything for a moment.

"Hi." I opened the door. "Come on in."

It was surreal to see Burke Morrison walking into my house, this space that had never previously existed with him. But in a way it was kind of . . . healing.

"Can I get you anything?" I ran through a mental inventory of the contents of my fridge. "Milk? Water? Old orange juice? Oh, wait, I think I have beer. Do you want a beer? They're warm."

He gave a laugh. "Warm beer would be perfect. Really hit the spot on a warm night like tonight."

I laughed too. "Well, I could put it over ice."

He winced. "Let's just keep it one kind of bad, not two."

"Right." I went to the kitchen and took two ominously named Flying Dog Raging Bitch ales out of the cabinet. I don't normally drink beer, but there's almost nothing I like more than beer cheese soup, so I try to keep it on hand in case the mood strikes me to cook.

"Glenn was in my neighborhood the other night," he called.

I winced and was glad he couldn't see me. How to play this? Nebulous. I needed to go for nebulous. So I could admit I was there if I had to, but not if I didn't have to. "I know," I said with loud confidence. "At that party."

"It was weird. He was out front for ages with the brake lights on. I wouldn't have known it was him if I hadn't taken the trash out and noticed his profile."

"Yeah, I dunno, I was just dead that night. I can't even remember what he said about your conversation." Good, right? Foggy enough? I could have been there or not.

I opened both beers and went back to the den, where he was standing in front of the fireplace I'd never lit.

I handed him his bottle and took a sip from my own. Yup, that was warm beer, all right. I changed the subject quickly. "So I ran into Lyle right after you left the other day. That was a salesgirl from Calloway's you saw him with."

"Yeah?" He looked surprised. "He introduce you?"

I shook my head. "He came out alone. And he had no idea you or I or anyone had seen them, so I know he wasn't making up a story. In fact, he didn't even realize who I was for a moment, even though he was looking me right in the face. Not that we know each other so well, but . . . anyway. He was actually in the shop because Dottie was insisting on buying him a watch and he didn't want her to waste her money, so he was trying to find a way to 'request' an inexpensive piece. It's nice, really. Actually the *opposite* of gold digging."

He took a drag of his beer. "You're very pretty still."

And, yes, it was that easy to get right to the heart of me. "Burke . . ."

"You always were."

I swallowed. "Thanks."

He set his beer down on the mantel and came over to me. "You know I can't resist you."

"I thought we decided this was a bad idea."

"I'm sure it is." He touched my cheek.

"Oh." I turned my face into his touch. A reflex. "As long as we've got that cleared up."

"It's been a long time for us."

"Yes," I whispered.

"Do you want me?" he asked, moving in to kiss my neck, my jaw.

"No." Lie. Stupid, lame, obvious lie. I should have popped a pacifier into my mouth, for all the sophistication of it. Then I couldn't resist banging another nail into the coffin. "Do you want me?"

"Yes," he whispered, tightening his hold on me.

My knees weakened. Literally. I don't understand the connection between the heart, the mind, and the physiology, but it's the physiology—which has no business in it whatsoever—that will give you away every time.

In the combination of sudden weaknesses, I curled my hands up over the backs of his shoulders and held on, effectively pulling him closer.

Which I couldn't admit I wanted.

But he knew.

Of *course* he knew. He *always* knew. He'd always been able to read me so well that any attempt I ever made at dignity or maturity or anything resembling resistance must have looked to him exactly like a child insisting he really was Batman because he was wearing the pajamas.

This was a defining moment for me. I had this split second to choose which direction I was going to go on the road ahead in my life. Safe and predictable? Or unquestionably foolish and dangerous?

With one option my life would return to normal eventually. Dottie's wedding would be over and time would turn this photograph to watercolor, and though I wouldn't forget this moment—and maybe I'd never stop questioning whether I'd done the right thing in walking away from it—walking away was the only sure way to avoid pain.

So I couldn't explain why, at that moment when I was so sure that disengaging and leaving was the only way to save my soul, I chose instead—on some level, I must have chosen it—to risk it all.

Almost as if acting from motor memory, I touched my fingertips to his forearms and skidded them up over the veins and skin that I'd never forget.

His shoulders were hard under my touch, the contours uneven with muscle and bulk. When he moved his hands to my lower back and tightened his arms around me, I felt a network of muscles and tendons shift in accommodation.

I looked at him in the dim light. The curve of his mouth, which had always been able to draw me in, no matter what he was saying or how much I tried to resist. I'd always loved his lips, his teeth: a movie star smile.

I was never able to resist it. Not since I was fifteen.

That smile had made me do the most idiotic things imaginable. Over and over. Often at his request, but too often born of my own lame attempts to get his attention.

I had it now.

"Tell me something, Quinn Barton." He moved toward me, slid his rough hands under my shirt, and held me firm at the ribs. "Did you miss me?"

"No." Lie.

He knew it too.

"Did you miss *me?*" I asked, sounding a lot more pleading than I'd wanted to. *I don't care*, I reminded myself with a conviction that wasn't my own. It was Dr. Phil's. Oprah's. Virtually any psychologist in a Google "local therapist" search would have wanted to slap the subservience right out of me. Every pro-woman, be-independent, to-hell-with-him adviser out there was collecting in my mind like a judge-y audience, a Greek chorus of, *What the fuck are you doing? This is not how you get a man!*

And that was true, the math formula was all wrong. Intellectually I knew that. People want what they think they can't have, and he had zero doubt he could have me, despite whatever protestations I made or how hard I tried to get away.

"Yes," he whispered, and pulled me closer, grazing his lips along my jaw.

My shoulders eased. This I was powerless against.

It was as if the stability of my knees and legs were directly proportionate to the distance I had from him. Get close enough and my bones dissolved; if he wasn't holding on to me, I would have collapsed like a broken doll at his feet.

So what could I say to *that*? What would Katharine Hepburn have said to that? *Well, Spencer*—or whoever Spencer Tracy was playing at the time—*that's all well and good, but it's too late. You blew it, buster.*

And then she would have marched off with Ralph Bellamy.

And *that* was the problem. There were a *million* Ralph Bellamys out there—nice guys, always ready to pick up the scraps the leading man left behind. Always willing to be *settled* for. To worship, love, and adore, for a lifetime of . . . what? Mediocre sex. Whitman's Samplers for Valentine's Day. Watching *CSI* every . . . whatever night that was on, in side-by-side La-Z-Boys?

Ralph Bellamy, or whatever alias his character might go by in my real life, was a *great* guy. No doubt about it. I'm sure I'd love him as my best friend's husband. He'd be a great neighbor. I could totally see having a friendly relationship with him at the bank or the grocery store, or at the mailbox every day when he delivered the mail.

But I would *never* feel the chemistry and passion for Ralph Bellamy's character that I felt for Burke.

Who *was* this guy, who could light such a fire in me, and then douse it so easily with a few words that translated to, *I don't really give a shit what you do, I'm a lone wolf in a wolf pack of one.*

I don't need you or anyone.

I knew he needed me. That asinine statement alone proved he needed me. There *are* no lone wolves! There *are* no wolf packs of one! Watch *Animal Planet* for seven minutes and you'll see some idiot animal wander away from the pack and get torn limb from limb by someone higher up on the food chain. That's what happens to "packs of one."

It made no sense.

And it made even less than no sense under the heat of his touch. He had to feel it too, didn't he? Could *one* person in a relationship feel that much more attraction than the other?

That was more math I couldn't figure out.

His hands tightened at my waist, gripping me possessively while he worked his mouth along my neck, my jaw, and finally my mouth, where I gave a token two seconds' resistance before giving in.

Okay, I know you're thinking I'm weak. And I am. But, I swear to god, it was like something supernatural happened around him. No matter what my resolve was, no matter how mad I was—or how *right* I was to *be* mad—he could level me so easily it was embarrassing.

His mouth found mine, and it was the same as always. As soon as he closed those lips over mine, it was *perfect*. Warm and familiar. The taste indescribable but exactly *right*. Every movement he made was expert, his tongue, his mouth, his hands, everything worked together like a perfect orchestra performing a symphony. This was my first kiss and, now, my last, and it was always the same. It was always exactly what I wanted. No one else could do this. No one else could *be* this. I knew his smell, his taste, the *feel* of him almost better than I knew myself. I would have known any and every square millimeter of every part of his body blindfolded.

In a sea of uninteresting offers, this was the only man I'd ever *really* wanted.

And that fact alone had screwed me over time and again. And again. And again.

Like now.

He started to slide my shirt up and I clamped my arms down, like a fussy second-grader who didn't want to take a bath. "*No.*"

He drew back, the smallest implication of a smile quirking his lips. "No?"

"We can't just . . . *do* this."

"We can't." It was a statement, not a question. A dubious statement. A statement he knew he could prove wrong in ten seconds or else lose Final Jeopardy. But he never lost. He could bet on this.

Anyone could bet on this.

An outsider would have to think I was easy. Daisy Mae, the town whore, who would blow the hot guy behind the diner with the hope of winning his heart, only to cater his wedding three weeks later, unacknowledged, in a stiff polyester uniform composed of drugstore clothes.

"I don't want to," I said, trying to add strength where I felt none, even though I knew I *should*.

Because if I gave in to him now, I knew how I'd feel later tonight. How I'd feel tomorrow. How I'd feel a week from now. Lost. Wondering. Hopeful but fearful. Ashamed.

Empty.

He was Pandora's Box and I was gnashing him open with my teeth, even though I dreaded all the things he'd bring out in me.

"Shut *up*," he said with a smile, like he always did, and kissed me again.

But something stiffened in me.

Shut up?

I knew he hadn't meant it *that* way. It wasn't a *Shut up, bitch,* kind of shut up. But that was where I'd gotten into trouble so many times before. It was a dismissal of my feelings.

"Wait, wait, wait." I drew back. "I'm not going to shut up. I think we need to talk first."

I expected defensiveness. Some asshole response that I could hang my *okay, then leave* hat on, but instead he said, "Okay . . . ?"

"Okay?"

"I've been waiting for this. I guess it's time. You want to talk about the past, right? Why I cheated on you?"

Chapter 21

Even though I'd known it was true, on some levels I hadn't believed it, so his words hit me like a blow. Then, immediately, I defaulted to the more comfortable thought that maybe he was being ironic, saying it because he knew I thought it was true, not because it *was*.

"I don't *want* to talk about it. . . ." But I wasn't going to let the chance go now that he'd raised it, and especially now that the question of his faithfulness had been resurrected again.

Even though everyone else on earth might have said it was never a question.

"This isn't easy for me, but, to be really uncool but honest with you, the truth is I've been thinking about it a lot. Chewing on it, you know? Wondering what the truth was."

He looked at the floor, but I saw his jaw twitch. "That probably would have been a good conversation to have at the time."

278 / Beth Harbison

"I know, I'm sorry, I just—it was so confusing and upsetting that I didn't know which end was up. I should have—"

"Quinn."

I looked at him. "Sorry, I was rambling."

"Please stop apologizing."

My heart was pounding like a scared rabbit's. "Okay, I'm so— Okay." Who the hell was I all of a sudden? This wasn't like me. My nerves were betraying me terribly. "Look, I have some questions about . . . everything. Frank's allegations. The business that made me call off the wedding."

He nodded. "I figured."

"Actually, I guess it all just begins with the one question."

"Right." He took a sip of the beer, swallowed, then let out a long breath before meeting my eyes and saying, "I'm not sure you're going to like what I have to say."

Dread snaked through me, then morphed into grief as sharp as a razor. There it was. There it was right there. *That* was what my nerves were about. Not the girlish attempt to dress up for my ex, not the sight of his beautiful face in the light of my porch, but the truth I must have known was underneath it all, had been underneath it all the entire time.

An outsider might not have been sure what Burke's response meant—after all, there were plenty of things he could say that I wouldn't like—but I knew exactly what it meant.

"Frank was telling the truth."

He gave a slow nod. "Probably."

My body went numb. It was like a replay of the wedding day inside of me. Shock, disbelief, anguish, anger, hatred, all wrapped in this tattered shroud of love and trust.

"I don't know *exactly* what he said to you," Burke went on. "You never said and I never asked him."

"You just"—I shook my head and shrugged—"weren't that interested?"

"In what *Frank* said? No. Your reaction was probably appropriate. At the time I didn't think so. I was marrying you, Quinn. I was ready to give everything else up and be yours alone."

"And by *everything* you mean *everyone*?"

He looked me in the eye. "There weren't that many."

Ugh. When I heard him say it like that, the shock was as sharp as if it were new.

"*One* was too many," I said, feeling both the desire to cry and let this out and the desperation to not let him see me lose my composure. Such as it was.

"I know. And I knew then. So there wasn't any point in elaborating, was there? I can't see that there is now."

I couldn't believe what I was hearing. "This was my *life*, Burke. This changed my whole life."

"Mine too."

"So I don't think there was *no point* in ignoring any of the huge disgusting facts that led to that."

He looked suitably chagrined. "What I meant was, the details could only hurt you more than you were already hurting."

"Then again, the facts might have been a *lot* less painful than the many, *many* scenarios I envisioned and tortured myself with." I stood up and started pacing in front of the sofa. "So why don't you just start at the beginning? Did you cheat on me the entire time we were together?"

"No!" He actually looked surprised. "Of course not."

"You'll have to forgive me if I don't see things to be as obvious as you think they are."

He gave a concessionary nod.

"How many other women were there? How long did they last? Years? Were there scores of them? More than five? More than ten? Did you ever see them before you saw me? Or leave me early to see them?"

"Slow down," he said, in what I recognized as his "soothing voice," but there wasn't a chance of soothing me right now.

"Fuck you."

"There was only one when we were engaged."

I wasn't proud of the fact that my first reaction was relief, since I should have been outraged at any betrayal at all. And I was. In that sense, yes, one was better than the cheerleading team that had been rapidly forming in my imagination.

But my second reaction, following the first almost immediately, was an even bigger horror. One woman. One girl. Whatever. *When we were engaged.* I almost couldn't put voice to the question. "Did you . . . did you *love* her?"

"Of *course* not, Quinn, I loved *you*." He sounded completely sincere. It made no sense to me. "I only saw her a couple of times."

I stopped and looked at him in disbelief. I wanted this moment to end. I wanted to go back and have this to do all over again so that I could *not* do it.

And those moments I was talking about earlier? Where *now* feels even sadder than a previous sad? This was one of those moments. Only an hour and a half ago, I'd been sitting on my front stoop with a lonely little melancholy and some niggling questions that turned out to be ice cubes compared to the iceberg I'd run into.

I resumed my pace. "Who was it?" I ground out, clasping my hands together so he couldn't see them shake.

"No one you know."

I looked at him sharply.

"I mean it," he said, looking me square in the eye. "It was no one I knew either. I met her at Shenanigans and, I swear, I don't remember her name."

"You don't remember the name of the woman who broke up our marriage?"

"*Her* name was Quinn. *You* are the one who stopped our marriage." Before I could lunge and kill him, he added, "Because of *me*. Because of what *I* did. No one else matters in this, or ever did, except for you and me. She was a prop at best. An experiment for me to see if I really wanted to get married."

"Yeah? Wow, the pain just goes on and on. Is this fun for you? Is this how you get your kicks, hurting someone who did nothing but love and *trust* you virtually her whole life?"

"Wait a minute." He got up and stood in front of me, his hands on my shoulders, while he looked into my eyes. "Consider this, just for a minute. It's possible that I'm enjoying this conversation even less than you are."

I scoffed. "Somehow I don't think that's true."

"You get to be mad," he said. "You get to hate me. You have one object of all your discontent and you can walk away from it if you want. You've done it before. *With my brother.* Without even looking back. Good on you." He nodded. "But *I* have to live with knowing I fucked up my own life too. I can't blame anyone else or get away from the motherfucker responsible, because it's me."

"Yup." And at that moment, I didn't feel bad about being with Frank at all. It felt like a completely different situation. A different world. A different family.

Burke had pushed me away all by himself.

"But worse, Quinn, I have to live with knowing I did this to you, that I put you through this, not just then but now too. And anytime in between when you might have felt pain over it. This is *torture* for me, Quinn, I *never* wanted to hurt you, and I couldn't have done a better job if I'd set out to do it on purpose."

That's when the tears started to come. I shrugged his hands off my shoulders and took a step back. "At least *on purpose* would imply some awareness of me. This just happening, just going on with some slut you used as a *prop* or however you termed it just tells me I was of no consequence to you."

"No, you were of *every* consequence to me. You were all I ever thought about, all I ever wanted. I was ready to marry you almost the moment I met you. But when it came down to it, when it was time to really take that step, I wanted to be sure I wasn't just under some spell of infatuation or something."

My jaw dropped and I splayed my arms. "Really? Seven years and you weren't sure?"

"Seven years of *no one but you.* Not even considering anyone but you. But I didn't want to make a commitment and find out it was based on an illusion or something." He shook his head, frustrated. "I'm not wording this right. But basically, I didn't want to have my parents' marriage all over again. I didn't want to become them, and I didn't want to change you into that." He put his hands back on my shoulders and held me steady as I tried to resist. "It wasn't the right thing to do, I *know* that. That's why I never told you. Because the truth sounds like a lie. But it made me realize even more how much I valued you. That I never ever wanted to lose you. I don't know what kind of man could have taken the chance on that by telling you the truth, but I couldn't."

"Frank could have."

"Frank never cared this much about anyone or anything in his life. Of course he could have risked the truth. He's always got a plan B. He's always either got backup for what he might lose or he risks it because he feels he can afford to lose it."

That was true, that was a perfect characterization of Frank. Except when it came to me. I truly believed one of Frank's only weak spots was me. I couldn't say why. But it had always been my feeling. "Then why did you tell him?"

Burke stepped back and raked his hand through his hair. "I didn't. He saw us."

"Where? Was it really at the farm?" I braced myself, though I was so wobbly at this point I couldn't say I was really *prepared* for anything.

"*What?* Why would you think *that?*"

Not a denial, I noticed. "That's what Frank said. That you took her there and she got stoned with Rob."

"She got stoned with Rob," Burke said dully, like he was

repeating a math question he wasn't even going to try to figure out. "At the farm. And I was okay with all that."

I gave a broad shrug. "Hey, you were okay with enough of the rotten parts that I don't know *what* to think. If you were okay with cheating on me, then I have no idea where you'd draw the line." Tears burned my eyes and I couldn't stop them even though they made me lose whatever small tenuous hold I had on my cool.

"Why would he say it if it wasn't true? I've never known Frank to be a straight-up liar."

Burke thought about this. "Maybe he imagined it was true. Extrapolated the truth out to include that. Or maybe he was just so sure you were wrong to marry me, in light of that he felt he had to add details he knew would send you over the edge."

That seemed plausible. And, though presented as noble, made me want to kill Frank for adding such a personally devastating story to what was already the worst news I'd ever received. "So never at the farm?"

"No," he said, looking into my eyes. "Never."

"Then where?" I asked, fearing it would be almost as bad. But what would be almost as bad? My bedroom in my parents' house? The roof of the shop? Nothing came to mind as nearly as bad as the farm.

He shook his head, like he knew there was no point in delving into the details, yet he had no right to refuse them to me now. "It was at that cheap motel by what used to be Price Club," he said.

Again, I had that feeling of relief, and again it was quickly replaced by another facet of grief and betrayal. This was some-thing I'd picture every time I drove that way now.

But there was no surprise there. I was asking for things that could only make me feel worse. He could have said *on Mars* and every time I looked at the night sky, I'd feel that little tremor of betrayal.

No good comes from learning the details in a situation like this one. None.

"So *Frank*," he went on, "knew I knew he'd seen me but that I thought he understood it wasn't going to happen again and there was no point in telling you. Instead, I guess he decided that the risk of losing his brother was worth it. Especially if you were the prize. So he told you."

I felt another resurgence of the old anger I'd felt toward Frank too. He'd waited and told me at the worst possible moment. Yes, maybe he'd hoped I'd come to my senses and realize the truth myself, but, good lord, what about giving me a week's notice? Even a day's!

Suddenly I just wanted to get away from these guys. Both of them. Their entire family. I didn't even want to finish Dot-tie's dress, though I had to. I wasn't going to let her down be-cause her grandsons were jerks. But I desperately wished I could.

"Go," I said to Burke.

"Are you okay?"

I looked at him with teary red eyes. Much like a stoner, come to think of it. "What do you think?"

"I don't want to leave you like this."

"Oh, please. Your time to care about doing the right thing passed a long time ago. Just *go*, Burke."

"All right, I will," he said, with a strange sense of nonsurrender. "But first I need to know that you understand what I'm saying."

"You need that, huh?"

"For your own sake, if not for mine. I need to know that you understand it meant *nothing*. *You* meant everything to me and I never got over that."

"Really? I'm sure your wife would have been surprised to hear that."

He winced. "You were gone."

"*And* forgotten."

"No. Never forgotten. I will never in my life get over losing you. I was young and stupid and immature and selfish, and instead of doing one of the millions of better things I could have done to make sure getting married was right for us, I did the cheapest trick in the book. There's no excuse, but I want you to at least know the reason."

I nodded, mute.

"I know you, Quinn. I know this tainted your whole view of everything we ever were together. But we were happy. We had fun. We loved each other. Even if you hate me now, even if you never talk to me again, don't punish that girl you were by believing she wasn't loved. She was. More than you'll ever know."

I was crying out of control now. "If that's the best I can do, then god help me."

"You can do much better than me, Quinn. You always could."

And at that, he turned and left me standing there, more heartbroken than I'd ever been in my life.

No matter how I felt about him, no matter how he felt about me, no matter what we wanted or how we tried to go about it, one question remained: Could I ever trust him again?

Chapter 22

Even with your best friend, it's not a particularly proud moment when you find yourself sobbing, in the middle of the night, about a guy who *done you wrong*. Despite the reality of the circumstances, I couldn't help but feel like a middle-schooler. Or at least like I *sounded* like a middle-schooler. I was aware that my feelings were legit.

It just became a matter of what I did with them.

I knew *that*. I just didn't know what I should—or *would*—do with them.

"He admitted he lied, he screwed around with another woman," I said to Glenn, putting voice to the horrible words I didn't even want to think about.

He put his hand on my shoulder. "I *know*," he said, with genuine sympathy. "But he also told you why. He told you it was because he was afraid of making a huge mistake—for *both* of you."

"Screw that!"

"No," Glenn said, looking at me seriously. "I'm not saying anything that you feel or felt is invalid. Honestly. So let's assume you're right, your heartache sucks and will be hard to get over, if ever."

"Fine." I raised my head to him. "So your point is . . . ?"

"What if he's just telling the truth?" He sighed and shrugged, as if, for a moment, he couldn't come up with other, or better, words. "What if he was just scared and fucking around to see how it felt and there was nothing more to it than that?"

I gaped at him. "Are you serious? *Just fucking around* like it meant nothing, and he could return to our relationship like it meant nothing? How much more does there *need* to be to it?"

He was *completely* unperturbed by my heat. He just shrugged. "Yeah. Wanted to see if the thing with you was real before he became his dad. Or his mom. Or whoever he relates to more. Whatever; before he had a potentially horrible marriage."

"Why would that be okay?" I asked, still incredulous. "On what planet would it ever be just fine for a man to cheat on a woman, or vice versa, on the eve of their wedding just to, what? Be sure he really wanted her?"

"Would you rather be with a man who lusted after other women and thought maybe there was something better out there all the time?"

I straightened my back. "Are you kidding? No, I want a man who wants only me."

"Of course, I understand that, of *course*." Glenn's voice was suddenly gentler. "I get that, I'm not on the bandwagon where all men are cheaters by nature and women have to accept it or be miserable. What I'm saying is that he was young—"

"Twenty-three."

Glenn tipped his face and raised an eyebrow, leveling a gaze on me that I totally recognized as impatient. "Oh, *twenty-three*. You know what? That's not old enough to get married no matter who you are."

"I was twenty-one!"

"And how'd that work out for you?"

I wanted to punch him. "Just fine, Dr. Phil."

"Is that why you're so upset right now?"

I considered for a moment, but the dull, throbbing pain inside of me took over. "No, I'm upset because he was unhappy—by all accounts he was unhappy time and again—and that was *still* better than being with me. At least to him."

Glenn paused. Thought. But it didn't seem like he was thinking about what I'd said so much as he was thinking about what to say to me. He thought he already knew the answers.

Maybe he did. But maybe he *didn't*.

"Quinn," he said, too patiently. "This was a *long* time ago. A *really* long time ago. And I *know* it was before your wedding and that you were devastated by the betrayal. I would have been too. *Anyone* would have been. Seriously, I'm not discounting that."

"Seems like you are," I answered, but there was a question in there too. *What are you getting at?*

"Quinn." He dropped his hands in his lap and leveled a very earnest gaze on me. "Men are different from women, biologically."

"No!"

Impatience snapped across his face. "I'm not being sarcastic or defensive. I'm completely serious. For men sex can literally mean nothing. For women, I know, it can mean close to nothing but it's always measured. Am I wrong? Have you not spent time considering every man you've slept with, even if it didn't end up being a *relationship*?"

"Obviously! I never just slept with a guy indiscriminately."

"*There* you go." Glenn slapped his hand on his knee. "That's *exactly* what I'm trying to say to you. You don't understand because you *can't* understand. Men feel emotions more acutely . . ."

"Oh, *please!*"

". . . *therefore* they avoid them much much *much* more strenuously. They will do anything to find out, or prove, that what they feel isn't real so it's not bound to them for the rest of their lives."

I tried to think of Burke in this context. Sweet, loving Burke—or so I'd thought—wanting desperately, deep inside, to get away from me and feeling that was the only way he could ever fully be himself. "I don't buy it," I said. "I'm sure some men are like that—I'm sure some women are like that too—but there's no way I can believe Burke was just *curious* enough all along to experiment with anyone and everyone else, even to my obvious detriment."

"I'm not saying he was *just curious*," Glenn returned, his voice hardening. "I'm saying on a very base level he was freaked out and did the number one, biggest dumbass thing he could. Name me one guy—one *person*—who is incapable of that."

"But—"

"I'm not *excusing* it," Glenn went on. "We all have free will, presumably we can all make the right choices over the wrong ones. But do you? Every single time, do *you*?"

"In a situation like that? Absolutely."

"What about in a situation that might matter almost as much?" he acquiesced. "Have you ever been too booked to sew an embellishment, or too tired to double-stitch a hem? Actually, I don't know enough about sewing for sewing analogies, so forget that. Have you ever put your trash bag by the door instead of taking it out to the garage because you just didn't feel like it?"

"Seriously? You think that's the same thing?"

"No, I don't think on a chart you'd put in front of a classroom it's the same thing," he said. "But I think to a panicked guy who's still young and who was raised by his grandparents because his parents' marriage sucked until his dad died and then his mother sucked so badly in general that she couldn't be bothered with him, yeah, maybe all of his values got jumbled up together."

I didn't have an immediate answer for that. It didn't mean I agreed, only that I heard him. Something in what he said made sense. Not the betrayal against me, of course, but I had to admit that I'd never really stopped to think about what Burke—and Frank— had experienced growing up. They *had* to be aware of a big sense of rejection from their mother, even if that wasn't what she'd meant to project.

It would be hard to trust women from there. Burke should have, of course. He knew me well, and from a young age, so I still wasn't willing to cut him a break, but this *was* stuff that mattered more than, say, being grounded and kept home from the prom in tenth grade.

And, really, if you were going to dive into the psychological implications, you could see how Frank had landed where he did too: he was the older one, thrust into the role of "parent" even from a young age when their mother left. Even if he wasn't aware of it, that had to be annoying for him as a kid, and for a long time; he didn't ever have the freedom to be wild and immature and irresponsible, because his brother and his mother took on that role.

For him to add on to that would have meant utter chaos. His grandparents couldn't have handled it. Even *I* remembered times in high school when Frank had handled Burke's antics himself, rather than turning them over to the adults.

Actually, the shakedown of this conversation was that I felt worse for Frank than I did for Burke.

"Am I wrong?" Glenn demanded.

I returned my thoughts to his point. That Burke had probably had some psychological jumbling going on, thanks to the way he was raised, his parents' terrible marriage, and so on.

But as much as I would have liked to let *myself* off the hook by letting *him* off the hook, I kept returning to the same point. "He lied to me. Repeatedly. In a lot of ways."

Glenn looked at me for a moment in silence, then threw up his hands. "Okay, that's who you want him to be. And who you want *you* to be. I'm not getting the feeling I'm going to be able to talk you out of that tonight, so, I don't know. Just promise me this. Promise me you'll *think* about what I said."

"Okay," I agreed. And it was easy enough, because I knew I'd be thinking of little else besides Burke for the time being, and that would include every possible way of looking at it until, finally, I would be close to madness.

. . .

Which I was sure *wasn't* what Dottie had in mind, having me come over to the farm to check her hip measurements, since she was sure she'd put on "enough to confuse my ass with a donkey" after attending parties in celebration of the golden anniversary of the Curry Comb Hunt Club.

"Three-quarters of an inch," I said, after doing the measurement for the third time. "And, honestly, that could be water weight, sluggish digestion, anything. The dress won't need alteration."

"But, by my measurements, it's a difference of three and a half inches." With that she took out her carpenter's tape measure and started pulling the metal sheeting tape out to wrangle it around her waist.

"Dottie, there's no way you can measure accurately with that." I put a hand out to stop her, and cut my finger on the tape.

"Oh, dear, are you okay?" she asked, gesticulating with the now-dangerous-seeming tool.

"Yeah, it's nothing. It just startled me." I pushed my thumb against my finger to stop the tiny drop of blood that was forming from getting bigger.

"Are you sure?" Anxiety rang in her voice, and she nervously unwrapped her third amaretto cookie. When I was a kid I could remember we'd make the wrappers into a cylinder, make a wish, and light them on fire—if the wrapper flew up toward the ceiling, your wish would come true.

I have no idea why my parents allowed this activity.

Anyway, the cookies weren't quite Oreos, but if she kept scarfing them down in her fret about her weight, she really could put on a couple of pounds. But her dress wasn't a fitted pencil skirt for a twenty-year-old body, so I had no doubt that it would be fine.

"I'm really sure," I told her. "And as for your hips, you're *fine*! This sounds like a case of prewedding nerves, nothing more."

"I *am* having some nerve trouble," she agreed. "Burke's been hinting around that he doesn't approve of this marriage."

Darn it. "Oh, I'm sure you're imagining that."

She pressed her lips together and shook her head. "I don't think so. I get a distinct feeling he's thinking I'm an old fool."

"No way," I said vehemently. If only he knew what his skepticism was doing. He wouldn't want Dottie to feel this way! I was sure of it. "If anything, I bet he's just feeling funny about life changing and you moving away and selling the farm. He is a creature of habit, you know. He likes things the way he likes them."

"That's so."

I nodded. "I'm sure that's all you're picking up on."

"Everything all right?"

I turned to see Frank striding into the room, looking seriously dapper in his business clothes, dark gray pants, and a simple crisp white button-down that was so well tailored I bet it cost more than many people made in a month.

"Dottie was just saying—"

"Everything's fine!" she trilled, and shot me a quick look. She was obviously embarrassed, and here I'd been about to announce her worries to anyone who walked in the room and asked what was going on.

Shamed, I tried to cover up. "We were just talking about how excited we are about the wedding."

Frank came to his grandmother, concern etched in his handsome face. "Gran, is something wrong?"

"No, no, I'm doing great. Just"—she gestured with the tape measure again and I saw it catch on his shirt, though she didn't—"hoping my darn foot will be good as new on time to walk down the aisle instead of hobble."

"You've been doing great," he said, shifting his arm so she wouldn't see the tear she'd just put in his shirt and freak out about that too. "I've barely seen a limp lately."

"It is better," she confessed.

I eyed the tear when he moved and noticed it was on the seam. Good. I could fix that in just a couple of minutes.

"Why don't you go up and get some rest?" Frank suggested to her. "You've been wearing yourself thin lately, and that's no good before a big event like a wedding."

"I am not a doddering old woman who needs to have an afternoon nap!" she snapped.

"You're a bride-to-be, though," I said. "And that is very high on the list of life stresses."

"All right, all right, I'll go up. But I'm going to pack for the honeymoon, not fall onto my fainting sofa."

We both laughed.

"I'm going to work from here," Frank said. "But I'll be back Friday. We'll knock out the packing in the tenant house pretty quickly. Let me know if you need anything in the meantime."

She laid a papery white hand to his cheek. "You're such a good boy."

Always had been.

As soon as she was gone, I said, "I can fix that. Take off your shirt."

"I don't want to put you to work for me." He looked at the damage, then added, "But I don't have much choice, I don't have time to go get another one."

He took off the shirt and handed it to me, leaving his tanned body looking pretty damn hot in those nice trousers and a tank top.

I went into my purse and took out my travel sewing kit.

He laughed. "Just happen to have needles and thread on you, huh?"

"Always."

"So what was really going on?" he asked.

"Nothing," I said. She'd stopped me from telling him once, it wasn't my place to tell him now. No point in adding drama to what would hopefully just be a happy day with no glitches. "We really were talking about the wedding." True.

He didn't believe me, though. He made a noise of uncertainty and sat down in the old wing chair a few feet from me.

It just happened to place him in exactly the perfect position for me to take in his entire form even in my peripheral vision while I sewed.

"So what will you do after the house is packed up and the wedding's over?" I asked.

"Breathe a huge sigh of relief, drink a scotch, and welcome normality back."

I nodded, watching my stiches carefully so there would be nothing askew. "I guess this has been kind of a pain, having to come do so much work here every time you have a free second."

"It's not the work," he said. "It really is sad. More so than I thought it would be."

"Yeah?" I looked up and met his eyes.

He looked embarrassed. "I'm not supposed to be the emotional one."

I smiled. "Wouldn't do to have anyone know you're human, huh?"

He kept his gaze fastened on mine and shook his head.

"I'll never tell."

A fraction of a moment passed. "You're the only one who could," he said softly.

"Could . . . ?"

"Tell. That I ever had any emotion at all."

It was true, the thing everyone said about Frank Morrison was that he was steely, unflappable. I knew better. *No one* is completely unflappable.

But maybe especially not Frank. He had a bigger heart than anyone, under there.

That was probably why he kept it so well hidden.

"I never thanked you for that," he said. "I mean for being someone I could trust like that when the rest of the world expected me to be something else."

I slowed my stitching. "Did I ever thank you for risking your family relations and putting your life on hold to drive me thousands of weepy miles just to try and make me feel better?"

"Actually, you did. Profusely. Repeatedly. To the point where I had to tell you to shut up a few times, as I recall."

"That's an exaggeration."

"Hardly. You didn't need to thank me at all, Quinn. It shook my world up a little too. In a good way."

I knotted the stitch and handed the shirt back to him, though I found myself curiously reluctant to. There was something so nice, so companionable about having this quiet moment with him in that old room, the only punctuation being the ticking clock.

But the tear was mended.

And the moment was over.

"Thanks," he said, then gave a quick laugh. "For everything. That and"—he gestured with his shirt—"this." He put it on and buttoned himself into perfect form again.

"No problem," I said. "And . . . no problem."

We looked at each other for a moment, and warmth tingled down my core.

Then, weirdly, neither of us said another word. He just left and I just watched him go.

Which was the note that led me, the next morning, to Day Drunk Day. The ubiquitous red envelope was fastened to the top of one of two red velvet bottle bags, and the instructions read:

Half and half. Have one glass immediately and one more within the hour. Have at least two per hour until five.
Refills are already in the fridge in your back storeroom.
Make sure you eat. That's there too. XOXO.

I pulled the velvet off the first bottle.

Champagne.

The second bottle was orange juice.

He wanted me to drink mimosas all day long.

Apart from a slowly sipped glass or two of wine when we were having cheese nights, I really rarely drank, and certainly never drank like this. Which, of course, Glenn knew. Ergo, this was definitely not like me to do.

I wasn't sure I'd follow it to the letter, but, given the night I'd had with Glenn, and the sleepless hours that had followed, I have to admit, a little breakfast cocktail didn't seem like that bad an idea.

"Good morning!" Becca's voice rang a few minutes later as she came in the door. I had just popped the cork and was pouring the bubbly into a chilled crystal flute Glenn had thoughtfully provided in the fridge, along with another bottle of champagne and an assortment of fruit and cheese, which I now had sitting on the counter.

"Morning," I said. "Care for a cocktail?"

"No?" She came over to me curiously. "But thank you. What are we celebrating?"

"I'm not sure. Freedom?" I was generous with the champagne. Three-quarters of a glass of champagne to one-quarter of a glass of orange juice. I took a sip. It was delicious. Champagne was always delicious. Orange juice was too, come to think of it, though I tended to avoid it since I'd gotten older and more diet-conscious. "Anyway I'm just shaking things up today, doing things a little differently."

"Oh, that makes sense." She nodded with more understanding than I was expecting. "You could probably use that."

"What do you mean?" Did *everyone* know I was a mess? Should

I just wear my high school cheerleader uniform every day and get it over with?

Becca looked chagrined. "I didn't mean anything bad," she hastened to say. "Only that, you know, you come in here every day and work such long hours, day after day." She looked at me with genuine concern, which was more crushing than if she'd rolled her eyes at me and called me fat. "You're young, you should be *living*."

I drank. Then said, "You're young too. Why am I the only one without a life?" The words could have sounded petulant or defensive, but I thought she heard them for what they were, a genuine question as to where I was going wrong.

"For one thing," she said, "I'm about fifteen years older than you, as you well know. And for another, I have kids. Obligations that cannot be shifted. If you got a wild hair and decided to go to Jamaica, you could easily get me to cover for you here. Then off you go. But when you have people depending on you for sustenance day after day, hour after hour, you can't even go to the grocery store without making sure you know where everyone is, what they're doing, and where they'll be when you get back. I'm not complaining, I love it, but those are the ties that bind. I'm not sure what's binding someone as young and beautiful as you to this life without ever taking a little break."

"I take breaks." I refilled the glass quickly. Seven-eighths champagne, one-eighth orange juice. It was already going to my head. "I was breaking just last night."

"Okay." Becca was never one to argue or impose her point of view on anyone too strongly. She'd probably only said as much as she did because she was feeling trapped in some way that she wasn't saying. Maybe a fight with her husband, or the still-chill nights of late spring were getting to her and she wanted to be in the tropics. "I'm a bit queasy this morning, but it still seems like fun to start the day with mimosas for no reason, so enjoy yourself!"

"Thanks." I drained the glass and felt pleasantly dizzy. "Want one?"

She looked doubtful. "I'd better not."

Fine. All the more for me. "You here all day?" I confirmed. She was here all day every Thursday, but I was just hoping there wasn't some kid thing going on . . . at least that she knew about now.

"All day," she said, and went into the back room, as usual, to look at the notes and see what needed stitching, packing, shipping, etc.

She was right. In theory, I could have gone across the world for two weeks and left the shop in her capable hands, and it would have been none the worse for it when I returned.

Apparently, in fact, my absence had little effect on anyone or anything. Witness Burke. He'd walked out of our wedding and right into another one. It hadn't worked out, granted, but he'd done it. Married some jerk with a boy's name and then divorced her. If it hadn't been her he divorced, would it have been me? Was he just bad at being married? What was the truth behind that anyway? Who'd divorced whom?

I took out a pad and jotted, *Ask who did who*, on it to remind me later. Then added, *whom?*

By noon, I was through the first bottle of champagne and was trying to pace myself by drinking flutefuls of water, alternating with the already-opened second bottle.

My pad, however, had gotten quite an extensive list:
Ask who did whom was joined by:

Who was btter in bed me or slut girl, been long time cn tell me now, right???

Get tambour lace for Trander drss

Did he KISS her?!

Hw old was wife?

Does he stll have ring from that wdding? Ugh!!

Steak/Cheese sub lttc, tom, mayo, onions with pepprs on side and swiss chese [Suddenly Puccio's Deli seemed like a good idea.]

Why is Glenn so high n mighty? Hes not with anyone! Ask! This could be bad idea to trst his plan!

703-555-6266 [number for the local beer and wine, which delivers]

Frank—remember That Thing he does. So hot.

Needless to say, it was a long morning. Probably more so for Becca than for me.

And for poor Linda Hyatt, who was in for her last fitting.

Linda had dated her fiancé for *years* before he'd finally proposed, patiently waiting through his dithering about commitment. When she'd come in to order her dress, it was after waiting a couple of *months* after his proposal, just to make sure he didn't change his mind "again" and cancel on her. Apparently that had happened more than once, always with excuses that made noise about the seriousness of the commitment and how he didn't want to hurt her and blah blah blah. So finally he'd gone an entire eight weeks or so without backing out and she had determined that to be enough time to finally believe him.

She was so excited that I had never had the heart to say anything about how much better she deserved than that. It wasn't my place anyway; I was hired to do my job, not be her counselor. A lot of ill-fated brides-to-be came into the shop, and it was my job to give them a beautiful dress—sometimes one I hoped they'd save and use for a *future* wedding, but I never knew most of the outcomes because that wasn't really any of my business.

Which meant that my current condition and the fact that Linda was tearfully explaining evidence of her fiancé's recent emotional detachment combined to make the perfect storm of sorts.

". . . He's just not always answering my texts," she said, looking to Becca with a tiny glimmer of what I recognized as tenuous hope in her eyes.

"He's probably busy getting ready for the wedding too," Becca soothed. "It's only a week and a half away."

"Yes . . ." Linda looked doubtful. "But . . . and I don't want to make him sound like a bad guy . . . but he's also not returning my calls. He says things like, 'It didn't sound like you needed an answer' or whatever, but, seriously, if I call at all, that means I want to talk to him, isn't that clear?"

From my vantage point, leaning on the door frame to the storeroom, I definitely saw the irritation cross Becca's face.

But her voice was measured and calm. "You'd think so and I'd think so, but maybe there's a good reason for him to seem so . . . short . . . with you. It might be a really good idea to talk to him so that you can go forward on your special day without a care in the world."

"Do you *really* think there could be a good reason for this?" Linda asked, the uncertainty ringing clear in her voice.

"*Absolutely*. You never know what's going on with other people, even the ones you're closest to, unless you ask."

I felt my grip tighten on the champagne flute I was holding. "That's for sure," I heard my own voice chirp. Somewhere along the way, my brain decided to take a break. "For example, he could be cheating on you, and if you don't *specifically ask him* he might not think it's something you'd, you know, *want to know.*"

Chapter 23

B oth sets of eyes turned to me, both alarmed, both for different reasons.

"You think he's *cheating*?" Linda asked, and I actually
saw the blood draining from her face. "Have you *heard* something?"

"Oh, she's *kidding*," Becca soothed, shooting me a look that
told me to shut the fuck up.

I took a couple of steps forward and set my glass down on the
counter. "No, I'm not. It happened to me. It's happened to millions
of women. Just watch daytime television. You think you're in love,
you think you can trust him, you think your life is going to be wonderful, and then—*boom!*—you find out you've been living a lie."

"Am I living a lie?" Linda asked Becca.

"No!" Becca looked back at me, and I clearly remember the
sharp question in her eyes. "Quinn's not . . . herself right now."

I gave a short laugh. "No kidding. I haven't been myself for years. *He* took that away from me." I pointed a finger at Linda. "I'm just saying be careful, don't let that happen to you."

"Weren't you sorting invoices?" Becca asked in a hard voice. "For the IRS? You ought to go back and finish that."

I looked at my empty glass. "Yes, I'll go back to my *sorting*." I picked it up. "But I'm just saying, Linda, be careful. Ask every question you can think of and listen to your gut." I gestured at her with my glass. "There's nothing worse than finding out when it's too late." I went back into the storeroom, possibly with a misstep or two along the way, and closed the door most of the way.

As I repoured my glass, I am ashamed to say I thought I heard some sniffling and the distinct sound of tissues being pulled out of the box, one after the other, among the soothing murmurs of Becca's voice.

Was it really so wrong to try to help another woman avoid the heartache I had suffered?

Maybe that was my true calling in life. Maybe I had gone through what I went through in order to *help others*.

That would kind of help make sense of it for me. I had been *chosen* for a purpose greater than doing Burke for the rest of my life!

I paused, thinking of how great it would be to do Burke for the rest of my life, and then sighed at the memory of his kiss.

But—I pulled myself back onto my high horse—he had cheated. It was indefensible. That was the bottom line. And the top line, and every line in between.

I had to find a way to get my message out to women.

Write blog!!!! I added to my to-do list. Then added—and later scratched through with *extra* vehemence—*Add to shops website!!!! Brilliant!!! Like insrance comp. that promises to shw u if u shld go w/ someone else!!!!*

As near as I can guess, that was around noon.

I'm guessing that because Deliah Carter's appointment was in the afternoon and I do remember her coming in. Deliah was big and proud. As in, very big, and very proud. And normally I'd have to hand it to her for that, because she didn't have the same vain insecurities many women have about body image and so on. She wore a size that, more often than not, must be specially ordered, and when she came into my shop that was the case.

And I'm not saying she wore a fourteen and I only sold up to a ten, because that bullshit drove me crazy. Fourteen is *not* "XXL," it's "average American woman," and I carried well into plus sizes.

But Deliah was a bit beyond that and when she first came in to order a dress I made the mistake of assuming she wanted to create a slimmer illusion. I'm not being sarcastic, by the way, it was definitely a wrongheaded assumption and I learned from it.

"Are you saying I should be ashamed of my curves?" she demanded, in a deep Mississippi accent.

For me, *curves* called to mind Nigella Lawson, who is one of the most gorgeous women on earth.

Deliah was no Nigella Lawson.

Still, I took her point. "Tell me what you want and we'll make it happen."

The smug look on her face was unmistakable, and utterly without humility. She liked those words. *Make it happen.* Deliah was proof that if you expected something of someone, they would rise to the occasion no matter how unlikely the odds.

So we'd worked together on her dress and it was coming together nicely. I had six months before her wedding—to a surprisingly hot guy, by the way, just FYI—so there was no hurry.

The problem was that she came in on Day Drunk Day to discuss the fact that she thought her bridesmaid dresses were too hot.

Well, she called them "slutty," but they weren't slutty. They weren't even particularly hot. I wasn't really sure what her problem with them was, all I was sure of was that it was the wrong time for me to discuss it.

"Lesley's dress, for instance," Deliah drawled to me. "It's, like, so tight around the waist that she can't hardly breathe."

This is probably a good place to mention that Becca was out on a reluctant and very late lunch break.

"Does Lesley have a problem with it?" I asked, trying very consciously to arrange my expression into that of serious concern.

Deliah narrowed her dark eyes at me and my impertinence. "*I* have a problem with it."

"What's the problem?"

"It looks too good on her."

I was so surprised by this bluntness that I laughed.

That pissed her off. "Um, *excuse me*, but do you think that's funny?" she demanded.

"Yes!" Now I couldn't stop laughing. "Of *course* that's funny! No one ever admits that!"

A normal person would have been disarmed by that and seen

the honest humor in it. But then again, a normal person wouldn't have complained out loud about the bridesmaid looking hot. She would have just chosen a hideous design and ghastly color in the first place, like most of them do.

Not Deliah.

"I don't think it's funny," she said, completely straight-faced. "I think you're being a jackass."

That made me laugh even harder. *Jackass!* It was perfect, or seemed so at the time. Not *bitch*, that was so easy. No threats to take her business elsewhere, this woman had the unexpected insult down to an art!

"I'm sorry," I said, and it sounded even more insincere than it was. But how could it not? "I'm just . . . it's a day."

"Are you *drunk*?"

I could have denied it, but what was the point? *"Completely!"* I waited for her condemnation. A haughty turn on her heels and a brisk lumbering out the door.

Instead, she was still for a moment, then held up her hand. "High five, girlfriend, what are we drinking?"

I went to high-five her and only caught half her hand, thanks to my double vision. "Champagne!"

"Bring it on!"

Thirty minutes later, we'd agreed that instead of altering her bridesmaids' dresses to make them all look like buffoons during the wedding, she could just have the pictures Photoshopped however she wished by the wedding photographer later. She needed, I pointed out in a moment of surprising lucidity, for her entire bridal party to look as good as possible because she didn't want all of her guests, for whom she was paying a *huge* price per head, to think she had no taste.

Therefore, I was neatly off the hook and she was more pleased with me than ever.

And having a woman as forceful as Deliah recommending you to her friends and acquaintances was like having Tony Soprano recommending a particular brand of quick-drying concrete—it was worth its weight in gold.

So up to then I had a mixed performance. Kind of okay, kind of horrible. Maybe I came out even, though, to be honest, I guess I still ended up on the lower end of that scale.

Still, my talk with Deliah had been so liberating that it was worth it. Or it felt like it was worth it at the time.

In fact, it felt *so* worth it that I poured myself a toast.

The subsequent events are a bit of a blur to me, I will admit.

I vaguely recall opening the door and shouting into the street, and to a few passersby, "I *hate* Burke Morrison!"

Then, not long after, "Burke Morrison is a fucking liar and cheater! Also, *never* get married!" which I'm sure was great for business.

At least for Taney's business across the street.

The showroom experienced a bit of a makeover, with the bride mannequin in a compromising position with the groom manne-quin in the corner (but, hey, it could have been the clichéd brides-maid mannequin, so I want credit for at least keeping it wholesome!), and I kind of remember thinking it was hilarious to turn the chairs upside down to see if anyone would notice.

As if anyone who would be in the store that day, or week, or month, would be capable of *not noticing* the chairs were upside down. Except me, of course. Because, tired from the effort of turning the chairs upside down, I actually tried to sit down. True story.

Sometimes we do, indeed, get what we deserve.

That was about the time when Becca returned and, rather forcefully I thought, put me in the storeroom with nothing but a Brita carafe full of water and a paper cup. She didn't even let me have my phone charger and I was down to one feeble bar.

I called Glenn. "This was a great idea!"

"What? I can't hear you, you're breaking up."

I moved two inches to the left. "Can you hear me now?"

"Yeah, that's better. What did you say?"

"I said this drinking thing was a *great* idea!" Of course, the words probably didn't sound as clear to him as they look in writing, but that was the gist of what I was telling him. I can't remember for sure, but it's not impossible that Fabio was mentioned somewhere in there as well, however. "Thank you *so* much!"

"How much did you drink?" he asked sharply. Suddenly he sounded like Felix Unger. And I wasn't even Oscar Madison, I was the bum who slept on the street outside their building but was never acknowledged on the show.

"I had company," I explained defensively.

"Oh. Okay. So this was a bad idea."

I sat down heavily on what looked like it would be a big soft pile of fabric but which crushed to nothing beneath my weight and sent the air from my lungs in an unattractive—and apparently alarming—rush.

"Quinn?" Glenn asked quickly. "Are you okay? Are you choking? Bang the phone if you're choking."

I started to laugh again, which probably sounded like phone-banging, so I forced out the words, "I'm . . . okay. . . ."

"Stop drinking," he said, like he was telling a dog to *stay*. "Do you understand me?"

"Obviously."

"What?"

That was the exact point at which I realized I'd had too much, but there was still a lot more, unprocessed, swishing around in my stomach. I made an effort to be clear. "*Obviously*."

I heard him groan. "This was a mistake."

"Obviously."

"Stay put, I'm bringing food over."

I smiled. "Obviously."

"Oh, my god, you are so incapable of working right now."

"Obviously!" By now I was laughing so hard it was silent, though he heard the sounds of my desperately hysterical gasps.

"Quinn," he said, so seriously it almost made me wet my pants. "Trust me on this. Everything you think is hilarious right now will not seem funny to you *at all* tomorrow or *for the rest of your life*. Please, please, please, just sit tight and let me bring some food over and try and rectify this hideous mistake I've made."

"Obvi—"

"No! No more. If you fuck up your business or personal life because of this, I will feel guilty for the rest of my life. Abort this mission! Stop now! The assignment is over, you passed with flying colors, give it a rest, stay where you are."

In short, *Anything to shut you the fuck up.*

"Okay," I said simply, swallowing a hiccup with some water.

"So you understand me," he clarified, as if speaking to an alien whom he couldn't be sure was truly comprehending the meaning of his strange earth language. "You know you have to sit *very still* in the storeroom and wait for me. You know there's *nothing to worry about* because Becca's out front taking care of business and you just have to rest and, sort of, sleep this off so you can be yourself again. You understand what I'm saying, right? How important it is for you to stay in the back?"

I hesitated, then said, "Obviously."

Three hours later he was still there and my buzz was not. It had been replaced by a horrendous headache and more shame than I could have imagined I could feel, even on the heels of the week I'd just experienced. So I had that to say for his big breakout plan: It certainly did make room for me to change.

I guess the problem was, he hadn't bet on me to change in any sort of *dramatic* ways.

Not that it was really dramatic, of course. I realized that by the thundering light of day the next morning. It had only been a temporary venting of emotion. Maybe healthy. Arguably healthy. But also maybe super-bad for business. That had yet to be seen.

Becca assured me, with eyes that kept sliding left and right instead of looking directly at me, that it hadn't been *that bad.* That she thought that, apart from a few people who'd been directly in the line of my fire, word hadn't gotten out to too many people that I was a psycho, incapable of running my own business, much less helping others create magical moments for the most special day of their lives.

And when it came down to it, maybe the fact of venting what had to be some long-pent-up feelings, ugly as they were, was worth the minimal risk of yelling crazy stuff into the street on a weekday when no one was really around and my reputation probably wouldn't suffer too much. Honestly, 70 percent of the people who might have been on the sidewalk on any given weekday would have been people who knew my history and understood exactly what I was saying about Burke (right or wrong); another 20 percent would have been commuters stopping through for coffee on their way to or from somewhere else; and the other 10 percent was divided among my customers and people who would never hear or care a damn about what I had to say about *anything*.

Not that I wanted to conduct business that way. I'm not saying it was a good idea, or desirable. It was definitely not a good PR trick. I'm just saying I did it, it was done, and I really hoped that, in the process of getting better emotionally on a personal level, I hadn't screwed myself over completely for the rest of my life.

So. With all that said, I really wish that was my primary concern. But the sad truth is that, during the episode and afterward, the main thing in my mind was Burke. Always Burke.

How did he feel?

What did he want?

Did he think about me as much as I thought about him?

Questions so old and repetitive that they almost bored me to death . . . yet they held a certain irresistible allure. Back when we were a couple, if I was feeling down or *meh* and I began to think of Burke and what it was like to be with him, every bit of my physiology turned on and I was right there, alive and present.

And that was what I'd been searching for ever since.

Now, if that's a cosmic connection of some sort, or body chemistry, or even just a willingness to be open to people, I don't know. All I know is that I was *not* interested in people, by and large, and there was definitely chemistry between Burke and myself. But that's not generally thought of as one of the more lasting things. So it had to be something more.

It had to be.

This was confirmed when Glenn called me later that night.

"I think you need to talk to Burke again," Glenn said.

"*What?*" I was still feeling woozy. "No, thanks!"

"You told Linda her fiancé was cheating on her and Deliah her bridesmaids were prettier than her but that it would make her look better than the opposite." He took a breath but only, I knew, so I could take a moment to reflect on what he'd said.

"I—" But he interrupted me right away, because it turned out he wasn't done. And I was glad, because I didn't have that much to say.

"No. There is no response. There is nothing you can say that's going to make me think, oh, you're right, you should be so concerned with Burke Morrison that you're yelling what a jerk he is out the door of your shop. There's just nothing."

"You heard about that?"

"I didn't hear *about* it, I heard *it*. *Everyone* must have heard it." There was clearly a smile in his voice. "It was drunken idiocy at its best. I thought you'd reflect on your past and your present and make resolutions about a strong new future. I had no idea you'd curl up like a potato bug into your own self-pity."

"Really? You didn't? No idea? Have you heard nothing I've said for the past few weeks?"

"You're right," he conceded. "All the clues were there. Your mental health has been clearly wobbly for some time now. So now we have to undo this huge clusterfuck of a mistake we've made."

I did appreciate him including himself in the clusterfuck, even though I knew a part of him was just vain enough to be miffed that his plan wasn't going as swimmingly as he'd thought it would. It has to be said, some of his crazy day plans had turned out pretty well, if only because they really had been so unlike me.

So the guy wasn't dumb. And he probably had better ideas than I did at this point about how to correct this catastrophe.

"So what do you want me to do?" I asked, thinking there was no way I could hit the road; I was still drunk, though less so. But having second thoughts and a headache didn't mean a person was sober.

"Talk to Burke," he said again. "Hammer it out and get *over* him once and for all. I've got to go, but I swear, Quinn, if I hear one more profanity-laced shriek from your direction . . ."

"You're miles away from me right now."

"Exactly. *That's* how loud you were."

I laughed. "Okay, point taken. I'll let you know what happens."

We hung up, and as soon as the connection was gone, so too was my conviction that he was right. Actually, maybe it wasn't even my conviction that was gone. I definitely wanted to feel better about things than I did right now. It was just that, while a moment ago I'd felt like, *Yes, I will call him and we will hash this out,* now I was all, *But what if he doesn't want to talk to me again because I've been such an immature idiot?*

He would certainly be within his rights to not want to talk to me again, particularly if he'd heard about my antics the day before.

But the bottom line was still the bottom line, and that was that I needed to clear things up with him. Actually—and, hey, maybe the fact that I came to this revelation proved that Glenn's plan had been sound on some level—what I really needed was to come to peace with the past. Not keep being pissed off about it, or even *more* fired up because I'd found out it was true. I just couldn't stand on that soapbox for long before it started to splinter under my own weight.

I'd done plenty of objectionable things myself. Maybe not *to Burke* but certainly *since* Burke. I'd done things I wouldn't want my mother to know about. And she was the one who always taught me to live in a way that left nothing deliberately hidden—to never say anything to anyone, and especially to never write anything to anyone (like in an e-mail or on Facebook) that I wouldn't want my grandmother or next-door neighbors to see. Because these days anyone and everyone could end up with access to communication you thought was private.

Admittedly, that lesson had come up with my mother when I'd written something about a teacher to Lincoln Stennet in third grade and he was a whiny little suck-up who showed it to the teacher and created this big situation where my parents had to come in for a conference and I had to pay penance by sitting in the Seat of Shame in the corner, five yards from the closest desk, for the rest of the month.

And all I'd written was that her breath smelled like old people, and it *did*. It was *horrible* to stand in front of her, especially if you'd done something wrong enough to warrant a lecture or you needed a long explanation for a math formula. That didn't get me a pass, of course, I was still in trouble. But the lesson was well worth the punishment because not only did I learn you couldn't trust that weasel Lincoln Stennet, obviously, but also that once you put something out there you're never entirely safe from it.

Lincoln went on to major in corrections, by the way, and is now the warden at the Lorton prison in Northern Virginia, so I guess his character was set up from the beginning.

The longer I sat there, thinking about my nefarious elementary school past and all the other things that had nothing to do with solving my problems in the present, the more uncomfortable I became. Because I knew what I needed to do, and ignoring it—*denying* it—wasn't going to make it go away. It was going to just feed the discomfort and make it worse.

I knew what I had to do.

So, not without a *lot* of apprehension, I took out my phone and dialed.

It rang so many times I thought he wasn't going to answer, and a part of me was relieved. *I tried*, it said. *This must be a sign*.

But then he did answer, right when I was sure it wasn't going to happen.

And that voice—wow, how that voice could still get to me. I

can't even describe it. "Deep" sounds so *Jim Nabors*, and it wasn't operatic like that at all. Just very masculine, with the slightest rasp of boyishness on the edge.

"Hi," I said uncertainly. God knows if he'd heard anything about my behavior.

Bad idea, I thought suddenly, painfully aware of my headache. *This was a stupid idea.*

"Hi," he said back, in an equally questioning tone.

Which could have meant anything or nothing.

Including that he didn't know who the hell I was.

"It's Quinn," I clarified.

"I know."

"Oh. Okay. Well. I'm sorry to bother you so late." I looked at my clock. It was 7:48. Those weren't streetlights outside, it was twilight. "But . . ." I was suddenly at a loss for words. But *what*? I had no right to ask him for anything. "I was wondering if maybe you could come over to the shop? And talk?"

There was a long silence.

So long I thought he'd hung up.

Then he said, "I don't think that's a good idea."

Only then did I realize I'd been holding my breath waiting for his answer. "Oh. O-okay."

He exhaled. "I don't mean to be hurtful, I just think we've said everything we can say. If we push that now, someone's just liable to get hurt."

Someone was already hurt, and he knew it. That was what this was all about. He just didn't want the liability for it anymore.

And I didn't blame him.

"It's probably best just to leave well enough alone," I said, as if I agreed.

"Right."

"So . . . I'll see you at the wedding, then." *This time I'll see you at the wedding.*

This time, since it's not ours.

"It's just a week or so away," I added, sensing, in the silence, that he was thinking of something else as well.

"Oh. Yes, I guess I will see you there."

"Assuming you don't stop it, since that's what you guys like to do, stop weddings, break dreams," I said, intending it as a joke but hearing its idiocy in real time, right along with Burke. God, what was *wrong* with me? Could I just push every bruise? Touch every nerve? Make sure no wound went unsalted? "I mean, god, I didn't mean—"

"I know what you meant," he said.

"Honestly, I was kidding, I just . . . wasn't thinking."

All it took was for Burke to do something slightly unpredictable— saying no when I really hoped for a yes—and I was completely rattled.

"Don't worry about it," he said. "I understand."

"I hope so. I really didn't mean to be insulting."

"I'll see you at Dottie's wedding, Quinn," he said pointedly. *And only then.*

I nodded, even though we were on the phone and he obviously couldn't see me. "See you then."

Chapter 24

I spent the next week trying to get used to my new reality, which was that my old reality was still exactly the same but now it was clouded by the knowledge that it was the same because *I* had doggedly remained the same, or at least kept my life so routine as to not really be able to distinguish one week from another in memory. In some cases, even the years were the same—I couldn't remember whether an event had occurred five years ago or seven, because the surrounding scenery in my mind was unchanged.

I can't say that Glenn's "days" didn't help. Certainly they had brought this truth into sharp focus for me. Of course, some days were better than others. Bikram yoga class had been interesting, and it was conveniently timed to allow me to sweat off five pounds of champagne from Day Drunk Day. Also, it effectively kept me in the back room finishing Dottie's dress the next day, nursing a hangover, while Becca dealt with the customers and just tried not to laugh at me every time I had to communicate with her.

No Caffeine Day was exhausting. Ask a Stranger for Directions but Pretend You Think You're in North Carolina Day was, I thought, covered by that stupid Improv Acting Class Day. Amish Day, when I used no modern conveniences except those that I absolutely couldn't avoid, made me laugh, and allowed me to get a lot of needlework done.

And I straight up refused to do Kiss a Stranger on the Cheek Day, and Glenn reluctantly agreed, persuaded by my argument that it was the kind of thing that could get a person arrested.

Two days before Dottie's wedding, a slight young woman with glossy dark hair, an exotic almond shape to her eyes, and deeply tanned skin came in and asked if I used Bell and Gardener threads.

"Yes . . . ," I said slowly, surprised. No one had ever come in here demanding a particular thread manufacturer for a dress.

She looked relieved. "Do you have any Ivory number four that I can borrow?"

This made no sense. "I'm sorry, I don't understand."

"I'm sorry, I work across the street"—she flung her arm toward the door—"and I'm making a dress that has to be ready in an hour and I ran out of thread because it got tangled in the bobbin." She shrugged helplessly.

Taney.

"Are you Taney?" I asked, trying not to look as if I were asking a movie star for her real identity.

She looked surprised that I knew her name. "Yes."

"I've heard a lot about you," I said, perhaps a little too bold. "You like making dresses?"

"Oh, yes." Her face lit up, completely innocent. "That is my passion." There was a long hesitation before she added, "But . . ."

"You know that's what we do here, right?"

She nodded. "That's why I thought you might have the thread." She looked around the shop with a smile. "I thought surely a place as fine and beautiful as this uses the best products."

That threw me off. "Thank you," I said uncertainly, and suddenly I didn't know whether to give her the thread or not. I didn't want to help her employer, but she was obviously the one who would take it on the chin if she "failed" to deliver on time. "I'll get the thread," I decided. It wasn't like I didn't have enough. I used it all the time.

I went in the back and got it, then handed it to her, holding her gaze for a moment as she took it. "Taney, do you enjoy working there?" I nodded toward her shop.

She looked down. "Yes, of course." But I knew she didn't mean it. "They have been very good to me."

What could I say? Nothing. Just the small, meaningless pleasantry of, "Good luck finishing the dress on time."

Which took me to Tell Someone Three Truths You've Never Told Before and One Lie Day.

The magnitude of both the truths and the lie hadn't been outlined, so I thought this would be easy, but I also recognized it as a potentially valuable breakthrough point. And even though all day I pretended to myself that I was trying to think of who I would choose to be the recipient of these revelations, I knew what I was going to do. Or at least what I was going to *try* to do.

Turned out I didn't even need to call him; he came to me, showing up magically and unexpectedly, the Brigadoon of men.

It was half an hour past closing time, and I almost didn't notice him out in the dark and did a double take that must have looked sitcom-like from the outside, with me inside under the lights.

He was leaning against his car out front, facing the shop. I opened the door and stood in the doorway, looking at him. "What are you doing, Frank?"

"Stalking."

"Any reason?"

He shrugged. "Came to make sure you're all right, since the talk of the town is you've popped your clutch. Apparently concern about that is another formula for an otherwise normal person to turn into a creeper."

I had to smile. "It can happen." Truth. Prior to Glenn's insane plan, I'd never *been* one before, and I didn't know if Frank knew about that, but I decided it was best not to acknowledge it. Just in case.

"I know it."

"Want to come in?"

"No."

I sighed. "Are you going to come in anyway?"

He heaved himself off the car and came toward me. "Can't see as I have much of a choice."

"No one's forcing you."

"Trust me, I've got no choice."

I locked the door behind him and asked, "Can I offer you anything? There's about half an ounce of orange juice and a pretty old leftover salad from Barker's Grill in the fridge." Truth. Lame, but true. And I wouldn't normally tell anyone I had gross old food in the fridge because I kept forgetting to take it out on trash night and I couldn't let it sit around in a trash bag inside before then.

"Tempting, but no, thanks."

I turned down the lights, but the alarm system had a default that always kept the place dimly lit so that no one would feel free to break in and feel his way around in the dark, taking stuff until the police arrived. Which, in our town, wasn't always all that fast. In some ways, Mayberry was alive and well.

"Let's go in the back anyway," I suggested.

He followed me back and I closed the door behind us.

It was no bedroom back there, with bolts and bolts of fabrics and supplies and unopened stock boxes, but because we also worked in the back, there was a comfortable sitting area with a long plush sofa, a couple of easy chairs, and a TV.

But we didn't get that far before I turned to him and said, "I'm sorry I've always let you down."

He laughed, clearly surprised. "What are you talking about?"

"You were always nice to me and I always let you comfort me and fix me and I never gave anything worthwhile back to you. I don't know why you're nice to me at all."

"Because I love you, Quinn."

This time I was the one who was surprised. "*What?*"

"You heard me. I'm not waxing rhapsodic about it, not hitting my knees and begging you to hand me a crumb. I don't want crumbs. I'd rather starve."

"I'm not offering crumbs, but still, I don't blame you."

He quirked a smile. "Good."

There were no words beyond that. Because there was nothing else to say. And there was *definitely* nothing else to do.

So how it happened that one minute we were making noise about all the *nothing* we had between us and the next his mouth was on mine and I was clutching his shoulders and pulling him closer, I don't know.

The urgency was immediate.

Ten minutes ago, I'd been the person I'd grown very familiar with being; practical, carrying on, a little limp maybe, but without dramatic ups and down. Now the man whose betrayal had been creeping around the back of my mind was nowhere, and here was Frank. His tongue was in my mouth, and I was parting my lips to bring him deeper but feeling like he could never get deep enough. I could not get close enough, I needed to *be* him in order to feel close enough. This wasn't the act of friends, not old friends, not new friends, not any sort of generic comrades. To anyone else in the world, we would have looked like lovers at an eagerly anticipated romantic reunion.

The soldier back from a long hardship deployment, maybe.

And that's what it felt like. It had been a decade since our two hot nights, and clearly neither of us had forgotten, and that amped up the urgency tenfold.

For all its wild inappropriateness—and there was no question that this kiss was wildly inappropriate, given everything between us that was too messy to overcome—it felt exactly *right*.

Every time our lips touched, I remembered his taste, and a single kiss brought back those nights I thought I'd all but forgotten. It was like having a favorite ice cream again or something. A flavor nearly forgotten but immediately remembered and loved.

The same was true of the smell of his skin. I am cursed with an unusually good sense of smell; if I weren't doing what I was doing for a living, I probably could have been a "nose" for one of the finest perfumers in Paris, and I could smell the soap on his skin, but also the *him* underneath the soap, and it wrapped me in a sense of peace and well-being. It was only the familiarity, I tried to reason; though our time together had been brief, he reminded me of running away from pain and feeling safe in the arms of a strong man. But it was more than that. I could feel it.

So much more that it scared me. Because there was no *halfway* with *this* man. No push-and-pull, no games. However nice he'd once been—and however nice he really still was—Frank Morrison was no boy, and he was not playing games.

So I was on a cliff.

"Stop," I said feebly against his mouth.

He slid his hands around my rib cage. "I don't want to."

"I do." I kissed him again.

"Do you really want me to?"

"You were never able to read me."

"Bullshit. I know you better than you know yourself. You just never allowed yourself to see that, when you were wrapped up in that other situation."

That other situation.

Burke.

How could it be that Burke suddenly had no pull on me? That thinking his name or picturing his face didn't matter in the heat of this moment?

In a way, that was a relief.

For a long moment, we just kissed some more. I couldn't stop. It was crazy. I loved it and hated myself for loving it and giving in to it. Even though it was ridiculous for a grown woman to have so little self-control as to be pining in different ways for two different men.

Right now, though?

There was only one man.

He ran his hands up under my shirt and unhooked my bra in a single movement. When he cupped my breasts with his heat, I was gone. There was *no* stopping this, and I knew exactly where it was going. Obviously even an idiot from another planet could have seen where this was going, and I was going with it.

He pulled my shirt off over my head, and I let my bra drop to the floor.

He bent down and kissed my shoulder, my collarbone, then took my nipple in his mouth and sucked, first one side, then the other. Normally this doesn't do much for me, and I don't know what Frank does right that everyone else did wrong, but it was like throwing gasoline on a fire.

Meanwhile, he unbuttoned my jeans and shoved them down over my hips and down my thighs until they heaped at my feet on the floor and I stepped out of them.

There was something incredibly hot about standing before him, all but naked, completely vulnerable, while he was dressed and working my body with his hands and mouth like I was just there for him to devour.

He moved me over to the sofa and I fell back against it, completely unresisting when he knelt in front of me and pulled my plain white panties off. (Had I known this was coming, I would have worn one of the cute pair I had from Victoria's Secret.) And then I was completely naked, completely at his mercy.

And he was not a sexually merciful man.

Lucky for me.

He put his hands on my inner thighs, parting them farther, opening me totally to him, then he kissed my stomach, my hips, my thighs, and everywhere but the place that ached the most for him. He was good at this, better than most, driving up the need until it reached a fever pitch. I didn't know what he'd been doing all these years—and I really didn't want to know—but he clearly hadn't been sitting around doing nothing but reading the *Financial Times*.

I arched against him, reaching to pull him closer until I felt his tongue flicker lightly against me. Then it was back to the tender spot between my pelvis and leg, where he ran his tongue slowly down, following the map closer and closer to my need until, suddenly, and without teasing, he took me in. And this time he did devour me. He held me in his hands at the hips and locked me in place with his mouth until I couldn't stand the anticipation anymore.

"I need you," I rasped, clutching at his shirt and tugging it to pull it off him.

He helped, and tossed it aside, then did the same with his jeans, leaving his briefs on as he knelt before me again.

I closed my eyes and reveled in it for a moment, before what he was doing could no longer be enough, and I pulled him up to me, catching his briefs with my toes and pushing them down out of the way.

He met my gaze and hesitated just for a moment before pressing into me, never losing eye contact. Then he moved down very slowly to kiss me, still looking at me, and me looking back. There was communication there, without a word. Understanding of something inside, though the questions of past and future remained.

There followed an intense moment I could neither define nor turn away from, before I threw my arms around his neck and pulled him closer, closing my eyes and willing him to fill me up and take me over.

We held fast and didn't let go, never losing that contact even when he moved me on top of him. I cupped his face with my hands, gazing at the man I realized I had so much more to learn about, and kissed each temple, the top of his head, then his mouth.

"This is amazing," I whispered.

He rolled me over again. "What about this?"

I smiled and felt my warmth wrap around him. "This too."

He kissed me and increased his power. I yielded, and touched my hands against his chest, feeling every movement flex in his muscles. It was easy to dissolve into this. It was what I wanted. It was what I wanted more than anything.

I had known this man almost all my life. Had he been my fate all along? Had life drawn us together over and over, only for me to focus on the wrong man?

There was no stopping now, there was no way I could.

I gave in to it.

Because the need to meld into him was overwhelming, and for moments it felt like we did just that, but ultimately I knew this action raised many, many more questions than answers.

We kept going. It was amazing, with dizzying moments of unity that made me feel like we'd transcended our humanness and gone into eternity.

And afterward I again experienced fleeting moments of harmony, but the voice in my head—or my heart?—kept interrupting them.

Say good-bye.

This nagging voice in my head began like a siren in the distance but grew louder and louder as the inevitable moment of parting drew near: How could we be doing this? How could we ever do it again? It was just too complicated. Too ceaselessly complicated.

Yet, at the same time, what would it be like to have this—to have each other—every single night?

After we lay there for I don't know how long, I made myself get up. It wasn't easy. I forced my movements, and then my words. "I have to go," I said. "Early day tomorrow." And there was the lie.

"Is something wrong?" he asked immediately.

I didn't turn to him as I put my pants on—a giveaway right there, I guess, but I didn't want to lose it in front of him. "No, not at all, but"—I forced a laugh—"this was an unexpected detour to-night."

"Yes." I heard him get up and could see him dressing from the corner of my eye.

This was wrong, this hurried return to normality, like nothing had happened. Making love like that deserved a long, warm, se-cure rest and recovery time, to let the spirit settle back into place. Not a harried pulling on of pants, an inside-out shirt, and a walk of shame to the car.

This was me, *I* was the one doing this, but I couldn't stop my-self. Everything in me said it was time to go. I wasn't sure what everything in me was reacting to, probably nothing more than fear or the weakness I felt for him under his touch, but I had to get out before I made a mistake I could never take back.

"So." I smoothed my shirt and grabbed my purse as he slipped on his second shoe. "I guess I'll see you at the wedding."

"Yes, you will."

We headed toward the door and I opened it, allowing him through first.

"Should be exciting." Who was I suddenly? A children's show hostess?

He gave a laugh. He was probably thinking something along the same lines. But he came over to me, wordless, put his hands on my shoulders, and drew me to him, kissing my forehead. "Good night, Quinn."

And, boom, just like that he had the advantage. Even though I knew he wasn't playing a game, and "advantage" would have sounded wrong to his ears, that was where we were. He had con-trol now because I cared in a way I had never quite cared before.

"Good night." I turned back and locked the door, then went to my car without looking at him again. It was only when I was safely locked in the private bubble of my car that I told him my final truth. "I love you."

In a way it surprised me as much as it would, undoubtedly, have surprised him.

Chapter 25

I'm sorry, I can't work here anymore."

I looked at Becca in disbelief. It was four hours before Dottie's wedding and I was in a bind trying to get everything together and take it to the church. "What are you talking about?" I asked. "As of *now*? As of *right now*?"

She looked pale. A moment passed when she pressed her hand to her month and looked like she was going to puke before she said, "I'm pregnant. Again. And I can barely get out of bed. I threw up all weekend long."

My sympathy kicked in. "Pregnant?"

She nodded, and there was very little happiness in her eyes at the announcement. "We weren't planning it. But this time I'm so sick." She paused again. "I just hope it's a girl."

"It will be great either way. As long as *you're* okay. So go home," I said, even though it was the last thing in the world I wanted.

Becca hadn't been here for three days, and prior to that, when I looked back on it, she *had* been acting a bit off. She must have been feeling crummy longer than she'd admitted.

"Thank you," she said, clearly not wanting to waste one more penny on explanations.

The bells over the door trilled, and I looked to see Taney coming in.

Oh, great was my thought. *Just add insult to injury here.*

"I'm sorry to bother you again," she said in her quiet voice. It looked as if she'd been crying. Her eyes were red and a little puffy, but it was her blotchy skin that gave it away. "I wanted to know if you were looking for any help here in your store?"

There was no way. Life never went like this.

"Help?" I asked, half expecting her clarification to include something snooty like, *Yeah, moving out, because we're kicking your ass in sales.*

But instead she just nodded. "I no longer work at the cleaner's," she said simply. "And now I have no work. I wonder if you need cleaning when you are closed?"

The timing was almost suspicious, but then I remembered that there had been a piece in the local paper on Dottie's wedding—she was a local celebrity, after all—and mention had been made of her dress being designed by me. That was only yesterday morning, but in the thirty-six hours or so since, I'd probably gotten at least a dozen calls for appointments.

"I need a seamstress," I said.

"How can that be? You are providing for the biggest wedding this year, with many people there. My employer—my *former* employer—says that you are much faster and better worker than I, so I did not earn a living wage."

That was it. He'd been trying to pull more work out of her and it had backfired. "I will definitely hire you," I said, then I mentioned an hourly figure that I guessed was considerably more than what she'd been paid at the dry cleaner's.

From the look on her face then, I knew it was true. "Oh, yes, *please!*" she said. "When can I start?"

And this was the thing. I knew she did superior work; that if I paid her well, she would put the detailing on my dresses that I thought was worthy of my name and my shop's name. I could be proud to send something out with her handiwork, versus that which I'd seen so many other times at the secondhand stores, etc.

So this was a blessing for both of us—for me because Becca was puking, for at least another few months, and for Taney because she was able to do what she loved to do—what she was clearly gifted at—and get paid what she deserved.

I'd mull over the serendipity later.

For now, all I could say was, "Start by packing that dress up with the tissue on the table in the corner. . . ."

"Are you nervous?" I asked Dottie, buttoning the tiny buttons up the back of her dress with my own shaking hands. I was usually behind the scenes, not at the wedding, so this was what weddings did to me now, they made me nervous. I was always afraid something unexpected would happen, and, in this case, I particularly hoped it wasn't going to happen to the dress. Somehow Dottie had put on some personal padding since our last fitting a week ago, and I really hoped none of the thirty-five buttons popped and set off a fireworks finale of flying plastic disks, leaving Dottie with a pool of silk at her feet.

"Missy, I have been here before!" she declared, then glanced over her shoulder at me. "Of *course* I'm nervous. Look how the last one turned out!"

There was an awkward moment in which I pictured her, the grieving widow, wishing she'd never loved so she'd never have had to feel the pain, before she laughed unexpectedly.

"Sorry, Quinn, gallows humor. I've always been guilty of it. I don't regret my first marriage and I sure as heck don't plan on regretting this one. Love's always a good thing, wouldn't you say?"

I thought about Burke and how my love for him seemed to have given me almost nothing but difficulty. "Yes," I lied. "That's all that matters at the end of the day."

I should have known better than to think I could fool her.

"Someday you'll mean that," she said, standing straighter and sucking it in while I did the buttons at her girth. "I know you don't believe it now, but you will."

"I do hope so, Dottie," I murmured, and Frank came to mind. I hadn't talked to him since we'd been together, endless nights before, so I knew it was as foolish to pine for him as it had been to spend so many years trying to change the past with Burke. Everyone was so tangled up inside this one story that I couldn't even make sense of it anymore.

Had it always been Frank?

Was it meant to be?

I didn't know.

"I do know, Quinn. I do."

I cinched the last of the buttons at her waist and said, "Turn around. How does it feel?"

She whirled to face me, the motion defying her years in a startling way, and for just a moment—one crazy moment—I saw a young, bright-eyed, happy bride in front of me. She looked beautiful, proving right every poet and cheap lettered wall-hanging that ever contended beauty was a matter of the light within.

Today Dottie was lit from within.

I don't want to overstate things, but it was like seeing those sun rays that pierce through thick puffy clouds and look like a postcard with a Bible verse on it.

In short, it was happiness.

So who could argue with that?

Taney came over then with Dottie's shoes and said, with more confidence than she'd shown in asking me for employment, "I think the match is *perfect*."

Indeed, the pale salmon–colored shoes were the exact antique pink as Dottie's dress and all the little roses I'd painstakingly hand-sewn onto it. And with her always-tan skin (outdoorsy, now, more than sexy), the dress and the shoes were the perfect soft pale punctuation to her look.

"Where's my hat?" Dottie asked, her cheeks positively flushed with excitement.

"Right here." I went to the pile of extras I'd brought and searched through for a moment, then carefully perched the old-fashioned riding hat—the same pale pink, of course, but with a tiny net of veil hanging down in front—atop Dottie's head.

The entire ensemble was a mishmash of styles and moods, but it all added up to be a perfect summarization of Dottie.

"You look *perfect*," I said, turning her to face the mirror we'd propped against the wall. I always made sure, in situations like this where there wasn't dressing-room lighting or mirrors, to bring a true mirror so as not to have the bride looking at herself at the mercy of a cheap carnival-quality mirror from a discount store, slapped on the wall because someone thought the wall needed something.

I'd learned that lesson the hard way with a bride who herself seemed awfully close to anorexic. She looked at herself in the cheap mirror pegged to the wall of a Civil War house that devoted 20 percent of its space to the business of "haunted house tours" and the other 80 percent to cheap office space for new or bad psychologists, massage therapists, etc.

She'd taken one look in the mirror and burst into tears, and as I went to console her and caught a glimpse of the bubble-butted pinhead that was my reflection, I realized immediately what the problem was. It wasn't until we'd found an undeniably slim-and-straight ten-year-old boy among the guests, and placed him in front of the mirror for the bride to see the distortion, that she finally stopped sniffling enough to see that there was a little bit of a discrepancy between reality and the mirror image.

But it was close. And I hadn't taken a chance since on being blamed for a delicate bride's misperception.

"What do you think?" I asked, standing beside Dottie and looking in the mirror at her.

I knew what she thought, it was written all over her face.

"I think I never imagined I'd be in this place again," she breathed, flushed like a schoolgirl. "I am so lucky. So *blessed*, to have found love again at my age." She glanced at me. "Never give up. He loves you."

"Who?"

"*You* know who."

I did. I thought. But did she? Were we thinking of the same person? And did it even matter?

I felt my face go warm. That was a loaded conversation we weren't going to have. "Today is *your* day. You look beautiful, Dottie."

She looked back at her reflection and took it in, shaking her head slightly. "It's like a miracle."

"It is."

There was a knock at the door and I went to open it. The maid I recognized from Dottie's house came in with a platter that held a large ice bucket with two bottles, and several champagne flutes. "As you asked, Ms. Morrison," she said, setting it on the table. "And there's a gift, as well, from Mr. Lyle."

Dottie went to the tray and took the small box from it.

"Would you like me to pour you a glass?" I asked her.

"Yes, please, dear. And there's some sparkling cider there for you." There was a pointed pause. "If you prefer."

I cringed, remembering Day Drunk Day. So that's who I was now. The person you subtly offer the *nonalcoholic* option to. I almost had to laugh, but instead I poured her a glass of Bollinger, and myself a glass of Welch's sparkling white grape juice.

I took the glasses over to her and watched her open the box, which had no stamp or label. She removed a pad of cotton and underneath there was a delicate gold chain with a Tiffany-set blue topaz on it. It was a modest stone, and the chain was a beautiful, intricate herringbone, clearly good quality but not without signs of age.

She took out the note and put on her glasses. "*Dorothy*," she read. "*I don't remember the whole saying, but I know you are supposed to wear something blue. But this, my love, is not borrowed. It belonged to my aunt and it was given to her by her love who sadly died in a war. We will live the love they didn't have the chance to.*" She gasped and held the note to her chest, then turned to me with shimmering eyes. "Isn't that lovely? He was raised by his aunt, you know."

"No, I didn't know that." I wondered why, but it didn't seem appropriate to ask that right now. "What a nice gesture. And a *beautiful* necklace. Do you want me to fasten it?"

"Would you?" She held it out to me and I went to fasten the clasp, but the necklace was small and Dottie's neck was less so, and the chain dug into her flesh. "Oh, no." Her shoulders deflated.

"Hold on, I have an idea," I said. I took my Swiss Army knife out of my purse, then took off my own gold necklace, which was newer and cheaper but had links. I pried a link open a couple of inches from the clasp and squeezed it shut again, then held it up. "Chain extender!"

She beamed. "Aren't you resourceful!"

I laughed. "I broke into my car with that knife once," I said.

"It's the greatest tool I've ever had." I clipped the chains together and was glad to see that the difference wasn't all that obvious with a few feet of distance. "Let's try this again."

She turned around and held her hair up and I put the necklace on her. "Perfect!" she declared, and turned around. The stone sparkled against her chest at the collarbone. It was perfect.

"What else could you need?" I asked.

"Actually," she said, "there is one thing. I wonder if you'd mind running over to the reception hall and grabbing a little bite of something for me? I'm feeling a little faint."

"You're probably revving high right now with nerves," I said. "You need protein. Have a seat and relax, I'll be back in a few."

As I was leaving, I saw three of Dottie's friends bustling toward the back room to join her. They were the old aristocrats from town, you could tell by their eclectic dress and hairstyles. The *real* rich, in my experience, tended to be the oddballs. I smiled to myself and took out my phone and pushed speed dial.

"Crazy Town, how may I help you?" Glenn answered.

"That bad, huh?"

"Your ex was here at the reception hall, on the phone with a lawyer, trying to make sure her assets were protected in case he was"—he lowered his voice—"a gold digger."

I thought about how happy Dottie had looked getting ready and how cruel it would be to crush her hopes. Over what? Money?

"I'm coming over," I said. "Can you set up a little platter of something for me to take back to Dottie? I think her nerves are getting the best of her. Meanwhile, I'll try to talk some sense into Burke, though I don't imagine that's going to be easy."

"You ain't kiddin'." He clucked his tongue against his teeth. "I'll set something aside for you to take back."

"Thanks." We hung up and I quickened my pace. Dottie wasn't a little old lady who couldn't take care of herself. And Lyle wasn't a gold digger, but even if he was, she was a sane adult who was making her own decision to marry him.

The place was bustling when I arrived. Glenn's staff was busy setting up the food, the ice fountain of champagne, the antique pink carnations on the tables. It was beautiful and dignified and 100 percent perfect. Man, I hoped Burke wouldn't ruin it.

You'd think he'd know what it was like to have someone step in and blow up your wedding.

Fortunately, I didn't have to work hard to get him into conversation, as he came to me the moment I walked in.

"You've *got* to talk some sense into her," he said without preamble.

"Who?"

"What do you mean, *who*? You know exactly who. My grandmother. She's making a huge mistake."

I collected myself for a moment, then spoke calmly. "I don't believe she'd agree with that. In fact, she looks happier than I've ever seen her. Happier than I've ever seen most people, actually."

"*All* I'm saying is that they should sign a pre-nup."

"And I see why you think that's smart; maybe I'd want the same thing if it were my grandmother, but that's only on the very off chance that he'd take advantage of her. I don't know Lyle that well, obviously, but I *really* don't think that's the case here. Maybe you should ease up and give Dottie the gift of her dignity today, huh?"

For just a second I thought maybe I'd reached him, then he shook his head. "Okay, this conversation is over. I've got things to handle, I don't need to argue with you."

"Fine." I started to turn and huff off, but stopped. "Let me just say one thing that I hope you'll take seriously. I mean, *really think about* before you fuck up your grandmother's whole life. Lyle is a nice guy, a great guy, I think he can make her happy, but"—I searched for words that wouldn't be demeaning—"I just don't think he has it in him to orchestrate the kind of plan you're talking about. I don't think . . . He doesn't seem all that *aware* of Dottie's net worth or the implications. I think he really loves her."

Burke scoffed.

"Great." I threw up my hands. "Well, have at it, then. Do the very thing to her that was done to me on *my* one and only wedding day. The circumstances were different, but we were both women who deserved to make our own choices. So if you blow this for her, don't strain your shoulder patting yourself on the back for it."

I started to leave but he said, "Quinn."

I raised an eyebrow at him.

"I hear you," he said, and a small bit of hope surged in me. "I'll think about it."

"Please do, Burke. *Please* do." I turned and went to Glenn, who had half an eye on me and half an eye on the Saran Wrap he was using to cover a pretty silver tray of canapés and fruit.

"Get through to him?"

"I don't know." I glanced back at Burke, who, for what it's worth, was not on his phone. "Maybe."

"You really think he's wrong about this?"

Glenn I could be blunt with. "I really do. Lyle's not the brightest bulb in the box. He doesn't have highbrow tastes, and, honestly, I think he probably works really hard to balance a checkbook so maybe he'd have a hard time managing a stock portfolio, you know what I mean?"

"He's stupid?"

I wrinkled my nose. "Maybe. Kind of."

Glenn laughed. "But a heart of gold, yes?"

"Yes."

He handed me the tray. "Sounds like just what she needs at this point in her life."

"Right! Let her be happy. Jeez. She's been alone for so long now."

He nodded. "Here's hoping today goes as planned."

"Amen. By the way, Dottie had champagne sent over but included a bottle of nonalcoholic sparkling grape for Drinky Mc-Dumbass here." I pointed to myself. "Thanks to Day Drunk Day."

He laughed out loud. "I know, I'm the one who sent it. She asked for apple cider, but I figured grape was funnier."

"Almost wine but not quite?"

He pointed a finger gun at me and clicked.

"Very funny."

"I know. See you at the wedding!"

I turned to go and was shocked to see Aaron across the room with an older woman who I took to be the grandmother he'd told me about. A friend of Dottie's, most likely, a guest who had brought her grandson as her date. Perfect.

"Glenn! Glenn!" I whispered as loud as I could.

He stopped and looked back at me.

Aaron, I mouthed, and nodded in his direction.

"What?" He came over.

"That's *Aaron*, over there with the older woman in blue."

"Who's Aaron?"

"The guy from Short Stops. You know, *the guy I told you about*."

"Oooh." He looked. "I see what you mean."

I nodded. "Work on that."

I took the tray back to the church, where Dottie and her clutch of hens were giggling like teenagers. She had no idea that Burke was on the warpath, and I hoped, so very much, that he wouldn't show up.

"Here she is, my hero!" Dottie cried when she saw me. "My goodness, I am starving."

"You are in luck." I put the tray down in front of her. "Glenn has outdone himself, I can tell. Everything is beautiful."

"Oooh, lovely!" She chose a square of ham and cheese, which I happened to know was one of the best things on earth, thanks to the brown sugar–cured ham Glenn used. "Mmm-mm. Doris, pour Quinn a sparkling juice, would you?" She gave her friend a Significant Look that I guess she thought I wouldn't notice.

Four glasses of champagne and one glass of grape juice were poured and we all raised our flutes to toast Dottie and Lyle's future happiness. And as time wore on and the women put on their makeup and gabbed merrily about events from long ago in their history, I felt more and more optimistic that Burke had heeded my advice and reconsidered his assault on the marriage.

He wasn't without romance in his heart, I knew that. Maybe he'd had character flaws that made him a lousy fiancé and, presumably, husband, but I knew—I *knew*—underneath it all he had a good heart.

So when there was a knock on the door in the midst of the revelry, I thought only that it must be the pastor, coming to alert us all that it was time to get into position for the wedding ceremony.

"I do believe it's getting to be about that time!" Adrianne Parker trilled to Dottie. "The bells are about to be ringing and *you* are about to be a missus again!"

"Lord help you," Lorel Beard chimed in. "If I hadn't seen your Lyle, I'd wonder what had gotten into you to make you do such a damn fool thing as getting married again." She giggled and raised her glass. "But I think I know *exactly* what's gotten into you. More power to you!"

There were shouts of "Amen" and clinking glasses, then Sukie Maynard went to the door.

Then there was a weird moment when I could feel, in my entire being, the pull between the lighthearted excitement of the women on my left, and a dark pull on my right, by the door.

I knew what it was, of course.

I'd felt this before. I knew exactly what it was.

Sukie came back to the group, looking confused. Not alarmed. Maybe I wouldn't even have gone so far as saying *concerned* to describe her expression, but she clearly knew something was *off*.

"Dottie," she said, but her voice was lost in the laughter, and she repeated, louder, "Dottie?"

Dottie looked up. "Yes, baby?"

"Burke's at the door," Sukie answered. "He says he'd like to talk to Dottie. Alone."

Chapter 26

June, Ten Years Ago

It wasn't as if Quinn wouldn't admit she was a romantic. She was *definitely* a romantic. But today was ridiculous, even for her.

Granted, it was her wedding day, so she was supposed to be on cloud nine, but she had the strangest sensation of walking through a dream. It was like a movie sequence about heaven—everything was perfect: her dress, the weather, the forecast for their honeymoon in Jamaica.

How had she gotten so lucky as to truly find the love of her life at such a young age and never have to go through the heartbreak that most had to suffer? All those songs, movies, books about it, and she'd slid into Burke Morrison's arms at fourteen and he'd never let go.

On some level she must have believed she didn't quite deserve the luck. That would explain the low hum of anxiety deep in the pit of her stomach right now. The niggling fear that this wasn't real. It was an elaborate hoax to set her up for a fall. By . . . God? It was silly. Maybe everyone felt this kind of fear, that complete devastation could hide in the shadows of perfect happiness.

"Quinn!" Karen, one of her bridesmaids, came tripping over with a glass of champagne and a giggle. "A little liquid courage for the bride!"

"She doesn't need courage," another bridesmaid, Rami, said. "She's only marrying the cutest guy who ever went to our high school. No offense, Quinn, I'm not after him, but you gotta know it's true."

"I don't know," Karen said, sipping the champagne she'd just brought over for Quinn. "There was Phil Edwards. Lee Holloway. Glenn Ryland. There were a lot of cute guys on the football team."

Quinn took the half-empty glass from Karen's hand. "I'm not into competition, thank you very much. You can take your Phils, your Lees, your Glenns, just leave my Burke alone."

"As soon as you get the ring on him, ain't no one gonna try and take him away," the maid of honor, Jackie, said. "So get your makeup on, girlie, and get out there to claim your man. You never know what's going to happen in the meantime!"

They all laughed, and Quinn went to the Jergens plug-in-light-up makeup mirror she'd brought, knowing the lighting in the church rectory was going to be so crummy she'd look like a clown in daylight if she relied on it alone.

"Are you nervous?" Rami asked, sitting down next to Quinn on the bench seat in front of the piano where Quinn had set up the mirror.

Quinn thought about it for a moment, swiping Great Lash mascara onto her lashes. Was she *nervous* or just eager to have it done so this crazy feeling that her happiness wasn't real would end?

"I'm not nervous," Quinn said. "I have never been as sure of anything in my life as I am that I want to be Mrs. Burke Morrison."

"That is *so* old-fashioned," Karen said. "Are you seriously changing your name to his?"

"Yes." Quinn felt a flush of anticipation. *Quinn Morrison.* She couldn't wait.

How many times, and in how many places, had she been exactly the clichéd schoolgirl scripting all the variations?

Quinn Morrison.

Mrs. Burke Morrison.

Mrs. Quinn Morrison.

Mr. and Mrs. Burke Morrison.

And, for a brief period during which she'd gotten grandiose ideas from watching too many Lifetime TV shows, *Dr. Quinn Morrison.*

Sounded familiar. So it must have been right.

There was a knock at the door, then it swung open and her mother came in, smiling. "You're looking beautiful," she said. "Don't go too heavy on the black liner, remember." She always said that. "Got your chocolate." She held out a Toblerone bar.

"Oh, *thank you.*" Quinn tore into it. Chocolate always made her feel better when she was nervous. Not that she was nervous, because she wasn't, but she'd still had a last-second craving for chocolate and sent her mother out to get it.

"You're welcome." She smiled, looking just the same for as long as Quinn could remember, and Quinn felt a pang of melancholy at knowing today was the day she officially grew up and was no longer a little girl anymore. "Now. What can I do for you?"

"Just tell me I'm going to live happily ever after."

"Of course you are," her mother said, then frowned. "Do you have any doubts?"

The laughter and chat of the bridal party filled the silence as Quinn thought about her answer.

"No," she said honestly. The room was large and, despite the party atmosphere of her friends, this conversation with her mother felt very private. "But this day just feels so perfect that I don't want anything to go wrong."

Her mother laid a warm hand on her shoulder. "Everyone feels that way on their wedding day. Like it's the biggest day of their life and nothing else can live up. But the truth is, it's just the first day of your *new* life." She paused and gave a small chuckle. "And that sounded even more hackneyed than I meant for it to." Her eyes met Quinn's in the mirror. "But it's true. Tomorrow everything is different. The same but different."

Quinn felt tears fill her eyes and put her hand on her mother's. "I'm so happy. Right now I'm so perfectly happy, I wish I could just freeze this moment and relive it over and over again."

"You can. Why on earth wouldn't you be able to? Every time you want a little lift, you remember your wedding day. I do."

"You do?"

"I do."

They both laughed.

Quinn took out her eye shadow palette and carefully brushed on some neutral browns. She didn't want anything too dramatic. With the black mascara and black liner—carefully and subtly applied, per her mother's instructions—she had enough going on.

As emotional as she was, she just hoped she wouldn't cry. The mascara looked great on but was notorious for being saltwater soluble. She didn't need wet black rivers running down her cheeks as she took her vows at the altar.

"Do you ever regret marrying Daddy so young?" Quinn's parents had gotten married when they were both twenty-one.

"Oh, I've *questioned* it a million times, and I'll probably question it a million more. Every time he irks me, I question it. But regret? No. Never."

Quinn swept some blush across her cheeks, then turned the lighted mirror off and turned to face her mother. "And you *know* he doesn't regret it!"

"I think he questions it himself sometimes, but no." She smiled. "I don't think he regrets it. But the person who doesn't question his or her major decisions is a fool." She hesitated. "Maybe a lucky fool, but a fool nonetheless."

"The music's starting, Quinn!" Karen called, then shrieked as Rami bumped into her and they both spilled their champagne. "That gives you about fifteen minutes until the final countdown."

Quinn took a bite of her chocolate. The champagne would be tempting if she didn't have to be sure she didn't trip, or slur, or otherwise make a fool of herself.

What was with these nerves she was experiencing?

Jamaica, Jamaica, Jamaica, she thought silently to herself. In twenty-four hours she'd be on a beach in Jamaica with Burke— her *husband*—by her side and all the fanfare would be over. They'd be baking under a bright Caribbean sun during the day, and making love to the sound of the waves lapping the shore all night. It would be pure bliss, the perfect cap to this beautiful wedding day.

Just thinking about it, the sun and Burke's hand in hers, made her relax.

It was just nerves, she told herself. She'd never been one to love being the center of attention, and that was the truth. Ever since she got engaged, she'd had a vague fear that she'd trip on her way up the aisle, or pass out on the altar, or do something else that made her look like a complete fool. The comparison would be even worse next to the always-confident Burke.

Fortunately, the always-confident Burke had never let her fall, literally or figuratively, so even if she started to, he'd catch her.

That was one thing she could always count on him for. He'd always catch her when she fell.

Wouldn't he?

She stood up and slipped her feet into her grandmother's satin wedding shoes. They were a tiny bit too tight, but still wearable, and they were so perfect with her dress that she figured she could make the short walk up the aisle and stand for pictures in them, then switch to the more comfortable, if ordinary, satin pumps she'd gotten from the Payless at the mall.

Everyone hushed and looked at her.

"Honey, you look beautiful," her mother said to her.

"You do!" Rami said. "I've been in the room with you for an hour, but suddenly you have bloomed into . . ."

"A bride!" Karen finished.

Everyone agreed.

Quinn took a steadying breath. "That's the idea."

There was a knock at the door and Karen went to answer it while Quinn took one last look in the mirror. A little bit of Cover-Girl pink Lipslicks and she was ready.

It was time.

Good-bye, Quinn Barton.

Hello, Quinn Morrison.

"Quinn?"

She smiled in the mirror. Quinn Morrison. It was really happening. Dreams really could come true.

"Quinn!"

Karen's voice brought her back to the moment.

"What?"

Karen's forehead was creased with worry. "Um. Frank's outside the door. And, um, he's acting weird. Not that I think anything's wrong or anything—"

Panic surged in Quinn's chest like a wave that had been building and was finally crashing on the shore.

"But," Karen went on, making—and failing at—a clear effort to sound casual and calm, as if this were par for the course. "He says he needs to talk to you. Now."

Chapter 27

Present

Well, I'm sorry, but my first thought when Sukie said Burke was at the door was, *Oh, fuck!*

This happily anticipated wedding, which should have gone so smoothly, was going to be stopped.

Or at least paused.

How had I hoped for anything else? Could a wedding within three miles of Burke Morrison ever work out?

It was odd that he'd be the one stopping it this time, but, at the same time, it made perfect sense. This was a perfect demonstration of the lack of regard he had for marriage.

Dottie began to get up to go to the door and I heard myself saying to her, "I think I know what this is about. Let me talk to him for a moment, Dottie."

Now, of course I know that I had failed in talking to Burke just an hour or so earlier, so there was no great reason for optimism, but with him at the door I was very clear on the fact that I was the only barrier between Dottie and him, which made me, perhaps, the only barrier between Dottie's happiness today and, at the very least, a great deal of stress.

Lord, believe me, I knew at the very least he'd be able to put a big damper on her day, so she could end up schlumping down the aisle after feeling pummeled, and I could not bear to let that happen.

I went to the door and opened it just enough to get through to the other side, which was a good thing, because he started to enter the minute it creaked an inch in my direction.

"Stop!" I rasped. "Don't go in there."

He looked impatient. "I have to talk to her."

"She's not dressed," I improvised. "If you go in there you're going to cause a much bigger—and much *weirder*—scene than you mean to."

That gave him pause. "How long will she be?"

"She's got a million buttons and nothing but arthritic hands to fasten them, so it's going to be a while. Come outside and talk to me." I took his arm.

He didn't move. "This has nothing to do with you. Stop trying to insert yourself in the middle of everything."

"I'm only trying to get you away from your grandmother's changing room before people start thinking you're a weirdo."

"There's nothing weird about me waiting right here to talk to her before the wedding."

I sighed. "Burke, you're in a church. Do you have respect for anyone or *anything*?"

"Of course! I just want to talk to my grandmother."

"Holy shit, Burke, stop being such a jerk." My stage whisper was not quiet enough. A few heads turned.

He kept his voice lower than mine. "You know damn well what I'm doing, I'm stopping my grandmother from making a huge and costly mistake."

"Have you considered what this is going to do to her, to this very special day for her, in the *very likely* event that she ignores your warning *again* and goes on with the wedding? You're just going to ruin her day! Is that what you want? To leave your mark in any way possible?"

At this point there was no question what the expression on his face was. Pure fury. "That's who you think I am? You think I just want to ruin her day at any cost? If it's not a warning to protect her assets, then maybe I'd just go on up and put a bag of dog shit on the altar and light it on fire?"

"You might as well!"

"What the hell is going on here?" a very welcome familiar voice asked. I didn't even have to turn around. I felt his energy right behind me and saw his identification reflected in Burke's eyes when they shifted to a spot over my shoulder and back to me.

"Did you call him?" Burke asked me.

I had to laugh. "When would I have?"

"Burke, what are you doing?" Frank asked, and I heard measured caution in his voice. He wasn't the hothead he used to be. He apparently wasn't even the hothead *I* was.

"Gran's not marrying a gold digger on *my* watch," Burke said simply, and gave a bold look to Frank. "How about on yours?"

"*Lyle?*" Frank asked incredulously. "A gold digger?" He straight-up laughed.

"I don't think it's funny."

"It's *hilarious*," Frank said. "Come on, have you *talked* to the guy? Even for five minutes? He's an idiot! He couldn't dig dirt out of the field, he's not digging gold from Gran!"

It was true, but even I felt a little prickle of discomfort at the label.

"Maybe that's his act. It wouldn't be a bad one, would it? Make everyone think he's just a moron who's incapable of anything?"

"There is no way that man has the cunning to execute a plan like that. What the fuck, Burke, don't you think Gran's worth marrying for *herself*? Any man would be lucky to have her!"

"I know," Burke said, softening only slightly. "But that doesn't mean that just any man knows that. Everything in me says that this guy is an opportunist. You can't make me believe that some-one his age, who looks like him, would pick an older woman with a lot of hard years under her belt unless it was for some other gain."

"I can believe it," Frank said.

"I can too," I chimed quickly.

Burke looked at us in disbelief, then settled his gaze on Frank. "Why don't you care about this? You didn't have any trouble stop-ping *my* wedding on some principle you'd decided on."

"Because you're wrong," Frank said. "Both times."

I agreed, but it wasn't my place to say. I didn't have a horse in the race this time, so I had no right to speak too freely. I took a step back so the brothers were face-to-face, without me standing—foolishly and symbolically—between them.

"What if I'm right?" Burke asked.

Frank shifted his weight from one foot to the other, a gesture of boredom. "What if you are?"

"I'm trying to protect her property."

"But it's *hers*," Frank said, and now the boredom was being replaced by ire. The edge to his voice was subtle, but I heard it clearly. "Look, Burke, I made this same mistake myself once. I'm not proud of it. *This*—the eleventh hour—is *never* the time to interrupt someone's life. The ramifications echo on much longer than you think." He glanced at me but didn't make eye contact. "I regret it. Do you really want to do this to Gran?"

"Burke," I said, more gently. "Men and women are different, so maybe you can't imagine what this is like, but a woman looks at her wedding day almost like the whole caterpillar-into-butterfly moment. Except she knows it's happening, and she looks forward to it and plans it. And every moment leading up to it is the slow part of the roller coaster, climbing up the hill to that ultimate thrill. Dottie's over the top now. She's already on the way down, sixty miles an hour on a wooden track. You can't change her mind, you *can't*, I *swear* it. All you can do is hurt her."

His determination began to wobble, I could see it. "I don't know . . ."

I looked into his eyes, imploring. I'd never willed someone to understand with so much intensity in my life. "*Please* believe me. You weren't in that room watching her get ready. She is happier than I've ever seen her."

"Leave it alone," Frank said, though his tone too had softened. "No matter how right or wrong I was last time, it was a mistake. Learn from that mistake."

I didn't look at Frank and he didn't touch me, but I could feel him as surely as if his hands were on me. "That should have been between you and me, Burke. And this is between Dottie and Lyle. You know that."

Burke pressed his lips together and looked down. Then, slowly, he nodded. "Okay. Okay." He put his hands up, the time-honored signal of surrender. "I think you're both wrong, but I hope you're right."

"You won't say anything to her?" I asked, trying to exact a specific vow from him.

He met my eyes. "I won't."

I smiled. "That's the right decision. I swear that's the right decision, Burke."

He shrugged. "So I'll go in and keep my mouth shut. I'm sure you two have a few words for each other." He gave a humorless spike of a laugh and nodded in the direction of the dressing room. "Scene of the crime and all."

Frank said nothing, but watched him with angry eyes.

"Thank you," I said, trying to soften the blows we'd both just leveled on him. "It's the right choice, I swear it."

He shrugged and went in.

Only then did I turn to Frank and face him directly. "I can't believe this. What happened to him? How could he have this stuff brewing and then just *blow up*? And *now*, of all times?" I shook my head. "What is *with* you guys?"

"Whoa, don't lump *me* into this!"

I looked at him.

He frowned. "The situation with you was completely different. I thought you knew and were ignoring it. I was *sure* you knew.

I couldn't understand why you'd be okay with it, but I tried to butt out. It wasn't until the very last second that I realized maybe you *didn't* know, and you *needed to*, Quinn, you really did. You can't deny it. Look at the way things went down then. Are you sorry you're not married to him?"

I didn't even have to think about it. "No."

"Wouldn't it have been harder to go through with the wedding, *then* find out and have to go through the mess of a divorce?"

"Okay, yes, obviously."

"There you go. Completely different situation."

"Fine."

"I did it because I loved you."

I met his eyes. "You kind of wanted to stick it to Burke."

"No," he said earnestly. "It was *only* because I loved you. I *always* loved you."

I sighed. "Then why didn't you ever say anything?"

"Because, Quinn, everyone knows that's not how the story goes. That's how the *movie* goes, the guy makes the big admission of love at the last minute and the girl cries tears of joy and they're off into the sunset together, via whatever mode of transportation is appropriate to the time period. But the *real* story never goes that way."

I liked that story. I wanted that story to be true. "How does the *real* story go, then?"

"In the real story, the bad guy gets his comeuppance eventually, and the sweet, beautiful girl gets hurt anyway. The prize for her virtue and faithfulness is zero at best, and pain at worst."

"What about the hero? The guy who saves her. What happens to him in real life?"

"In real life everyone thinks he's a jealous dick and judges him for that, and he walks away, trying to tell himself he did the right thing and the rest doesn't matter." He cocked his head and looked into my eyes. "He tries to forget the girl and hopes she finds a better man."

I smiled. "But who's a better man than the best man?"

He looked confused for a moment, then realization came into his eyes. "You mean me?"

"Yes." I nodded. "I think I do."

He gave a sad smile. "You can do a lot better than me too, Quinn. It's time for you to get your whole fairy tale, not settle for the cranky, unromantic businessman who hasn't even thought about love or marriage in a decade."

"Seriously. You're out of the game."

"I was never even in the running. I'm not flowers and chocolates, I'm pragmatic. I could never make you happy. Find a good guy who has nothing to do with this messed-up family so you can be *happy*, Quinn."

I looked at him for a long moment. He was serious. He was utterly and completely serious. He would give me up at his own expense, in addition to mine, and tell himself he was doing it for me. That it was in my best interest.

"Are you *fucking* kidding me?" Using both my hands, I shoved him. He nearly lost his footing from the unexpectedness, but steadied before going down. "You'd let me go, no, you wouldn't even give us a *chance*, all because you're so sure I should be off with some, I don't know, poetry-spouting lute player?" I shoved him again. "Are you fucking *kidding* me?"

He grabbed my hands. "Stop it. No, I'm not fucking kidding you. I'm trying to do the right thing."

"Then you're a fucking moron! What the f—" I shook my head. I had to avoid screaming *fuck* inside of the church. It was bound to carry over the organ music that was beginning to swell, like some discordant performance art of melody and vitriol.

"I'm *sorry!*" He was apparently unconcerned about the act we were accidentally putting on. "I was trying to do the right thing. Give me a break, I'm not good at this, *as I just told you.* If you want to give it a shot, I'm *more* than willing to give it a shot."

"Define *a shot.*"

"Not a shot," he said, and paused. "A cannon. The whole thing, all the way. Marry me."

I stopped. "*What?*"

He stopped too, in front of me, and knelt before me. "I don't have a ring, obviously"—he took my left hand and kissed my ring finger—"but if you'll marry me, I'll spend the rest of my life doing whatever it takes to make you happy."

The idea thrilled me. No two ways about it. *Thrilled.* Deep inside, I knew this was the right choice. It always had been. "Okay. Fine!" I said, my voice contentious but my heart filled. "Whatever you say, apparently you're *always* the one who knows best."

He smiled. I loved his smile. "I am this time." He stood up and took me in his arms and kissed me. And it was as if all vestiges of Burke and the past had disappeared. Like a haunting smudged away.

"You better be," I said with a smile.

"I did do one thing I think you'll like, though," he said, a little too casually.

I looked at him, but he wasn't looking at me. "What's that?"

"Bought the farm."

I frowned.

He glanced at me. "Literally. Grace Farms."

I stopped again and gaped. "*How?*"

He'd bought the farm. He owned the farm. He wanted to marry me. I wanted to marry him. I was going to have the life I'd dreamed of after all.

"Come *on*," he said, with that smile I knew and loved so well. "The 'Wedding March' is starting."

Goes to show, you never know. As Dottie would say, we'd worked out our demons. Not quite in the way I would have expected, and I'll never know if it was the way *she* expected, but she didn't look all that surprised when we made our announcement a week later.

Her wedding was perfect, by the way. Went off without a hitch. True to his word, for once, Burke kept his mouth shut.

The reception was beautiful too. Glenn and his staff did a great job, not surprisingly.

But the best moment of the reception, for me, came at the end when Frank and I were leaving together and went to say good-bye to Glenn.

He handed me a small red envelope and said, "Your final task."

"Oh, no." I laughed. "How embarrassing is it going to be?"

He smiled. "I think you can handle it." He winked.

On our way out, Frank asked, "What was that about?"

I shrugged. "Let's see." I stopped and opened the envelope, then took out the familiar little red card. It said:

Quinn,

You did it. You tried every one of my assignments and did a great job with most of them (though there were a few notable exceptions). And I can see your life has changed. Maybe not in the direction we both thought it might originally but you're definitely moving forward now, in a way you've needed to for a long time.

So your final assignment is a simple one but it's going to take forever: be happy. No matter what it takes. No matter how embarrassing it might be sometimes, no matter who or what you might have to forgive, no matter how hideous the color of the hat that makes you smile, be happy.

I'll be watching you and giving you a boatload of shit if you fail. And next time, Day Drunk Day will seem like a cakewalk compared to what I'll have you do.

Love always,

Glenn

P.S. Marry the guy, would you? The right one this time. And soon! These old fogies aren't going to eat even half the food I prepared! Besides, you suck at being single and bitter . . .

7-16-13
4·30-22
33
2